HOW-MAN HAS A SECRET IDENTITY, OF COURSE. IT'S so secret, even he doesn't know what it is. So instead, he pretends to be Glenn Hauman, a mild-mannered publisher of soft-core anime and the occasional tentacular effort. His most successful book would have Multiple-Man, had it not been for the injunction filed against it by the real Multiple-Man.

—David Gerrold's "The Killing Croak"

BLOOD POOLS ON GLENN'S PILLOWCASE WHILE I stand frozen and stare down at his corpse. I want to say this was an accident. I didn't come into Glenn's sty of a dorm room looking to split his skull like a rotten melon. It just worked out that way.

This is a debacle, but I need you to know this: It's all Glenn's fault

—David Mack's "The Look on Your Face"

BARON HAUMANN WAS A VERY TALL MAN WITH unruly brown hair but a rather kempt beard. He was dressed in the fashion of the day. The most amazing thing about the corpse was that in both hands he held those new fangled electric light bulbs which were still lit and glowing. They gave the whole scene a very eerie feeling.

"Good lord," I gasped to Holmes.

—Kathleen David's "The Case of the Industrial Revolution"

# THEY KEEP KILLING
# GLENN

### Edited by
## PETER DAVID and KATHLEEN DAVID

CRAZY 8 PRESS

# CONTENTS

*Introduction* ...................................................................................vii

*They Keep Killing Me: A Foreword of Last Words* ........................xi

*The Killing Croak* by David Gerrold ...........................................1

*The Look on Your Face* by David Mack ....................................13

*Revenge of the Clipper Kin* by Joe Corallo ................................21

*"Is It You?"* by Robert Greenberger .........................................31

*The Hardwicke Files: The Case of Hauman's Comet*
  by Russ Colchamiro .....................................................41

*House Hunting* by Keith R.A. DeCandido ...............................55

*Patient Zero* by Dean Scott .....................................................63

*Buried in Books* by Mary Fan ..................................................77

*The Case of the Industrial Revolution*
  by Kathleen O'Shea David ...........................................89

*For Whom the Bell LOLs* by Setsu Uzumé .............................103

*Too Damn Tall* by Lorraine J. Anderson ................................113

*There's No Such Thing as Glenn* by Hildy Silverman ...............125

*DuckBob: All In* by Aaron Rosenberg ....................................137

*R is for Roadster* by Blair Learn ............................................147

*The Long and the Short of It* by Brett Hudgins .......................157

*The Marathon* by S. Brady Calhoun .......................................171

*For Cockeysville* by Michael Jan Friedman .............................185

*Rhino* by Amy Lewanski ........................................................201

*Waking Things* by Jenifer Purcell Rosenberg ..........................211

*The Day of Killing Endlessly* by Paul Kupperberg ..................223

*That's All, Folks* by Peter David .............................................239

*Post (Mortem) Script* .............................................................247

# INTRODUCTION
## by Peter David

I MUST ADMIT, I AM NOT ENTIRELY CERTAIN HOW this came about.

It began at a Farpoint convention, an annual *Star Trek*ish convention held in Hunt Valley, Maryland every year. Most people, if they've heard of the convention at all, remember when it was nicknamed Snowcon back in 2003 when a massive snowstorm paralyzed the entire area and the convention wound up going another two days. Armin Shimmerman wound up conducting a class on Shakespeare while Erin Gray led yoga workouts in the lobby.

A group of us Crazy 8 authors were conducting a panel (this was last year, not back in 2003) and we were talking about this, that, and the other thing. And somehow—and I don't remember exactly how or why—the subject of killing Glenn Hauman came up.

Now my guess is that you know who Glenn is if you picked up this book. But on the off chance that you do not, I will quote from his Wikipedia entry:

> Glenn Hauman is an American editor, publisher, writer of novels and short stories, book illustrator, and comic book colorist. He has worked in a variety of roles in print and electronic publishing, including software and website development, as well as his TV and novel work within the *Star Trek* and *X-Men* franchises.

I have known Glenn for many decades and he's as close a friend as he can be, considering I've never been to his house.

One of my earliest memories of Glenn was when he responded to a famous bit of the Flying Karamazov Brothers called "The Challenge" (since then redubbed "The Gamble") in which one of the brothers will juggle three random objects provided by the audience. Glenn came up with a meticulously designed object: a six-pack of Coke with rope slithered through the flip-tops so that juggling caused the cans to pop open and Coke to gush everywhere. And of course since the weight kept shifting, it was impossible for the juggler to get a consistent feel for it. On stage, the juggler admitted that it was, to use his word, "diabolical."

So anywhere, at Farpoint for some damned reason or other, we started tossing around ways to kill Glenn. And I, because I'm an idiot, said, "We should do an anthology. 'They Keep Killing Glenn,'" a variation from an episode of *Torchwood* with a similar name.

Immediately it was decided by everyone else that that was a great idea and I should edit it.

I said, "No, that's a terrible idea" with the same force that I had said it years earlier when, at an X-Men creator meeting, I said, "If I'm Magneto, I don't bother fighting Wolverine; I'd just rip out his skeleton," and every writer and the editors said, "Great! We have to do that!" and they did despite the fact that I kept insisting I was just thinking out loud, not pitching an idea. And they went and did it anyway.

Kind of the same thing here.

I must admit, I'm somewhat stunned at the number of writers who wanted to contribute and the numbers of methods they came up. We had to have a checklist to make sure there was no overlapping of means for his passing.

All of the Crazy 8 members participated in this insanity, plus we got some relatively prominent others on board.

As for Glenn, he has remained remarkably sanguine about it. Me, I have a sufficiently fragile ego that if people came up with over two dozen ways to off me, I'd be convinced that the world hates me and would wind up in a fetal position in a corner somewhere. But Glenn has taken it remarkably in stride—which makes sense since he has a very long stride.

And so without further ado, or even a don't, let's see just how many lives Glenn actually has.

—Peter David
Long Island, New York, 2018

# THEY KEEP KILLING ME: A FOREWORD OF LAST WORDS

I, Glenn Hauman, being of sound mind and body, do hereby declare . . .

. . . no, that's not what I'm supposed to be putting down here. I'm supposed to be describing what it's like to be the subject of this here comedy anthology. (At least, everyone else calls this a comedy anthology. I think it's a horror anthology, but they claim I'm biased.)

I mean, what can I say about these people and their stories that I haven't already detailed in a file that will be sent to the authorities should I go missing for an extended period? "It's an honor to be eviscerated! I look forward to being brutally stabbed seventeen times"?

Why me? Some people are roasted by their friends, I'm getting impaled on a spit and shoved into an oven. Is it because now that Mary Fan is part of Crazy 8 Press, I'm no longer needed as a shabbos goy, and I was lucky to live this long? Good grief, multiple fifteen-year-old girls have submitted manuscripts—what did I ever do to them? A couple of thoughts occur to me on my impending demise:

First, it's just funny to pick on the big lumbering guy, it always has been. Think Bull in Night Court, or Peter Boyle in Young Frankenstein, Jaws in Moonraker, John Cleese in something like a third of his roles, Groot, Lurch, even Worf gets this treatment on occasion (and Morn certainly does). Seeing a big guy bump his head against a low-hanging chandelier is always guaranteed to get a laugh; I'm convinced some of you are now doing it on purpose. And it's funny to punch up. If you've ever said "How's the weather up there?" you've done it yourself—and you're unlikely to get pushback, as it's not as funny to punch down (considering the height of some of you midgets, WAY down) and we just don't want to be seen as mean.

To a certain extent, every tall person deals with this in real life. We can either go around being scary and as a result being isolated, feared, and occasionally chased with pitchforks and torches, or we can go, "No! No! Friendly giant! Friend! FRIEND . . . !"

Second, I like to think that this entire exercise is to writers what "The Aristocrats" is to comedians. If you're not familiar with "The Aristocrats", it's a joke that usually starts with a man going into a talent agency and saying, "Have I got an act for you!", finishes with the agent saying "That's a hell of an act, what do you call it?" and the man replying "The Aristocrats!", and stuffed in the middle is the most profane, ridiculous, obscene material your mind can come up with. It's a chance for comedians to top each other, show 'em what you've got.

And so it is here. My "good friends" Peter and Kathleen David (who might want to get someone else to start their car tonight) have collected a literal murderers' row of authors who are devoted to telling a story of my demise, each of them trying to outdo the other. It's like the grisliest version ever of Name That Tune:

"I can kill Glenn with a flower vase!"

"I can kill him with a toothpick!"

"I can kill him with an eyedropper full of water!"

"Okay . . . Plan That Manslaughter!"

Third: Various editors have thought I've been dead for years. That IS what they mean when they refer to me as "the late Glenn Hauman" and "Glenn is late again", right?

Fourth: The common advice given to writers is "kill your darlings." With that in mind, I must be truly beloved by these mooks. You've heard it said: Friends will help you move. Real friends will help you move a body. These people wanted the dead body to be mine.

I haven't even been allowed to read their stories yet, I'm going in blind. I don't know who's really ripped me apart, defiled my corpse, and has my veins in their teeth, or who's been respectful and gentle. (Not a single one of them, I'm guessing.) However, I have been informed by many of the authors that this was the easiest story they ever wrote. They just sat down at the keyboard, and an hour later thousands of words had appeared.

Fifth: Let's face it, I probably had it coming.

But for me, there's another weird reason . . . I already have a reasonably good idea of what's going to kill me.

I have an autoimmune disease. It's not a big deal, for the most part, but it is a chronic ongoing grief that requires medication and monitoring for the rest of my days, although I'm lucky enough to not have only a specific number of days left. It comes and goes, so sometimes I have good days, others I wake up and out of nowhere I feel like death microwaved. And it's simply not going to get better, you can't muscle your way through it. It's not my fault, there's nothing I can do to prevent it, and there's only so much I can do to alleviate it. There's no cure. There's an increased risk for some cancers, and there's lots of other little things so that over time, it's the most likely thing to cause my death.

But now? Now I have twenty-one excruciatingly detailed other ways to die that are far more entertaining.

And I find that I'm oddly grateful for that. There's something . . . well, fatalistic about knowing what's going to kill you, even if you don't know when. Instead, I have a variety of exits off this highway to choose from again. It's liberating. Death is inevitable (probably) but knowing how you go shouldn't be.

Anyway, I'm rambling a bit and I know you want to get to what you really came here for . . . you bloodthirsty sickos. No sense putting off the executions any longer.

Anybody got two coins for my ride?

—Glenn Hauman
Live from Death Row

What can I say about David Gerrold that I haven't already said in endless court filings and depositions?

Despite a long and varied career as a novelist and screenwriter, winning Hugos, Nebulas, and writing for Sliders, Babylon 5, and Land Of The Lost, he shall be forever remembered for writing that TV show with the Tribbles, accidentally becoming the first person to describe a yiff pile years before the term was coined. (Go ahead. Google it. I dare you.)

By the way, he's actually been done with the War Against The Chtorr series for years. He's not releasing it just to piss you off. Yes, you.

To him I bequeath the piles of his unsold books still sitting in my garage, minus attorney fees.

# THE KILLING CROAK
## by David Gerrold

SEE THAT SHINING CITY ON THAT HILL?

That's Futuropolis, a marvel of modern society. It gleams and sparkles in the morning sunlight. Its people are proud and joyous, for they live under the protection of one of the greatest superheroes of the 21st Century—How-Man!

How-Man is a strange visitor from another world, his powers derived from the bite of a radioactive scorpion, while simultaneously exposed to a near-fatal overdose of green gamma rays under a yellow sun. The only thing that can weaken him is an exposure to Gorgonite, an impossible mineral that comes from the bizarro universe—more about that shortly.

Under How-Man's vigilant protection, Futuropolis prospers. Its most dangerous criminals are teenage jaywalkers, dog-owners who don't pick up after their pets, and three crazy cat-ladies who have been carefully spayed and neutered.

How-Man has a secret identity, of course. It's so secret, even he doesn't know what it is. So instead, he pretends to be Glenn Hauman, a mild-mannered publisher of soft-core anime and the occasional tentacular effort. His most successful book would have Multiple-Man, had it not been for the injunction filed against it by the real Multiple-Man.

What is How-Man's superpower?

Sidebar: *Everyone* has a superpower. It is built into the laws of super-physics in this particular universe. Most people are unaware of their superpowers. Some have an inkling. Others have discovered their powers by accident.

Examples:

Richard Waiver exists in an emotional sparkle-sphere. He is unaware of it, but the charismatic ripples are such that people want to be in his presence. Richard never has to sleep alone. He has bedded men, women, and a variety of confused animals.

Derry Freedlander gets television parking. Wherever he goes, there is a parking place directly in front of the building, restaurant, or store. He does not have, nor does he need, a blue handicapped sticker.

Marsha Pflug is unable to cook a bad meal. If there is nothing in the house but a can of soup, a can of tuna, a bag of rice, and some frozen vegetables, she will create a Spanish-style jambalaya that would have Guy Fieri begging for the recipe.

Dorble Sanders gets caught by red lights everywhere. He cannot get on the road without there being detours and traffic jams blocking his way. He has never been on time for anything. Arriving late at the airport, missing the flight, he was not onboard when the plane crashed and burned.

Missy Solemnis has never had acne. She has unblemished skin, flawless teeth, and perfect nails. She has never had an orgasm.

Every superpower has a cost to it. The greater the super-power, the greater the burden. The universe demands a balance. It is the Law of Conservation of Coincidence.

The same applies to Supervillains. The greater the villain, the greater his or her weakness.

Supervillains gather in the bizarro universe to arrange vendettas, feuds, and Dungeons and Dragon campaigns. They recuperate from past failures and plan new efforts. Most use their various ill-gotten gains to hire C.A.S.T.L.E. to Construct Awesome Super Terrific Lairs Everywhere. (Listen, somebody has to build all those various fortresses and hideouts and underground lairs. Do you think that volcano just hollowed itself out?)

They also participate in the S.S.S. program—the Supervillain Support Seminars. The supervillain coaches encourage various master villains, journeymen villains, and wannabe bad guys to share their fears, their goals, and their nefarious challenges. Over and over, a common theme appears in their conversations. They all aspire to make a name for themselves. They all aspire to become legendary.

There are few truly legendary villains. There is Yehudi the inescapable, responsible for a million lost buttons in the wash, ten million unmatched socks, and the inevitable failure of the light that's supposed to go off when you close the refrigerator door.

There is Chuck, the bad luck fairy—the creator of the polymorphic error. You go to change the battery in the remote control and the knob on the battery drawer falls off. You go looking for the screwdriver and you cut yourself on the scissors. You go looking for the bandaids and when you open the medicine cabinet a dozen things fall out, some of them going down into the open drain of the sink. At the end of the day, you still haven't changed the batteries in the remote. That's Chuck, the bad luck fairy.

Most people haven't heard of the legendary supervillains—which is why they are able to continue their nefarious efforts. But every supervillain wants to brag of his or her greatest successes. It's part of being a supervillain. And every wannabe villain aspires to the same success. For example, there was Micro-Mite, who proved that even the smallest incident could topple a government. Micro-Mite was responsible for the ill-fitting tape on the door of the DNC headquarters in the Watergate Hotel on June 17, 1972.

Micro-Mite had inherited his superpower from his grandfather, the original Micro-Mike. His greatest success had been to start a fire in the number two coal bunker of the Titanic. Because of the strike by coal minors, the great ship did not have enough coal aboard that they could stop for the night and then restart the boilers the following morning. It had to proceed at full speed through the Atlantic ice fields. It was a gamble on

Micro-Mike's part, but the sinking of the great ship ensured a legendary reputation for the entire family.

Never mind that. This is a different story. Among supervillains, there is one challenge that remains unmastered—the conquest of Futuropolis.

There is one superhero who has never been beaten.

How-Man.

How-Man's eternal vigilance is an impossible obstacle to even the greatest assaults of the most notorious supervillains.

How?

Precisely.

How-Man's superpower is tautology.

Whenever a supervillain arrives in Futuropolis, How-Man is there with his inevitable questions: "How? Why? What's the point?"

These are questions that the average supervillain never considers.

"So, after you destroy the Earth, then what?"

"So, after you kill SuperDuperMan, then what?"

"So, after you own all the gold in the world, then what?"

"What will you have that you don't already have? How many secret lairs do you need?"

Any supervillain capable of conversation greater than "Ugh. Me kill now," will hold up a hand, stop the fight, and say, "Let me get back to you on that."

See, here's the thing.

How-Man understood that you can stop a millipede dead in its tracks by asking it in which order it moves its feet. There's a story told about W.C. Fields, who began his career as a juggler. After a performance at the Palladium Theatre in London, the London Times gave him a laudatory review, praising his juggling skills. That night, Fields tried to watch himself juggle and he dropped his balls everywhere. He had to stop watching and just juggle.

Knowing this distinction—that you cannot observe and do at the same time—How-Man had stopped over a hundred and forty-three attacks on Futuropolis with just a well-timed question. "Why? What's the point?"

This had also reduced his sex-life to zero—at least until his wife convinced him to stop bringing his work home with him.

Some of the smarter supervillains, those who had actually given some thought to their processes, actually enjoyed their conversations with How-Man. When he would say, "Tell me more about that," they would happily expound. At length. Until their emotional energy had been completely dissipated. Like a writer who shares the details of the story at a cocktail party, there is nothing left for the return to the keyboard—the supervillains retired, exhausted, unable to generate any more enthusiasm for destroying the Earth, killing SuperDuperMan, or just irradiating the nation's gold supply.

How-Man had found the fatal weakness in supervillainy.

There is this about supervillains, they are desperate for validation. This is why no supervillain ever kills a hero immediately, not without first explaining the details of his or her dastardly scheme—the validation comes when the hero declares, "You're insane!"

"Yes, of course. Thank you for noticing."

But, despite their collective respect and admiration for How-Man's skill at deconstructing their agendas, every supervillain from Lethal-Man to Honey, the Badger Woman, wanted him dead. The continuing presence of How-Man in Futuropolis existed as a painful thorn in the claw of the supervillain community.

See, it's about context.

Were it not for How-Man, Futuropolis would be just another shining city on a hill. There is no shortage of shining cities. There is no shortage of hills on which to put shining cities. But there is a limited number of superheroes in the world—individuals who have discovered and mastered their innate superpower. And wherever there is someone with a superpower, the universe demands a supervillain of equal power. Everything must be balanced. Everything.

The stronger that How-Man becomes, the more necessary it is for the universe to find a supervillain capable of challenging him, keeping him so engaged in the eternal struggle between good and evil that he cannot unbalance anything else in the cosmos. The universe has its own agenda, you know.

A word about How-Man now.

In his secret identity as Hauman, he is of unassuming appearance. That is, if you ignore the wart, the hump, the incessant drooling, and the bald spot so bright it has an albedo visible from space.

As How-Man, however, costumed in day-glo orange spandex and a shining purple cape, he is an impressive figure. More than one observer has said, "Oh, for God's sake, have you never heard of a dance belt?"

That is another of his secret strengths. Once you have seen How-Man ready for action, you will never get that picture out of your head. That sight alone was enough to send several supervillains fleeing back to the bizarro universe in a state of shock and awe.

So, yes—the supervillain community has put How-Man at the center of its metaphorical dartboard. And several literal ones as well.

It was Flandry Soyce who gets the credit for finally bringing How-Man down. More famously known as Screech Girl, Flandry Soyce gained her unique power as a small child. She had been practicing her voice lessons when she was struck by a rare bolt of polarized red lightning during a magnetic storm under a full moon. It transformed her vocal cords into a weapon of terrifying power. In the years that followed, as she reached maturity, and as she developed and trained her ability, she was able to create a screech that when focused could stop bullets, shatter glass, crumble brick, melt steel, and curdle molten lava. Screech Girl had emptied bank vaults all across the continent, eventually turning most of her wealth into Lootropolitan Bitchcoins.

This particular incident began at the weekly potluck dinner of Supervillains, the Super Sunday Supper Squad meeting at the Fortress of Magnitude. Hellfire brought spicy barbecue ribs, measuring at 5,000 Scovilles—that was the "mild" recipe. Tengu-Tengu, also known as Double Demon, brought a tangy Japanese seaweed salad. Maxwell's Demon brought Baked Alaska, with real Alaska as its primary ingredient. Phase-Man brought a delightfully acidic sorbet. The Harangutan brought an unusual nut dish, but she did not reveal the source of the nuts and no one wanted to ask. Screech Girl arrived with her usual tuna casserole again.

After the meal, over the usual cheese and whine, as the super-villains compared their various plans and goals and challenges—also their various upsets, failures, and disasters—the name of How-Man kept coming up. Finally Screech Girl said, "We cannot beat him with our abilities, we will have to counter his."

"Well, duh," said Captain Obvious, who wasn't quite obvious enough to know that he was tolerated more than appreciated. His super power was unconscious irony. He had brought a container of cole slaw picked up from the local outlet of KFC. (Yes, even in the bizarro universe.)

Ignoring the obvious, Double Demon replied to Screech Girl, "But we have no Gorgonite. The last of it was used as bait when we enfolded SuperDuperMan into the spectre sector."

"And how well did that work? He escaped out the back door!"

"Well, there's always a back door. Just ask Back Door Man." (Also known as Ben Dover in real life.)

"And all the Gorgonite remains in the spectre sector. We have no way of retrieving it. Back Door Man won't do it."

"So what else is there?" asked Hellfire, his flaming aura reduced to just a bare sizzle. "How do we fight naked tautology? Or even well-dressed tautology?"

Micro-Mite spoke up then. "Does anyone remember Swift-Boy?"

"Wasn't he the crippled kid who transformed into a super-hero by shouting SWIFT?" ("Speed-Wit-Intelligence-Flight-Tambourine!") (There wasn't a good super power that started with a T, so he had to settle for standing at the back of the group, shaking a pathetic excuse for a musical instrument.)

"No," said Micro. "I'm thinking of the one from the unex-purgated version of Gulliver's Travails. Remember how they stopped the Gulliver monster before he stomped Lilliputz to smithereens? While he was napping, they tied him down with ten thousand little ropes."

"Didn't the monster eventually break all those little ropes?"

"Yes, finally. That's how they knew he was a monster. But if they'd had stronger ropes—" Micro scratched his antennae. "No, wait. That wasn't my point." He stopped in confusion. "I need a bigger brain."

"Oh, I get it," said Captain Obvious. "It's the ropes. Instead of one big rope, you use lots of little ones."

"But we don't have lots of little supervillains," said Micro-Mite. "I'm the only one."

Screech Girl interrupted with a quick burst of white noise. (She was capable of many different colors of noise, but as a supervillain she was also a bit racist.) "The ropes," she said, "are a metaphor. When we deconstruct the cultural subtext of the narrative, it becomes immediately apparent that the Lilliputzem are meant to be understood as advocates of the entrenched system of tyrannical patriarchy." To their surprised looks, Screech Girl said, "I'm not just a supervillain, you know. I have a Masters Degree in Forensic Literature. Life is about a lot more than building secret lairs, killing superheroes, taking over planets, and irradiating Fort Knox."

"And your point is—?" prompted Hellfire, whose life had been primarily about heating his secret lair, fighting the Iceman, and conquering the uninhabited day side of the planet Mercury. Fort Knox was not on his bucket list.

"The point is, we have to think outside the box."

"Does it have to be a box?" asked Micro-Mite. After a particularly bad experience while trapped in a metal Altoids container, he had developed an aversion to small enclosed spaces.

"Okay, it can be a bottle," said Screech Girl. "We'll think outside the bottle."

"Um, no. I think I prefer thinking outside the box. I had a bad experience in a bottle too. Some children were collecting fireflies and—"

"Okay, okay. We'll just go outside and think."

After the group regrouped outside, she continued, "My point is that our traditional ways of fighting superheroes don't work. We've been fighting the wrong battles on the wrong battlefields with the wrong weapons. That's why we always lose. We need to do something for which there is no defense."

"And that is . . . ?"

Screech Girl smiled. It was an evil smile—a leer of exuberant nastiness, because that was the only kind of smile that Screech Girl was capable of. It was hideous and produced the desired effect in the others at the table. They recoiled in disgust.

She smiled once more, it was too good an effect to waste—and then, having finally shocked the others into awestruck submission, she told them.

It took a while to put the plan in action. It required time and energy and money. Especially money. Lots of money. But supervillains tend to have access to unlimited amounts of stolen coinage, and after manipulating the value of bitchcoins into the realm of quadruple digits, Screech Girl was able to—

Well, you'll see.

Three months later, while enjoying a pleasant spring day in New Jersey, one of only four that would occur in this particular year, How-Man was confronted by a phalanx, a legion of pudgy little men in gray suits, all of them holding thick bundles of documents.

Subpoenas.

"What?" said How-Man. "Why?"

"This one," said the first lawyer, "names you in a class action lawsuit for emotional damage to fifty-three supervillains."

"This one," said the second lawyer, "names you in a class action lawsuit for discrimination against supervillains."

"This one," said the third lawyer, "names you in a class action lawsuit that you and other superheroes exert a magnetic attraction for supervillains, drawing them to Futuropolis like moths to a flame, causing undue emotional damage to the citizens of the city."

"This one," said the fourth lawyer, "names you in a class action lawsuit that you and other superheroes exert an a magnetic attraction for supervillains, drawing them to Futuropolis like moths to a flame, where they cause undue physical and financial damage to the commerce and industry of the city. It also includes a restraining order."

"This one," said the fifth lawyer, "names you in a class action lawsuit that you and other superheroes, because of your magnetic attraction for supervillains, and the resultant emotional, physical, and financial damage you have caused to the residents and businesses of Futuropolis, you have placed an undue burden on the financial resources of the entire insurance industry. It also includes a restraining order."

"This one," said the sixth lawyer, "names you in a class action lawsuit that your presence in Futuropolis, and the attraction you hold for supervillains, requires an extreme investment in emergency management resources, inflating the local and state budgets, causing an unfair tax burden to individuals, businesses, and corporations that function in the city and state. It also includes a restraining order."

"This one," said the seventh lawyer, "names you in a class action lawsuit that your activities as a superhero create an inflated perception of heroism, creating an emotional black hole for young minds in the educational system, and a lifetime of self-esteem issues, when they realize that no matter how good they are at algebra, they will still never be a superhero."

"Wait. No restraining order?"

"The judge threw it out. It was a stretch anyway."

"This one," said the eighth lawyer . . .

It went on all day. And all night. And all the following week.

The lawyers kept arriving. They came by the carload, they arrived by the busload, they arrived with truckloads of documents. They came from the airports and the train stations. They Ubered and Lyfted and they poured out of the subways in an avalanche of gray suits and paper.

How-Man had to rent a warehouse to store the boxes of subpoenas. It was a big warehouse and it still wasn't enough. More and more arrived every day. They came in through the doors. They came in through the roof. They came in through the bathroom window.

The total weight of paper was more than even the bedrock of New Jersey could stand. The total number of pending lawsuits was so extreme that the state judicial system ground to a halt. The state grumbled under the strain—and when critical mass was finally achieved, the ground heaved, a massive belch of tectonic disgust.

It was a lawquake, 6.7 on the Richter Scale.

The warehouse trembled.

And then it collapsed in a terrible thundering slow-motion crash of noise and dust and smoke. It smelled bad too.

It collapsed on How-Man.

All the boxes and boxes of documents came tumbling down in an unstoppable avalanche of legal-length 20-pound stock.

How-Man was buried under so much paper, he couldn't move, couldn't breathe, couldn't escape. It took him seven years to die. (Superheroes do not die easily.)

His last words were, "What? Why?" The *how* of it was no longer a question.

And then . . . nothing.

There was much rejoicing in the bizarro universe. For the first time in living memory, a superhero had been defeated—supervillains had finally won a victory.

But victory is short-lived.

In the realm of superheroes—as well as in the realm of super-villains—no death is permanent.

Everyone gets resurrected. And most of the time, they come back with more power than before. Sometimes they even come back with a blue glow around them.

The rubble trembled. A cloud of dust drifted upward. Bricks and steel moved.

And there, at the center—

How-Man was back.

But he wasn't How-Man anymore.

How-Man the Gray had come back as . . .

Who-Man the Wight.

This time, his questions would be even more penetrating—they would be existential to a fatal degree.

The next supervillain to arrive at Futuropolis was a kaiju-sized figure, a skeletal form that towered thirty feet high. Had there been meat on its bones, it would have weighed nine tons.

It was met by a dazzling vision floating three meters above the ground.

"Who?" the vision demanded in a voice that echoed with profound sepulchral doom. *"Who are you?"*

"Huh? What?"

"No. Who."

"I am the Doctor Who Sues. I am The Malicious Malevolence."

"No, that's your name. *Who are you?*"

"Tremble before me. I am the Tyrant Rex of Judicial Terror!"

"No. That's your function. *Who are you?!*"

"Um . . . I'm not sure I understand the question—"

"Yes. That's the point. *Who are you?!*"

"I am the—um, I'm a harbinger of doom, the destroyer of ambition and aspiration—?"

"No, that's your intention. Try again. *Who are you?!*"

"Wait! What? Your question makes no sense."

"No. *You* don't make sense. How can you *be* anything—how can you *do* anything? If you don't know who you are, then you don't know what you want!"

Okay, one more try. "Who I am is what I do!"

"What you do defines who you are, but it doesn't answer the question, does it? Now begone and don't return until you can speak the truth of who you are!"

"Wait! What?" A very confused Doctor Who Sues demanded, "Tell me this. *Who* are you?"

"I am The Query. I am powerful and unending. I am the inquiry that can never be completed. You may call me Who-Man! And I stand here in defense of Whomanity!"

And as Doctor Who Sues began her cautious retreat, Who-Man added this: "Oh, and one more thing. Lawsuits don't work against me. Because I am not a superhero. I am simply a manifestation of existential dread. You will die, but the inquiry will remain as a continuing process—*who are you?!*"

The Query hung in the air long after the spectral villain had fled back to her boneyard in the bizarro universe—that place where everything is for sale, but the value of nothing is known.

Oh, and one more thing.

Most of the citizens of Futuropolis emigrated within months. They didn't want to stay in Whoville either.

But that's another story for another time.

What can I say about David Mack that I didn't already tell the ER doctors?

David's been wanting to kill me for decades, ever since our days together at NYU. I don't know why. Okay, maybe there was my introducing him to that girl that stole his heart and stomped that sucker flat, but it spurred him into writing his way to a lot of his Star Trek career, including his New York Times best-sellers, where he first got the nickname "the angel of death." For years, we have maintained detente, as we both have vast amounts of incriminating information about each other—but since that truce seems to be out the window, I can now reveal that the big bad "angel of death" is actually a great huge softie with a weakness for kittens and bunnies, and would wear more pink if only it didn't clash with his skin coloring.

To him I bequeath the plague. No, not back issues of NYU's humor magazine, actual plague. Feel that tickle in the back of your throat that you always thought was alcohol burn? That's how you know it's working.

# THE LOOK ON YOUR FACE
## by David Mack

I'M PRETTY SURE THERE ISN'T A JURY ON THE FACE of the earth that'll convict me, but why take the fucking chance? I've got to make this shit disappear.

Blood pools on Glenn's pillowcase while I stand frozen and stare down at his corpse. I want to say this was an accident. I didn't come into Glenn's sty of a dorm room looking to split his skull like a rotten melon. It just worked out that way.

This is a debacle, but I need you to know this: It's all Glenn's fault.

Okay, it's *mostly* Glenn's fault. All right, at least sixty percent.

Not that it matters. Like so many disasters I've endured since I met him here at NYU, it might have been his fault but now it's my problem.

I check his bedside clock. Its face is partly obscured by one of his discarded socks, but I can see enough to tell that it's 7:43

a.m. I don't have time to deal with this right now. I've been awake all night and I'm not thinking straight.

Six hours ago, Glenn came home from his internship at DC Comics. I have no idea what the hell he does there. I'm not sure he did, either. What I know is that he has—had?—a computer and I don't, and that's how we ended up in this mess.

I'm struggling through my sophomore year at NYU's film school. It's the most brutal year at NYU film, the one during which the program tries to weed out everyone who isn't one-hundred-percent committed. I'm up to my neck in classes and production work, sleep-deprived, and perpetually broke. I've been running for months on whiskey, cigarettes, and anger. All of which is to say, I've been a ticking time bomb since September. And Glenn finally set me off.

The clock flips to 7:44. I have forty-six minutes to get to my 8:30 a.m. class, Surrealism in Film, and turn in my latest paper, "Luis Bunuel: Lunatic or Madman?"

I've been up all night writing it on Glenn's shiny new Mac II personal computer. Last night I'd begged him to set up the machine for me so that I could work through the night and, I hope, avoid flunking out of college. Glenn had taken a moment to fiddle with its settings before inviting me to sit down to work while he plodded off to bed. Foolishly thinking that he'd had my best interests at heart, I'd labored through the darkness of the small hours.

Shortly after dawn, my essay of surrealist film criticism complete, I'd entered a simple command into Glenn's computer:
*Print.*

A cryptic error message appeared on the screen, accompanied by the voice of HAL 9000 from the film *2001: A Space Odyssey*: "I'm sorry, Dave. I'm afraid I can't do that."

Exhausted, strung out, overcaffeinated, and short on time, the last fucking thing I'd wanted after spending a whole night contemplating surrealism in film was to be upbraided by the voice of the most psychotic computer in cinema history.

"Glenn!" I roared.

I stormed out of the dining room, down the hall to Glenn's dorm room. We live in what NYU calls "special interest" housing:

two-occupant bedrooms, with women's dorms and bathrooms on one corridor and men's lining the other. At one end are a communal kitchen, dining room, library, living room, and elevator lobby. All on the 11th floor of the East Tower of the Third Avenue North student residence hall.

Glenn had seemed almost amused as I shook him awake.

"Wake up, you bastard! I've got to print my paper! But your dumb fucking machine won't print! Why won't it print?"

He laughed at me, so I shook him harder.

And I heard his head bang against something.

He stopped fighting me. His body went limp.

Blood stained his pillow. I realized that some piece of junk, some toy or geek gadget he'd left on his bed when he crashed the night before had been obscured under a dirty T-shirt. I'd smacked his noggin against it with my full caffeine-plus-nicotine rage.

I stepped back from the body. Looked at the room's other bed, wondering if Glenn's roommate Andy had witnessed my crime. To my relief, Andy was not there. A small stroke of luck in the middle of a giant clusterfuck.

Now it's 7:47, and I'm in some serious shit. I've killed Glenn before he could tell me how to fix the printer error.

I wrap his split-open head in a bunch of his dirty clothes. Luckily for me, Glenn has a reputation for keeping odd hours— sometimes he sleeps all day, sometimes he's gone for days at a time. That works to my advantage. But I can't risk Andy or anyone else coming in and finding Glenn until I figure out what to do with his body. At six-and-a-half feet tall, he'll be hard to miss.

It takes all my strength, but I roll the lanky bastard over so that his blood will pool inside his head wound instead of spilling everywhere. I cover his head with the already bloody pillow.

*Halfway there*, I figure.

I force his arms and legs into a fetal tuck, and then I bury him in his own dirty laundry. Sure, it'll start to smell in a few hours, but this is a college dorm, and it's Glenn. I figure I've got at least forty-eight hours before it gets bad enough to raise suspicion.

I steal one of Glenn's floppy disks. I copy my essay from his Mac. If I skip my shower and run like a motherfucker, I can print my paper at *The Washington Square News* production office, get to class on time, and live to bullshit my instructors another day.

Which is a lot more than Glenn will be doing.

When you need to get rid of a body, always call an Italian.

It's after midnight. Glenn's been dead for about seventeen hours. Most of the 11th Floor's other occupants are out enjoying their Friday night. The rest are gathered with Glenn's roommate Andy in the living room, watching movies and smoking weed.

I regard the mound of Glenn's dead body with my film-school buddies Frank Jannuzzi and Vinny Yacavino. I feel like a shrimp standing next to them. They're both a few inches taller than me. Frank is a hefty sonofabitch, but Vinny is all muscle.

"Jesus," Vinny says. "What a fuckin' mess."

"You really fucked up," Frank says to me.

My temper frays. "Gee, you *think*? Help me out here. The fuck are we gonna do?"

Vinny shrugs. "Maybe we can make it look like an accident."

"Did you sleep through the class on *film noir*? If you want to make it look like an accident, you have to set it up that way ahead of time." I look to Frank for some semblance of insight. "How do we get Glenn out of here?"

Frank crosses his arms on top of his belly and shakes his head. "I don't know, man. It's not like we can just stuff him down a trash chute."

Vinny leans in, curious. "Why not?"

I side-eye him. "Cuz he won't fit, for one thing."

"And it's not like it goes to a furnace," Frank adds. "Some janitor would find the body in with the trash."

A sound from down the hall startles me. I go to the door and check. No one is coming, but my paranoia grows worse with each passing moment. Frank and Vinny watch me, probably to see if I start to have a nervous breakdown. "All right," I say, "we need to be fast. How do we get the body out of here without getting caught?"

Vinny nods toward the window. "Chuck him out."

Frank beams at the idea. "Yeah! It'll look like he jumped."

I shake my head. "Forget it. Won't work."

"Sure it will," Frank says. "We're on the eleventh floor. That's plenty high enough for a fatal drop."

"And if I'd thought of it this morning when he was still warm, it might've worked. But coroners can tell the difference between injuries caused before and after death. Try again."

Concentration creases Frank's forehead. "Can we open the elevator doors? Drop him down the shaft?"

Vinny dismisses the idea with a wave. "No, they'd still find him when he starts to stink. And the elevator lobby's too exposed. Someone going to the can might see us."

With a heavy sigh, Frank checks his watch. "I can't believe I'm giving up my shoot time for this bullshit."

My first instinct is to apologize for fucking up another film student's precious and limited production time. Then an idea blossoms in my imagination.

"What kind of gear did you sign out for the weekend?"

"Standard beta rig," Frank says.

"Any lights or stands?"

"Sure. Full grip kit, cables, some one-Ks and Inky spots."

Now the gears of my imagination are turning. "And how did you move all that shit into your room?"

"I signed out a—" He pauses as understanding widens his eyes. "—a gray cart from the front desk."

"You see where I'm going with this, right?"

Frank nods and looks pleased with himself. What we're doing is heinous, grotesque, and criminal, but there's nothing film students love more than solving logistical problems on a shoestring budget. He gives Vinny an encouraging slap on the back. "C'mon. We're gonna get a cart and grab the gear from my room, then bring it back here."

Vinny wears a dubious expression. "Someone'll see us."

"What they'll see," I tell him, "is film students hauling their gear through Greenwich Village in carts at odd hours. Which is the same dumb shit they see *every* day."

No one on the 11th floor so much as bats an eyelash when Frank and Vinny come back with a rolling gray bin loaded with video gear, lights, cables, and gleaming metal stands. It's a given of life at NYU that film students routinely impose their art upon other students' residential spaces. One either learns to live with it or else one drops out or commits *seppuku*.

My pals reach Glenn and Andy's room as I finish stuffing Glenn's body, his soiled linens, and his blood-drenched pillow inside his oversized laundry bag. It's another bit of good fortune that Glenn liked to send out his laundry only twice per semester, and for that purpose he has this nylon bag . . . which happens to be more than large enough to hold his corpse.

I help Vinny and Frank unpack the video gear from the cart in a hurry. As soon as the three-foot-deep cart is empty, we tilt its angled front forward until the edge meets the floor. I hold the cart in place while Frank and Vinny shove Glenn's sasquatch-esque body into the cart, and then I let his weight settle the bin back into its upright position.

It takes a few minutes for us to cover the body with the film gear. Once everything is in, I check the hallway. Seeing no one there, I give the guys the all-clear sign and we move out.

It's almost a perfect exit. As we stand with the cart in the elevator lobby waiting for one of the two elevators to arrive, Glenn's roommate Andy shuffles past on the other side of the glass doors. His eyes are bloodshot and heavy-lidded. I tense to return whatever greeting he might extend to us, but he ambles on by without seeming to notice our presence.

The elevator on the left opens. We get in with the cart. Frank presses the button for the lobby. No one else gets in between the 11th floor and the ground. I give silent thanks for the fact that NYU is too cheap to pipe insipid *muzak* into its elevators.

On the ground floor, we stick to the pathway that circles the dorm's courtyard, on the far side from the other residential towers. As we pass through the building's main lobby, the security guard never lifts his gaze from his sports magazine.

Lower Manhattan in 1988 is a strange place at most times of the day or night, but it's especially surreal in the small hours of the morning. From one block to the next we pass crack whores working their favorite corner and frat boys vomiting on another. Dive bars sit tucked into basements beneath apartment buildings. Avenues yawn empty for miles, then surge with cars.

It's after two in the morning when we reach the East River. An icy wind off the water stabs at us while we seek a remote spot beneath the Williamsburg Bridge.

Since this is my body to dispose of, Frank and Vinny task me with rounding up cinder blocks from the construction site a few dozen yards away beneath the bridge. Because Frank is a generous soul, he consents to let me waste a shitload of his gaffer tape lashing cinder blocks to Glenn's arms and legs. To prevent the laundry bag from becoming a corpse-flotation device, we toss it, the linens, and the pillow into the river with a cement wedge of their own for ballast.

After I tape four cinder blocks to Glenn, I cast a questioning glance at Vinny. "Think that'll do it?"

"What do I look like? A hit man? I'm a fucking film student, just like you." He beckons Frank. "Let's finish this. I'm freezing my balls off out here."

Frank and Vinny each grab one of Glenn's arms. I lift Glenn by his feet. Together we tote the cement-laden body toward the river and struggle to lift it over the iron railing.

Glenn coughs out a mouthful of blood.

Vinny yelps, Frank howls, and I make a sound like Jerry Lewis achieving orgasm—as we all drop Glenn to the ground, well short of the water, as if he'd suddenly grown fucking porcupine quills.

"The fuck?" Vinny snaps, pacing like a nervous tiger in a cage.

Frank looks ready to shit himself. "He's *alive*? Jesus!"

I kneel beside Glenn. "Hey! Can you hear me?"

"Yes," Glenn says, his voice hoarse. "And your shouting isn't helping my headache." He looks at the cinder blocks gaffer-taped to his limbs. "What the hell is this?"

"Sorry," I say. "We thought you were dead." I choke up, partly out of guilt, but then my mood turns from maudlin to manic, and I start to laugh. "You fucker. You have no idea how close you came. I cracked your goddamned head open. We were three seconds from sinking your dumb ass in the East River, all because your piece-of-shit computer malfunctioned."

Glenn's pained grimace widens into a grin. "No malfunction.

I changed the system error sound, then I unplugged the printer."

"What?"

The big galoot chuckles under his breath. "Figured you'd finish right around the time I had to get up." His chuckle becomes a chortle. "Better than an alarm clock."

"Are you fucking serious? You did this *on purpose?*"

A dopey grin. "It was worth it just for the look on your face."

I stare at him for all of three seconds. Then I turn to Frank and Vinny. "Lift on three."

They take his arms. I grab his legs. We heft Glenn toward the railing.

His mirth turns to panic. "Wait! Stop!"

None of us speak as we dump Glenn into the river.

I know this is murder. I know my motives are petty.

But as I watch Glenn sink into the black water, I feel as if I truly understand him for the first time.

*You're right, Glenn. This is worth it just for the look on your face.*

What can I say about Joe Corallo that would possibly get him out from under the fatwa?

Joe is a queer cisgender white guy who tries to keep his privilege in check. (I'm not telling you this to mock him, just trying to beat him to the punch because he'll tell you. At length.) He writes for Geeks Out, ComicMix, and is the editor on Kim & Kim and co-editor on the Planned Parenthood benefit anthology Mine! He watches every single Hallmark Christmas movie he can, often multiple times. I'm sure he would like me to list his youth and good looks, but—ehh.

To him I bequeath my last check at the Malibu Diner. Pay at the front register, please.

# REVENGE OF THE CLIPPER KIN
## by Joe Corallo

IT'S 1989. GLENN HAUMAN IS FRESH OUT OF COLLEGE and working as a mild mannered production grunt at a major metropolitan funny book publisher. While he is still learning the tricks of the trade, Glenn must remain ever vigilant, for he and he alone is the last line of defense against the scourge of spelling mistakes, gruesome grammatical errors, and continuity catastrophes. He may be young, but he runs a tight ship.

Many comic pages are passed off to Glenn and thoroughly eyed over. You may have even read some of them. One of those comics was a soon-to-be cult classic that we'll just call *The Doomed Men* by a writer whose name we'll take for granted and an artist that goes something like Donald Chase. The first arc of this series has seen these Doomed Men battle with the Clipper Kin, strange beings from another dimension with giant scissor hands. They really don't make a lot of sense, but hey, it's comics!

It didn't seem any different from the other comics that have bounced around Glenn's brain. Just pencils, inks, colors, and lettering arranged in such a way that a story is told. Hopefully a damned good story. Maybe a word is misspelled, or a word balloon is going to get cut off in print. By the time this reaches Glenn there should be almost no errors left to be found. *The*

*Doomed Men* #22, the thrilling conclusion to the Clipper Kin saga, would reach Glenn with a mistake though; a big mistake. A mistake that would come back to haunt Glenn nearly three decades later.

"Hmmmm," Glenn ponders to himself as he pours over the pages of *The Doomed Men* #22. "Don't quite get what the big deal is about this book. Kind of just weird for the sake of . . ."

Glenn pauses. "Wait a minute!" Then lets out a big sigh. "Ahh, Christ." He starts flipping through the Rolodex in the corner of his desk then picks up the phone. "Bob? Yeah. We have a problem."

Storming through the halls of a major metropolitan funny book publisher holding a portfolio folder, Glenn Hauman couldn't look more determined. He found a mistake, and he doesn't take that lightly. Bob wouldn't take that lightly either. He's a top tier editor that only knows the meaning of the word nonsense because he needs to for his job.

Though tall and awkward, Glenn moves through the building and into Bob's office with such grace that Bob could have sworn that his office door had been shut, but before he realizes what's happening Glenn is sitting in front of his desk with the pages.

"The riddle, Bob. It's wrong."

"Your mother ever teach you to knock first?"

"Not when it's this important."

"Yeah yeah, let me see." Bob says as he gestures for the pages with his right hand and doesn't break eye contact from the memo on his desk he's just about finished reading. A few seconds later, Bob sets his sights on those pages.

"*The Doomed Men* #22. People really like this stuff, huh?"

"Don't ask me, Bob. I just make sure they're printer ready."

Bob flips open to the pages Glenn noted and starts reading.

"The Clipper Kin have the Doomed Men right where they want them, " Glenn explains. "The only chance the Doomed Men have is to answer the riddle of the Clipper Kin. Which they do. But it's wrong, Bob. The answer is wrong."

Bob looks it over with his eagle eye. "Yes and no," Bob says as his right index finger carefully maneuvers around the page.

"See here? One of these guys always lies, and the other always tells the truth. We adjust the tail on this word balloon right here; easy fix."

"Well, yes, but I just wanted to run it past . . ." Glenn begins to say before getting cut off.

"Yes, yes." Bob replies as his attention to this matter is waning. "Run along and get it done."

Glenn rushes off so fast he forgets to shut Bob's door. As Bob marches towards the door to his office and grabs a hold of the knob, he leans forward a bit and shouts out, "And you knock first next time, Hauman! You knock!"

By that afternoon, the page had been fixed. The Doomed Men defeated the Clipper Kin justly and properly. The series would go on to thrill and baffle audiences for decades as Glenn Hauman would go on to thrill and baffle the greater geek community in new and exciting ways for decades as well. Few would ever know the story of how Glenn stood up to the absurd and made this strange comic make slightly more sense than it otherwise would have. The Clipper Kin know though. It's something they haven't forgotten. And something that Glenn will be remembering when he least expects it.

It's the present day, or pretty close to it. Specifically, it's a chilly afternoon in the fall that is quickly rolling into evening out in Northern New Jersey. Glenn Hauman has the house to himself, spare a couple of cats, as his wife Brandy is away on a business trip. The Diet Mountain Dew cans have begun piling up as he's powering through updating a client's website while he's checking in with a printer.

"Yeah, the con is next month." Glenn says, "50 copies. Yeah, we got plenty of the other books. Just need to restock on that one. Maybe. Let's touch base after the con. I'll bash on some numbers."

The doorbell rings.

"Gotta go. Yeah, it's the same card on file." Glenn hangs up as he walks over to his front door.

Glenn looks perplexed as he approaches the door and notices that no one is there. After a moment he realizes he should probably look down. It's then that Glenn notices the modest sized box addressed to him. He picks it up and starts examining.

"Hmmm, no return address."

He starts feeling the chill of the early evening and decides it's time to get back inside to further examine the box. Glenn lumbers into the dining room and sets the box down before plopping into a chair in front of it. After digging through his pockets for a few seconds, he gets a firm grip of his car keys and starts cutting through the tape on the box carefully; a ritual he's clearly performed countless times and takes some level of pride in his surgical precision.

Carefully, Glenn opens the top of the box to find some brown paper crushed in at the top protecting its contents. Much to his surprise he finds those contents to be multiple copies of a new printing of *The Doomed Men* Volume 1. Leaning back, Glenn takes the top copy out the box and begins to flip through.

"Didn't know they were doing a new printing. Not liking the glossy paper." Glenn mutters to himself as he's going through the book. "They finally made that color correction. That's good."

Then Glenn gets to the riddle of the Clipper Kin. He reads it all again and savors it.

"Ah yes, the riddle of the Clipper Kin. Technically, if I didn't solve this then they would have beaten the Doomed Men. Being technically correct is the best kind of correct, after all."

Glenn continues to talk to himself, as many a cat owner do.

"You know, I still owe Don Chase a call anyway. He should know more about this new printing."

Picking his iPhone back up that's still warm for his last call, Glenn opens up Don's contact information. After a couple of rings, a familiar voice is heard through the phone.

"This is Don."

"Don, it's Hauman. You have a minute?"

"Oh, yes. This about Baltimore?"

"Partly. You still up for sharing a table?"

"Yeah, that would be great. You'll be helping me set up then Thursday night?"

"Sure thing! Now, I had something else to ask you about."

"Of course, Glenn! What is it?"

"I just got the new printing of *The Doomed Men* Volume 1 in the mail. I never got comps of the other recent printings, but it didn't have a return address so I don't know who sent it."

Glenn hears nothing as Don pauses for seconds. "Don, you still there?"

". . . Yes." Don eventually gets out. "There is no new printing though."

"What do you mean?" Glenn exclaims as he grabs the copy he was flipping through with his free hand and starts waving it about, much to the alarm of his cats. "I'm holding it in my hands right now."

"Glenn, I'm sorry but there definitely is no new printing. I would know. I drew the damn thing."

"You and I both know that it doesn't always pan out that way in this business." Glenn says in part out of indignance, but also in the hopes of lightening the mood.

"Yes, that may be true, but I'm sorry Glenn there isn't a new printing. I don't know what to tell you."

"Then how do you explain this book, Don?"

"Like I said, I don't know what to tell you. I'm sorry. See you next month at Baltimore?"

Glenn lets out his patented long exacerbated sigh. "Yes, of course. See you then."

The two hang up. Then Glenn sits back down and stares at the mysterious box.

Glenn plops down in his living room wielding a wireless mouse in one hand and a Diet Mountain Dew in the other. He feverishly looks through tab after tab on his laptop as he desperately tries to get information on this mysterious new printing of *The Doomed Men* Volume 1. Each click leaves him with more questions and less answers. Google, Amazon, Twitter, Comic Vine, it's nowhere to be found.

After taking a break to feed his increasingly vocal felines, Glenn sits back at the dining room table to see if he can find the answers he's looking for in the book itself. He starts going through the credits trying to see if there may be a clue in the publisher credits.

"No . . . nothing there."

In his frustration he begins flipping through the book thinking that perhaps he could find something different. Maybe these are uncorrected preview copies. That might explain why this new edition isn't available yet. If that is true though, why would Glenn Hauman be receiving these in the mail? He hasn't been working on comics with this major metropolitan funny book publisher in quite some time.

Glenn was perplexed to the point of nervousness. He decided the best course of action would be to get some fresh air and pick up more Diet Mountain Dew to feed his jitters. After standing in front of his car for nearly a minute contemplating if it was worth it to take the drive and likely sacrifice his parking space (it's not easy to find parking in North Jersey) he ultimately decides to go for it.

An increasingly frazzled Glenn Hauman lumbers through the supermarket. Though he's been up and down these aisles countless times, he's rarely ever been this distracted before. After losing himself in thought a couple of times on the way, he finally reaches his destination. The real question is, does he go for cans, twenty ounce bottles, or a two liter? Once he determines what will get him the most amount of Diet Mountain Dew for the least amount of cost (on this day it's a box of twelve cans) he heads to the register. Okay, maybe he got a box of chocolate covered graham crackers too. Brandy's out of town anyway, after all.

Opening the passenger seat of his car door, Glenn drops in the couple of items he picked up at the store. As he walks around the car to get to the driver's side door, he realizes he had missed a call from Don Chase. After sitting down, starting up his car and setting up his phone, Glenn calls Don back.

"This is Don."

"Don, Glenn. You rang?"

"Oh, yes! Glenn, what you told me seemed so off that I made a few calls. There is most certainly not a new printing ready. In fact, when I talked to the collected editions editor, they told me it was funny I had called because they wanted me to write a foreword for the next edition for the big anniversary next year!"

"Great, Don . . . great. I'm happy for you, don't get me wrong, but I don't know what I have sitting on my dining room table."

"You keep your books on the dining room table?"

"No, Don, I just . . . look, thank you for letting me know. I appreciate it. Gotta find parking now. Bye!"

"Ahh, Christ." Glenn lets out under his breath as he sees his parking space, and many others, have been taken. After taking a lap around the block, Glenn finds a space that's not as close to his liking, but it'll do. Lucky for him, he only bought the essentials earlier.

Once he manages to unlock the front door which was more difficult than it should have been as he refused to put down his groceries to do it, Glenn marches straight to the kitchen. He fills a plastic Tiki cup with ice, unloads a whole can of Diet Mountain Dew in it, and opens up the box of chocolate covered graham crackers to have one or two before bringing them into the dining room to continue working.

As Glenn makes his way into the dining room he tries to think of what all of this could mean as he sips his drink and hopes it will focus him. Glenn Hauman will find himself very focused in mere seconds, but it won't have anything to do with feeding his Diet Mountain Dew addiction.

The Tiki cup that Glenn was holding slips from his hand and bounces around his feet spilling the entirety of its contents. The box of chocolate covered graham crackers hit the floor on its side with only a few casualties sliding onto the floor. Glenn has walked in to something he never thought he would—*The Doomed Men* books have all been cut up as if by giant scissors with a message on the wall made up from the cut up paper reading, "Revenge Of The Clipper Kin."

At first Glenn recoils, shivering. He slowly approaches the paper clipping sign on the wall and touches it as if he didn't think it could possibly be real. Nervous, he decides it would be best to think further about this elsewhere. As he has this thought, he realizes he left his phone and car keys in the kitchen.

Not knowing what to expect, Glenn walks back towards the kitchen. As he turns the corner, he's terrified to discover two Clipper Kin slowly moving towards him. These featureless ruby red marionette dolls with giant shiny obsidian scissorhands begin to extend their arms far as if about to take flight. They reveal more messages clipped out in paper. The one to Glenn's left reads, "You solved the riddle and we lost," as the message from the one on the right reads, "We waited so long. We will now have our revenge."

Despite how absolutely horrifying this otherworldly experience unfolding in front of Glenn's eyes is, he can't help but think to himself how these Clipper Kin have stronger motivation and clearer goals than the ones that appeared in *The Doomed Men*. Conceding that his phone is a lost cause, Glenn thinks of the spare set of car keys he has in his basement office and decides to make the only decision he thinks he can. He rushes out of the room, slams the door behind him, and makes his way to the basement entrance.

As Glenn rushes towards the basement door, large shut obsidian scissors cleave through the door and begin to open up. He shuts the basement door hoping it will buy him some time, and tosses folding chairs and other cumbersome items behind him to create some obstacles. All the while, the haunting sound of giant scissors opening and cutting over and over can be heard throughout the house.

Rummaging through his desk, Glenn is getting closer and closer to finding his car keys. He has some minor comfort in that there are a couple of doors and some objects in the way before they could even get to him. But now Glenn is holding his keys, and the Clipper Kin are not to be seen. Perhaps he'll make it out yet. That is, until he hears the basement door come crashing down.

Glenn remains perfectly still, and it takes him a moment to realize he started holding his breath. Seeing no other option in front of him, he ducks behind the couch in his basement office and waits. Maybe they won't notice him, he thinks to himself. After all, what can he do? And after a couple of minutes, he thinks it may have even worked.

Slowly and quietly, Glenn gets to the door to his office, and opens it. He looks around and sees the basement door had fallen down the stairs and that the Clipper Kin have made a mess, but they appear to have gone deeper into the basement as the sound of their giant scissors are feint. To Glenn's right is an exit from the basement to the side of the house. He could slip out that way and bolt to the car. After thinking on it for a couple of seconds, Glenn acts. He ascends the stairs quicker than you'd think, even given the situation, and makes his run for it to the car.

After he passes a few houses, Glenn looks back to make sure he's in the clear. While he doesn't seen any Clipper Kin, he can still hear their scissors opening and closing. At this point he doesn't know if he's just imagining in or not. It doesn't matter anymore though; he's reached his car.

The door shuts faster and harder than Glenn meant it to and startles himself. He instinctively makes sure the doors are locked two or three more times as he starts the car. While he's in the middle of switching gears from park to reverse, giant scissors pierce through the passenger side door almost making it to Glenn.

Panicked, Glenn rushes out of the car forgetting it's still in reverse. His car slowly backs into the car behind it, setting off the car alarm as Glenn doesn't bother looking back this time. No one has ever witnessed Glenn running this fast in his adult life.

The haunting sound of those scissors fills Glenn's ears as it gets louder and louder. He doesn't know where it's coming from anymore, just that he has to get away. Suddenly, Glenn can't feel his legs anymore. He's stopped running and he doesn't understand why. It feels as though he's sliding. Then he realizes as the front of his body leans all the way forward and is crashing down that the Clipper Kin must have gotten him from behind. There's nothing he can do now except to wait for his upper half to crash into the sidewalk and to briefly contemplate how this chain of events was definitely above the paygrade of a production assistant.

What can I say about Robert Greenberger that hasn't been written on a high school bathroom wall?

You've already seen some of my backstory with Bobby G.B. in the previous story, and I'm hard pressed to write anything mean because he's so . . . nice. I mean, a real sweetheart. Everyone says so. Heck, he was even willing to take the blame for After Earth tanking at the box office. And if there was any dirt that could be used on him, it would have come up during the cutthroat political campaign for becoming a member of the Fairfield, CT Parking Authority. (Vicious campaign—bicycle tires flattened, flowerpots knocked over, ivy replaced with rhododendrons. Chicago machine politics has nothing on these guys.)

To him I bequeath my copy of Issac Asimov's The Sensuous Dirty Old Man.

# "IS IT YOU?"
## by Robert Greenberger

"IS IT YOU?"

The tall, bearded man looked over his shoulder and saw that an older black woman was addressing him. She was smartly dressed as if she were attending church although it was only Thursday. They were standing in the broad passageway of the Pennsylvania Convention Center, near the passage to the adjacent Philadelphia Marriott Hotel.

He was wearing Jedi robes, being photographed as part of SciFi.com's coverage of the 59th World Science Fiction Convention, otherwise dubbed Millennium Philcon. The place was cavernous, with one attendee quipping it was large enough to house several zeppelins. The multiple levels were filled with attendees in various outfits, everything from t-shirts and shorts to chainmail armor. As a result, he looked as if he fit in and she, in her floral print dress made of some stiff satin, sensible black flats, and large dark purse, seemed overdressed.

Her question interrupted the photo shoot and he looked at her, realizing this was an odd case of mistaken identity.

"You're . . . him," she said, her voice rapidly filling with awe, her eyes glistening in the light. He saw her breathing was growing heavier and she seemed on the verge of . . . something.

It was then he recalled that the facilities were not entirely given over to the science fiction convention but also a religious meeting of some sort. The denomination escaped his recall but it dawned on him that she was clearly unaware of the weekend's main event. Instead, she was a believer and saw what she wanted to see.

What she saw was a tall, brown-haired, bearded man in robes that would not be out of place in the Middle East, specifically Jerusalem. Back in New York, he and a colleague were similarly shaggy in appearance and differentiated themselves as Big Jesus and Little Jesus. Add in the Jedi attire and he could see how a religious person would see the Messiah and not Obi-Wan Kenobi.

"You've come back," she got out in a timid voice. "Just like the Good Book promised."

He had no idea what to say, unwilling to shatter her belief. That he had nothing to say was a rarity and that caught his attention.

"I don't know what to say."

"I am in your presence, that should be enough," she continued.

He shifted from foot to foot, growing increasingly uncomfortable with the encounter. At that moment, he regretted wearing the robes, wishing he had dressed as an Orc or a Vulcan instead. At least Vulcans had pointed ears to avoid any confusion. Indeed, their general Satanic appearance might have caused the woman to steer clear of him.

"You've graced our meeting with your presence," the woman said. Each utterance seemed carefully considered and practiced in her mind before she spoke. "We . . . are honored. No, we're blessed."

She wasn't meeting his eyes although now she looked directly into his face. She didn't notice the amused photographer behind the imposing figure or the passersby, some in alien garb, pirate gear, and one remarkably faithful Denslow Tinman.

Wishing to be rid of her, the man gestured vaguely in the air over her head. "Be well, my child."

She uttered something unintelligible and hurried off, not looking back.

He exchanged shrugs with the photographer, had his picture snapped, and went on to tell any and all about the odd encounter for the remainder of the weekend. It was certainly a highlight for him and a great story about how worlds collide.

What Glenn Hauman didn't anticipate was what happened when she too told of the encounter.

The woman hurried back to her congregation, come by bus from Georgia. Once Alva Payton found her fellow parishioners, they could tell something was wrong. They made her sit and their leader, Pastor Thomas Wells, got her a cup of water. Finally, she managed to explain that she had been out in the hall, coming back from the Ladies' Room, when she saw Jesus.

The pastor raised his eyebrows high in surprise while some of the others exchanged glances. Clearly, she had seen something or someone, but Jesus? That didn't seem right. If the Son of God were to walk among them, why not in their meeting rooms, and why just to Alva? They knew she lived and breathed the Gospel of the Lord, more so than most folk, but did that earn her something special? Could it have been a hallucination? It was awfully hot and the ride in the un-air-conditioned bus had left several feeling poorly. They silently communicated these questions among themselves as Alva once more repeated her encounter.

The Southern Baptist Congregation had come to Philadelphia to attend "For His Glory," to listen to James G. Merritt, a minister and denominational leader, among other notables. They had saved and fund-raised for a year to make sure the largest contingent possible could attend.

While Alva had been out, the others had commented on the costumed heathens. Several of the congregation had been invited by others to actually protest the ungodly actions later. Two had readily agreed, intending to crash several of the science fiction panels after the midday prayer service.

"He blessed me. Me," she repeated.

The pastor prayed it had been something innocent and nothing to worry about.

One parishioner, though, William Johnson, was frowning. Something felt wrong about this report. He muttered, "Yet for us there is one God, the Father, from whom are all things and for whom we exist, and one Lord, Jesus Christ, through whom are all things and through whom we exist."

Alva looked up at him. "Corinthians."

William, a black man past sixty, going to fat with a belly sticking over his belt, straining at the buttons of his crisp white shirt, nodded. He ran a hand over his balding scalp, still sweaty from the late August heat, and just shook his head. Like the others, he wasn't thrilled to be sharing the convention center with these godless people but he was content to let them be, refusing to join the protests. If God needed him to act, he'd know when.

"You sure about this, Alva?"

"I know I saw our Lord and Savior," she replied, her voice firm.

Johnson was less than convinced and set out to see this "lord" for himself. He exited the conference room and was bombarded with colorfully clad men and women, more than a few in shameless attire. He had heard there was some freak show sharing the convention center but hadn't known just how many would be out and about. He studied his surroundings, making certain he could find his way back, and explored the rest of the second level.

Like his own Baptist meeting, there were meetings in the smaller rooms, some sort of blasphemous art show in another, and many people of all ages who should have showered before going out in public.

Johnson didn't like what he saw, not at all.

He also didn't see Jesus. His presumption was that if their Shepherd had presented Himself to Alva Wells, a nice, but somewhat blundering woman, He would make His presence felt elsewhere. The faithful were plentiful at the meeting and Jesus would surely want to speak to all His believers, not just one woman.

In the distance, he saw the robes Alva had described but the man was not bearded, had short hair, and couldn't possibly be mistaken for Jesus. Still, Johnson hurried to get closer and see if this was some form of pretender. He felt out of place in his black suit and did what he could to avoid coming into contact with any of these people. He suspected most were not of the faith and dismissed them from his thoughts. His quarry, though, might be something different.

He drew closer as the man in the beige and taupe robes was chatting to someone in a quiet voice. They were discussing some book or movie, nothing holy at all. Then the other called him "Thomas," and Johnson nodded, ruling the man out as just someone in a costume.

However, Alva said she had seen Jesus, or a man who looked like Jesus, so where might he be?

Nearly an hour later, after growing weary of the hunt, Johnson began heading back to the meeting in defeat. As it was, he had missed a lecture that had intrigued him, putting him in a foul mood. That was when he spotted "Jesus." The imposter had his arm around a far shorter woman, acting in a most familiar way that did not seem at all holy. Yes, he could see how someone like Alva might mistake this man for Jesus, there were enough similarities, although he spotted something she had clearly missed:

He was wearing a plastic sleeve with a name badge.

Why would the Son of God need a name badge?

"For false Christs and false prophets will arise and perform great signs and wonders, so as to lead astray, if possible, even the elect," Johnson said to himself, quoting Matthew and growing angrier with every step.

This false Jesus, this blasphemer, needed to be dealt with before other poor souls like Alva were taken in. She had merely received a useless blessing; others could be dealt far worse. He could speak to the pastor, but that man only talked of peace. Sometimes lessons had to be harsh and painful and this felt like one of those times.

The false god's name was Glenn. He would remember the name and the face, find him later, and deliver that lesson.

Whenever the meeting broke up over the next few days, Johnson said he was going to stretch his legs, get some exercise. While others went out into the streets or over to the Reading Market to seek food and souvenirs, he stalked the convention center. Each day there seemed to be more people, and more dressed in foolish or outlandish attire. It practically hurt his eyes to look upon the garish colors. As he walked, his look of disapproval clear on his craggy face, his eyes scanned for the false god.

At least once, he spotted this godless Glenn, no longer dressed as Jesus. In fact, once he was in a jacket, shirt, and tie, looking more businessman than freak. Still, he had fooled Alva, who continued talking about the encounter, and could be fooling others. The lesson clearly needed to be delivered.

On Sunday—the Lord's Day, of course—he crossed close enough to this Glenn to overhear him tell of the encounter. It wasn't with reverence but with humor.

"She truly believed me to be Jesus. What could I do? I genuflected over her head, told her to go and sin no more and she left, happy."

The gaggle around him tittered, clearly enjoying this woman's humiliation. It made Johnson exceedingly angry and he decided today was the day he would act. Glenn needed to learn his lesson and what better day than the one where people sacrificed in the name of God?

His hand patted his pocket. The slight bulge was comforting.

Glenn made his farewells and walked down the corridor, hurrying off to some other event. Johnson followed him, ignoring all the others around him in these crowded hallways. There seemed to be some shift in the schedule. People were pouring out of rooms, while others lined up to gain access. Glenn turned right to enter one of the rooms and Johnson tentatively followed. The sign outside proclaimed that in a few minutes there would be a concert with David Honigsberg and Friends. So far, no one was there to see this performer, a name Johnson didn't know.

Glenn was looking around, checking his watch, then some electronic gadget. So preoccupied was he that Johnson was able to size him up in private. He was tall and on the lean side. Dressed in what were clearly casual clothes, he less resembled Jesus than some aging hippy.

Slowly, Johnson withdrew the folding knife, the one his grandfather had given him, claiming it had been in the family for generations. If true, it could be traced back to the days of slavery before they were freed. The weapon would now deliver a different kind of freedom.

"You think it's okay to fool a woman like Alva?" Johnson's voice was steady and clear. Glenn looked up from the gadget and over to Johnson. He bore a grimace of confusion, which made sense.

"I'm sorry . . . ?"

"You led that poor woman astray; let her think you were something divine."

A look of recognition crossed Glenn's face. "I'm sorry if you think I did something wrong."

It was then Glenn spotted the switchblade, not yet opened, in the man's beefy fist. His eyes darted toward the door, behind Johnson, who was now approaching. The eyes went wide and he stammered something unintelligible.

"She couldn't sleep on the bus," Johnson declared, "she was so exhausted but excited to be here. To hear the Gospel and discuss the Lord's good works. We had high hopes, but you went and gave her a thrill. A false thrill, making her believe she had a divine encounter."

"I know; she mistook my *Star Wars* costume for something else. I'm really sorry but you don't . . . "

"You were laughing about it, laughing at her gullibility. How many others did you dupe?"

Glenn started at that. "Dupe?"

"Making others think you were Jesus and blessing them and then laughing at them behind their backs."

"I wasn't laughing at her, but the situation was funny. Mistaking my Jedi robes for Jesus."

"It's not funny to me and certainly wouldn't be to Alva if she ever finds out."

"Really, I didn't mean anything by it," the imposter stammered.

That's when the blade silently popped into view, fluorescent light gleaming off it. Glenn took a step back, bumping up against the walls, eyes once more looking at the door. The performer and audience were nowhere to be found.

"Why?"

"'For the Lord your God is a consuming fire, a jealous God.' And you pretended to be something you're not," Johnson replied. He was feeling clear-minded and righteous, ready to do the Lord's work.

"But I told you, it was a case of mistaken identity. You don't have to hurt me over a misunderstanding."

Johnson neared, tightening his grip. He liked the look of fear in the taller man's eyes, the quick breathing. He studied the long torso and determined an ideal spot to strike. It wasn't going to be all that different from slaughtering a hog like he had back on his daddy's farm all those years ago.

"I can't have you fool anyone else."

He lunged forward, Glenn twisted, and the blade sliced neatly through the shirt, the skin, and into the soft tissue below the rib cage. Glenn let out a yelp.

"I won't have you laughing at Alva," Johnson said, neatly adding a second cut, deeper than the first and just above. He had hoped to go right for the heart like his daddy taught him, but he underestimated how tall Glenn was. This time, the yelp was extended and higher. Glenn weakly waved at Johnson, his longer arms only managing to ineffectively brush against the older man's arms.

A third stab was lower, making Glenn bend over. This time he said nothing, his arms trying to defensively wrap around his bleeding belly. The blood was oozing through the torn shirt, beginning to drip onto the faded brown carpet.

"H-help . . . " he cried, but couldn't muster much volume so only Johnson heard him.

" 'Behold, I am bringing punishment upon Amon of Thebes, and Pharaoh and Egypt and her gods and her kings, upon Pharaoh and those who trust in him,'" Johnson added as the fourth and deepest slice opened up his target's abdomen.

Glenn toppled over as Johnson stood watching. He then murmured a prayer and quickly left the room. He'd let the concertgoers find out what true vengeance looked like.

A day later, Johnson impassively watched the news report about the mysterious convention murder as he packed to go home. The rest of the meeting had been good and he felt at ease. He had come to hear the word of the Lord, had done work in the Lord's name, and had protected a friend's reputation.

Overall, he thought the weekend had worked out wonderfully well.

And then Jesus walked in, and He looked pissed . . .

What can I say about Russ Colchamiro that the 60 Minutes expose didn't cover?

I've often said that Russ looks like Richard Gere, except shorter, doughier, and with close cropped hair to hide . . . okay, maybe not so much after all. Russ doesn't have the worst reputation in New York real estate, but that's because it's a business that includes Jared Kushner and Donald Trump. A nice quiet guy living in a NYC suburb with his wife and 2.4 kids, Russ has everything a man could want—except for respect, friends, and a Hugo award.

To him I leave yet another cover to his novel Crossline. He changes the cover once a year or so, about the same time he changes his toothbrush.

# THE HARDWICKE FILES:
# THE CASE OF HAUMAN'S COMET
## by Russ Colchamiro

AS A PRIVATE EYE WHO WORKS BOTH SIDES OF THE Universe, I'm a woman who gets called into cases of every stripe. I usually don't get involved in Earth business—too much baggage, too much drama—but sometimes I can't help myself.

I've done a few jobs with Renfro before—long story for another day—so when I got word through back channels that he was asking for me, I figured, what the hell? I could use a break from the usual. So I start with the obvious questions.

"What do you mean Halley's Comet has been suspended from orbiting the Universe? How is that even possible?" I say.

I can think of at least nine reasons, but I want to hear it from him.

Drudge, his executive assistant, answers for him. "Hauman. Glenn . . . Bloody . . . Hauman."

"Sorry," I say, "but who and what is a Hauman?"

Renfro stands from his mahogany desk, leans against the large window, and gazes out at what the locals call the Space Needle. We're in Seattle. It rains here. A lot.

"Who is Glenn Hauman?" Renfro asks, twirling a cigar he's

not technically permitted to light indoors, but will anyway.
He's a nebbish with thin brown hair and delicate features, who
despite being just 38 years old dresses like his grandfather, in a
dark, three-piece suit, and a shirt and tie buttoned to the neck so
tight his eyes bulge. "Who is Glenn Hauman?" He turns to face
me. "I'll tell you who Glenn Hauman is."

Renfro's stare is blank, but behind those beady little eyes
burns a rage so fierce he can barely articulate himself. "Drudge,"
he says, and waves his cigar hand, "tell her."

Drudge composes himself. "Glenn Hauman is the devil himself. He is the bane of our very existence. He is, and pardon me
for being a tad indelicate, a bastard. An oafish, giant-headed,
ridiculously bearded bastard."

"Uh-huh," I say, and place my fedora on my knee. Classic
client. They want me to know how upset they are so I'll take
them seriously. Oaf. Bastard. Got it. "Can you be a little more
specific?"

"Miss Hardwicke," Drudge continues. "Renfro Incorporated
has been in the celestial branding, acquisition, and consignment
business for the better part of forty years, dating back to Renfro
Senior, who practically created this industry himself. We have
branding agreements with dozens of comets, and pending
contracts for three more. In fact, they're on this very desk for
signature right now."

He taps the desktop for effect. In case I was confused which
desk he meant.

"Four," Renfro corrects.

"Four, correct, sir. My apologies. My point is that—and being
a woman of, shall we say, galactic origins—I'm sure it would
come as no surprise for you to learn that securing these contracts
does not come easily."

He's right about that. I know more about the comet industry
than I'd like to, but it's an occupational hazard. When you're a
private eye from Eternity—the realm responsible for the design,
creation, and maintenance of the Universe itself—dealing with
comet designers, construction managers, and, of course, branding firms is unavoidable.

"This is great, fellas, but what's he done? Hauman. What's

your beef with the big oaf? And what do you want from me?"

"What's he done?" Renfro paces his office. "What's he done? Have you heard of a science fiction writer by the name of Gavin Berrold?" I shake my head no. "Gavin Berrold is a semi-successful writer of silly stories and TV shows about spaceships and time travel and dinosaurs and that sort of nonsense."

Drudge weighs in. "I liked that episode he did with the little furry critters that nearly took over NASA. *The Problem with Prodos*. Those little guys were cute."

Renfro shoots Drudge a look, then continues. "It turns out that this Hauman doofus fancies himself a publisher of sorts, and, by hook or by crook, befriended Berrold, who's looking for a late career resurgence. They've partnered on a series of children's books, the first of which is called *Halley's Comet is My Best Friend*."

I still don't see where this is going, but I indulge him. "And . . . ?"

"And?" Renfro mocks, as if I'm missing what he believes to be obvious. "And . . . ?"

"We hold the trademark on Halley's Comet," Drudge says. "We are the legal owners of the name."

"I still don't see the holdup."

"The holdup," Renfro repeats, "is that we own the name!"

"Yes. You said. Twice now." I like to rile him up. Makes it worth the trip. The veins in his neck start to throb.

"We've filed an injunction," Drudge says. "Hauman and Berrold are legally bound to cease and desist all production and marketing of their book. The name belongs to us."

"You'll have to forgive me, fellas, but what's the difference if they publish their book or not? In what possible way does that affect you?"

That one sets Renfro off. "That's not the point! The name is ours, we said he can't use it, and that's that!"

I've never seen Renfro so upset. Hauman's really gotten under his skin. Now I want to meet him, just to see what the big oaf is all about.

"Don't you have lawyers for this kind of thing? If you hold the trademark, this should be a pretty simple case, no?"

Drudge grumbles. "The bastard sued us right back."

"Sued you? For what?"

"For fair use infringement. He claims that Halley's Comet is in the public domain, and therefore he and Berrold are legally entitled to use the name free and clear."

"Hmm. Yeah. I could see that."

"Hardwicke!" Renfro shouts. "Stop taking his side!"

I chuckle. I can't help it. "Take it easy, Eddie, take it easy. I'm on your side. But even if he's suing you back, what's the hold up?"

"The judge slapped an injunction on us! He's suspended Halley's Comet from orbiting the Universe until this is resolved! I'm losing a fortune!"

I've seen planets born and die. I've tracked killers and arsonists. I've been kidnapped, trapped off-world, and even worked a case where two energy waves barreled across the Universe on a collision course that almost initiated the next Big Bang.

But even this is a new one on me.

"So what you're saying is that this guy, this Glenn Hauman, is legally preventing one of the most famous and recognizable comets in the Universe from cruising the cosmos . . . over a children's book?"

Renfro looks to Drudge. Drudge looks to Renfro. They both look away. Then they look at me. Renfro offers a slight, reluctant nod. "That's the gist of it."

"And you want me to look into Hauman and Berrold and see if there's anything I can dig up on these guys to get them to drop their claim?"

"Yes," Renfro says. "As soon as possible."

I make my way to the window. Gray clouds stretch across the region. Lots of grass. Lots of trees. Lots of rain. The Space Needle stands out among the green. Apparently, there's a restaurant inside. Back home I've got two missing persons cases and an unsolved murder I'm supposed to be working on. But sometimes I need to mix things up.

"Okay, fellas. Hauman sounds like a character. I'll check him out."

Renfro flies me first class to New York. Airplanes are so painfully slow and crowded, I don't know how Earthlings tolerate it.

Then I hop a yellow cab from JFK Airport into Manhattan and stop at a dump called the Malibu Diner. It's got a maroon awning out front, dim lighting, and worse food—by magnitudes—than many of the prisons scattered throughout the Universe.

I order a cheeseburger, medium rare. It's awful. Yet the place is packed. Go figure.

I'm in a booth, near the back, where Hauman is with his friends, three science fiction nerds who are vigorously debating which version of some TV series called *Star Trek* is the best: TOS, whatever that means, *The Next Generation*, *Voyager*, *Discovery*, or *Deep Space Nine*.

I can't follow the logic of their arguments, but that's because they're yelling so loudly at each other and interrupting so often their voices muddle together.

And then Hauman leads me where I want to go. He is in fact a large oaf of a man, nearly six-foot four with long, shaggy hair, a barely kempt beard, and thin glasses.

"So," he says to his friends, all middle-aged white guys with varying degrees of white and/or thinning hair, "have I told you the latest on my lawsuit?"

His friends let out a collective grumble. "Here we go," the grumpiest of them says. I heard one of the others call him Drick. Or Drack. Maybe Mack. It's hard to hear.

"Glenn," the guy they call Aaron says, munching on a chicken finger that looks like it was cooked under someone's armpit. Smells like it, too. "You told me already. Yesterday. And the day before that and the day before that. There are many layers to your lawsuit. We get it."

"Yes," Hauman interjects, "but did I tell you what happened *last night?*"

The group sighs again, shakes their heads. "No," they mope.

"Well here's where it gets *really* interesting," Hauman says, appearing quite pleased with himself that he has another reason to pontificate about the lawsuit. "There's a provision in Washington State—where Renfro filed his suit against me—which states . . . *fff-fff-fuh* . . ."—I think Hauman just chuckled, but I can't tell; he mumbles more than speaks and seems to consider half-constructed thoughts to be fully articulated discussion— "that the rights holder to the name of any unclaimed celestial body has the first position against any counter claims of owner- ship . . . or fair use."

"We know," Mack says, spreading butter on his toast. "You've told us this story about *eleven . . . THOUSAND . . . times!*" He pounds the table. Plates and silverware rattle. Temper on that one.

"Ah-ha," Hauman replies, then leans back in his chair, which I'm half surprised hasn't collapsed by now. "But my business entity is a different thing . . . *fff-fff-fuh.*"

"Glenn," the third friend says to him. Raphy something. He's been quiet up until now. His voice is soft. He has an accent I don't recognize. "What are you talking about? Different how?"

"Sure, sure. While Renfro is registered in Washington, my business is registered in New Jersey. And New Jersey has very clear provisions on this sort of thing. The law states that *any celestial body* that's part of the lexicon is fair use, and that its name and likeness can be repurposed in any format, at any time, for any reason. . . by any*one.*"

"So let me guess," Aaron says. "You're claiming that the New Jersey state law takes precedent, and he's claiming that Wash- ington law does?"

"Exactly." Hauman adjusts his glasses. "But there's another provision Renfro and his lawyers have completely overlooked . . . *fff-fff-fuh.*"

"Glenn!" Mack shouts, his face beet red, his eyes bulging. "For once in your life. Can you just"—he slams his fist on the table after each word—"finish"—*slam!*—"a complete"—*slam!*— "freaking"—*slam!*—"SENTENCE? WHAT . . . PROVISION?"

"The provision. Oh, yes, the provision. This one's Federal. Big F. It states that in fair use naming disputes in cases of celestial bodies, an injunction can only hold against a publishing entity if there's clear and unambiguous evidence showcasing malice of intent. And *that's* what's interesting. Malice of intent. So Ren- fro would have to prove that Berrold and I *intentionally* tried to damage the reputation of Halley's Comet through the publication of our books."

"How can they prove that?" Aaron asks.

"Ha HA!" Hauman boasts triumphantly, pointing toward the dirty drop ceiling. The air conditioning unit in the far corner is dripping on the floor. "They can't."

"But they're trying?" Raphy surmises.

"Oh, yeah. Indeed they are. And they're spending a fortune to do it. But the judge sitting on our case has already dismissed the first three portions of Renfro's claim against us. One more ruling and we're in the clear. But it's the big one: State versus Federal. Renfro's got a team of lawyers, I have one guy. But we're holding our own, which should tell you something. My lawyer is confident we're going to win. And when we do, we'll be able to sue for court costs plus penalties. That money will allow me to pay my attorney and then fund me long enough to publish as many copies as I need. And that's when the gravy train starts. With the TV options we're discussing for an animated series, this could be worth millions."

I hang back as Hauman and his nerd herd filter out. They mill about outside the diner for a few minutes, then go their separate ways.

Hauman is on his own, heading toward his car. I seize the moment.

"Hauman!" I shout. "Glenn." He doesn't hear me, which is a surprise considering the size of his ears. "Yo! BIG GUY!" I shout this time.

Hauman stops at his car, turns around. He's at least a foot taller than me. I don't know him, and I work for Renfro, but I kinda like Hauman. He's got a gentle spirit. He seems to mean well. He's sort of an idiot, but he means well.

He eyes me suspiciously. "Yes?" He raises an eyebrow, but with the glint of a smile.

"I'll get right to it," I say. "I'm an . . . associate of Edgar Renfro."

He rolls his eyes, steels himself. "Oh, joy. And you're here because . . . ?"

The traffic is loud. I can barely hear myself think. "Mind if we sit in the car? I've had a long day already."

He hems and haws, then agrees. He opens the door. We sit.

"So you're here to what?" Hauman starts. "Intimidate me? Threaten me? Bribe me?"

There's a lot of ways I can go with this. Being a private eye forces you to improvise more often than you'd think. But a big part of closing almost any case is forgetting what you think is right and fair and finding ways to get people to tell you things they might not otherwise want you to know.

"You've got this all wrong, Mister Hauman."

"Glenn," he says.

"Okay. Glenn it is."

"And you are . . . ?"

"Hardwicke. Angela Hardwicke. Private Eye."

"Oh, great. You're . . . what? Tailing me? Digging into my life?"

I'm not in the mood to debate with him, and from what I've heard already, he loves to debate. Ad nauseam. I don't have that kind of time. Or patience.

"You've got this case all wrong, Glenn. Renfro isn't the man you think he is."

That's both the truth and a lie. Renfro is exactly the man Hauman thinks he is, in that Renfro can be a sniveling, greedy, entitled sap who will never back away from his claim. But he's also kind of a sweetheart, if you can get past the sniveling, greedy, entitled part of him that dominates his personality when he doesn't get what he wants. You really have to want to look for it.

"Uh-huh," Hauman says. "So what kind of man is he then?"

"Do you know much about him?"

"You mean, besides the fact that he knows he's wrong, he's suing me out of spite, that his claim is bogus, and that he doesn't need the money?"

"Let's put the money aside for a minute. I'm sure it's actually more important to you than him. No offense. He's rich, and you seem to be struggling financially."

Hauman nods.

"It goes back to childhood. Renfro's never been much of a

talker. Even when he was a kid. His parents worried that he might be mute, as he barely spoke until he was almost five years old. His father, Renfro Senior, took it especially hard. That maybe his son's silence was his fault somehow. That he'd failed his boy."

Hauman's listening. Good. He's on the hook.

"But then news came that Halley's Comet—the famed comet that only passes by the Earth once every seventy-six years—was due to come scorching across the heavens for all to see. That did it for little Renfro. Once he heard about Halley's Comet, he couldn't stop talking about it. To his parents, it was nothing short of a miracle."

"Okay." Hauman is starting to unclench. "He has an attachment to Halley's Comet."

"It goes a lot deeper than that," I say, "but, yes. Taking advantage of this miracle, Renfro Senior saw Halley's Comet as his son's salvation. So he immediately started to invest in the celestial markets, bought a high-powered telescope, and had a contractor build a deck on the roof of their house so they could have a viewing party to watch Halley's Comet as it zoomed by. It was all young Renfro could think about. No one had ever seen him so excited."

"I'm assuming there's a catch," Hauman says.

"Unfortunately for Renfro . . . and now for you . . . there was. Halley's Comet was due to pass by the Earth on February nine, nineteen eighty-six. Only . . . young Renfro came down with an epic case of food poisoning. Violent. Persistent. He was either vomiting in the toilet, or in his bed, with the shakes and chills, his fever so intense the sweat soaked right through the mattress. He could barely stand."

Hauman sighs. "Let me guess. He missed Halley's Comet."

I nod. "He missed it. It broke his little heart. Traumatized him. His father said that no matter how long it took or how much money it cost, they were going to claim that comet once and for all, and once they did, they would never let it go."

How much of what I'm saying accurately depicts Renfro's past and how much is pure fiction, I can't tell anymore. The last time I worked for Renfro things got a bit heated. So I trust that the kernels of truth will find their way out and let the story linger.

Hauman ruminates awhile. "It's really not about the money for him," he says finally.

"No. It's not." It's actually very much about the money, but Hauman doesn't need to know that, and it's not my role here to advise him otherwise.

"It's not about spite, either," Hauman surmises.

"In this case . . . no. I don't believe it is." That part's debatable, but I'm okay with it.

What's also true, however, is that Renfro isn't beyond getting physical. Sending me to get close to Hauman—sort of an advanced scout—is Renfro's way of determining whether he needs to send in muscle. That's why I agreed to take this case. Renfro and I have history—I actually owe him one—so I'm trying to save him from his worst impulses.

I have no desire to see Hauman end up with any broken bones . . . or worse. But if he doesn't come to his senses, there's only so much I can do. Renfro is my client, after all.

"I know this project is important to you, Glenn. And between you and me, your claim is legit. But you're facing that classic conundrum. Do you want to be right, or do you want to be successful? And in this case, I see no way of being both."

He looks at me in silence—I can see his mind working—until he lets out another long sigh. He wipes a smudge from his glasses. I think he made it worse. "He's never letting go of this?"

"No. He's not."

"And even if I win in court . . . ?"

"He'll appeal. No matter how many times it takes. He's not giving in, Glenn. He will never let this go. Never ever."

Hauman nods like he's listening to a song, looks through the windshield. He watches two jaywalkers cross against the light, nearly getting themselves killed as several cars barrel around the corner. The pedestrians just make it.

"Renfro'll never give up. I get that." Hauman starts the car. "But the thing you don't know about me is"—for the first time I see a fire and determination I hadn't realized was there—"neither will I."

Every once in a while—not often, but sometimes—the Universe has a funny way of pulling two opposing forces into a state of perfect harmony.

This is not one of those times.

With Renfro and Hauman both having accepted that they were in the right to such a stupendous degree that the other could be nothing but wrong, there was only one surefire way to end their conflict.

I called in a favor to some of my pals back home and arranged for them to establish a launch pad on the Moon, encased in a protective shield. Renfro and Hauman thought I was joking when I first brought it up, but when the Galactic Courts took over their case, and had us transported to Earth's satellite, neither Renfro nor Hauman were in a laughing mood. But they seem to have gotten over it. Mostly.

"Gentleman," the Cosmic Magistrate says at the edge of the runway, "what we have here is a failure to communicate—a dispute over the naming rights to Halley's Comet. It's not much of a comet, as far as these things go, but you both have your reasons for placing your claims, as foolish as they might be."

In the distance, the Earth hovers against the black of space. It's actually a gorgeous planet, if you ignore the people populating it.

"Mr. Renfro, the Galactic Court acknowledges your claim to Halley's Comet. But we cannot see fit to rule in your favor, as you have violated the spirit, if not the direct law, that regulates this situation."

Hauman puffs out his chest. He likes that one.

"On the other hand," the Magistrate says, "Mr. Hauman's claim of fair use, while on point in many respects, does in fact violate several regulations on Earth and in the Galactic system."

Renfro shoots Hauman a look of *I-told-you-so-so-nyeh*.

"Despite our best efforts, you have refused to settle out of court, and there seems to be no end to this nonsense. So it has come to this."

The Magistrate points to an oblong airship, built for space travel. "Mr. Renfro . . . you will pilot *The Savant*." The Magistrate then points across the platform, to a slightly smaller, sleeker airship, though no less nimble. "Mr. Hauman, you will pilot the *Balkan Breeze*. You will both take your respective airships into the Solar System. While you are in flight, a comet will pass through our orbit. Halley's Comet, to be exact. We've made special arrangements, so that your airships are equipped to match the comet's speed and trajectory. The first one of you to land your airship on Halley's Comet will thenceforth control the rights to its name."

Renfro turns to me. "When I said find dirt on Hauman, this isn't what I had in mind."

"I hear you," I say. "But you also asked me if I had any juice with the Magistrate, and to get him involved, if I could. I do. . . and I did."

"But I don't know how to fly that damn thing!"

"Maybe." I gesture to Hauman. "But neither does he. And one way or another you've been in the celestial business almost your entire life. You live for the cosmos. He just publishes stupid little books about them—and poorly at that."

"True, true," Renfro says, unable to hold back a smirk. "Yeah. I can take this guy. I can take him good." He then looks at the distant Earth, and gulps. "Can't I?"

"Sure. Why not? Besides, this is your chance to be the first man in human history to come face to face with Halley's Comet. Your dream come true."

The Magistrate clears his throat then. "Mr. Renfro, Mr. Hauman . . . it's time."

They eye each other and nod, the only recognition between them that maybe they've taken this whole lawsuit just a bit too far, and that it may not end well for either of them.

"Hauman," I call. "Glenn." He turns back to me before taking the onramp to his airship. "You don't have to play this out. Berrold is lucky enough to have been left off the official docket, or he'd be here, too. You can drop the suit, forget your books, and write a new one. You can write about *this*." I gesture to our place on this barren rock in the recess of space. "What a story. You're truly the Man in the Moon. Well, on the Moon. But close enough."

"I intend to," Hauman smirks from behind his glasses. He

can actually be quite imposing when you get close enough to him. "But why would I drop the suit? Renfro is an entitled mop who hides behind his lawyers. I may not have his money or his empire, but we in the Hauman clan have this unique fashion of surviving the strangest of circumstances. *Fff-fff-fff.* For instance, did I ever tell you about the night my mom was driving along the Southern State Parkway when a stalled truck—"

"I'm out," I say. I just can't listen to another of his convoluted stories. "Good luck."

Renfro and Hauman climb into their airships and emerge within the cockpits.

The Magistrate leads me to a third airship and pilots us far away from the Moon. He addresses Renfro and Hauman through their com systems.

"Gentleman, are your systems online?"

"Good to go," Renfro says.

"Me, too," Hauman says.

"Excellent. Before we begin, I'm offering you both one last opportunity to settle this case. Any takers?"

"Nope," Hauman says.

"Never," Renfro says.

"Very well." The Magistrate leans over to me. "You can never say I didn't make the offer."

I nod. "So noted."

From a point far beyond the Earth, I watch as a tiny ball rockets toward us. But as it approaches at breathtaking speed, that tiny ball grows larger, larger, and larger still until in full view we see Halley's Comet barreling toward us. Or, to be more precise, toward them. Toward Renfro and Hauman.

The Magistrate and I are far enough away—a safe distance. And then it occurs to me. "Can their airships actually fly?"

He looks at me and smiles. "Nah."

"Then what are we doing here . . . ?"

From *The Savant's* cockpit, Renfro's eyes light up in horror.

From the *Balkin Breeze*, Hauman's do the same.

The Magistrate takes us farther out of orbit—out of the path of impact—as the great comet scorches toward the Moon

"Renfro and Hauman are possibly the two most aggravating,

stubborn blowholes I've presided over on either side of the Universe," he says. "They both wanted to wrap their arms around Halley's Comet, keeping it all for themselves." The comet refocuses its trajectory just then to a specific point on the Moon. "Now they can."

And with a galactic WHAMMO, they do.

What can I say about Keith DeCandido that I didn't declare the day I married him?*

I suspect his choice of story comes from living in my basement for six months, a living arrangement as grueling for me as it was for him. Before him, there was a tall gorgeous blonde living in the basement, then he came along, untied the straps, and let her go. Reviewers of his books have described him as "the second coming of Peter David" but I don't think he looks anything like Gwen.

To him I bequeath a carbon monoxide detector. Batteries not included. Intentionally. To be delivered on the condition that you get a haircut, you damn hippie.

*No, I'm not kidding. Reader, I married him. Papers filed in New York and everything. It's legal now.

# HOUSE HUNTING
## by Keith R.A. DeCandido

"I DON'T LIKE THIS PLACE."

Brandy put her head in her hands. They'd only just walked into the house.

The real estate agent pursed her lips. "If you'd just take a look at the open floor plan, Mr. Hauman, you'll see that—"

Glenn let out a sigh. "I just had to duck to get in the front door. I'm sure all your clients who *aren't* 6'7" think the open floor plan is just ducky. But my wife and I are looking for a place to spend the rest of our lives, and I don't want to spend it bending over every single time I walk in the front door. Pass."

Giving the agent an apologetic look, Brandy said, "I'm sorry, but—"

The agent held up a hand. "No, no, it's fine. I really do understand. I've got four other places for you to see today anyhow."

Glenn muttered, "Hope they're not all built by architects from Hobbiton. Ow!" That last was from when Brandy smacked him on the arm.

"I don't like this place."

At least this time, Glenn waited until they had looked at the entire house. Glenn fit in the doorway, he had no complaints about anything else, and Brandy adored the newly remodeled kitchen, which had everything she wanted.

Glenn himself had barely acknowledged the kitchen, as his involvement in that particular room would be limited to grabbing cans of Pepsi out of the fridge and loading the dishwasher. Both those appliances were present and accounted for.

But then they looked at the bathroom. Immediately, Glenn stepped in the shower. He barely fit in the tub, and the shower head was at the same height as his neck. "I'm not stooping down every time I wash my hair."

"Look, I know it's annoying, but—" Brandy started, but then Glenn stared right at her.

"Fine, how would you like it if you had to climb up a step or two to sit on the toilet?"

Brandy just stared at him for a moment, then turned back to the agent. "I guess we won't be making an offer on this one, either."

"So I see," the agent said brusquely. "Let's move on to the next one."

"I don't like this place."

Even Brandy had to admit that this two-story house was problematic. The ground floor was magnificent, a beautiful kitchen, a huge dining room, a spacious living room with plenty of space for that giant flatscreen they had been drooling over.

Upstairs was another matter. Where downstairs had ten-foot ceilings, the upstairs—which consisted of two bedrooms and two bathrooms—had seven-foot ceilings. For the 5'2" Brandy, it wasn't an issue, but Glenn's head was almost scraping the ceiling—and it did scrape the light fixtures.

The agent sighed. "Maybe you could convert the space down here to a bedroom, and—"

"The reason we need a two-bedroom is because the second bedroom will be my home office. I can't work when I feel like I'm Gulliver trapped in Lilliput."

"I'm really sorry," Brandy said, "but he's got a point."

"Fine. I'll try to find something more Brobdignagian for you."

"I don't like this place."

"Oh, come *on*!" Brandy and the agent said that simultaneously.

"You fit in the doorway," the agent said. "And the shower." She pointed upward. "Ten-foot ceilings, for pity's sake! What's the damn problem?"

"No, that's all perfectly okay. I just don't *like* the place. Don't like the ugly kitchen, don't like the closed floor plan, don't like how tiny the back yard is, and I don't like Victorians as a rule."

Brandy shrugged. "We need to both like it. Do you have any other places?"

Tightly, the agent said, "I do have *one* other place. Wasn't planning to show it to you at first, but thinking about it . . . " She pulled out her cell phone. "Let me just make a quick call."

The agent stepped away as she pulled her smartphone out of her purse.

Brandy looked up at Glenn. "Maybe this next one?"

"Maybe this next agent. She's getting a little snotty."

"I guess, but we're being picky. We want to spend the rest of our lives here, we have to both love it."

"Why doesn't *she* get that?" Glenn shook his head, then frowned. "Is that Latin she's speaking over the phone"

"Oooh, I like this place!"

Brandy had to admit that she was iffy about this last house at first. It was on a hilly back street, in a cul-de-sac, with no other houses around. The yard was a bit overgrown, but that just meant the two of them had to do some landscaping work on it. It was very old, but it seemed to be in good working order.

The kitchen was to die for. It had plenty of room, an island, a breakfast nook, a huge gas stove, and tons of counter space. The ceilings were all eight feet, which was plenty, and the rooms were all spacious. There were two bathrooms, one with a tub, one with a shower stall, but both were spacious enough to fit Glenn's outsized frame. There was even a two-car garage, which meant they could park their car in it *and* have room for storage.

It was also at the very bottom of their price range, which was a bit suspicious.

"The previous owners sold it rather unexpectedly after only living here for six months. It had been on the market for years prior to that. Like I said, I wasn't going to show it to you, because nobody ever wants it. I'm surprised you like it so much."

"Why's it so cheap?" Glenn asked.

"Well, the wiring is a bit substandard, and a lot of the fixtures and such are pretty old. The previous owners were saying they wanted to upgrade it all, but they never did before they sold."

"I like it," Glenn said definitively. "It's got character. And I fit in it!"

"Well, it's kind of a mess," Brandy said with a chuckle, "but it's a mess we can clean up. Maybe if they come down another ten thousand?"

They made an offer on the house, and immediately started making plans for sprucing it up.

They never met the previous owners. According to their attorney at the closing, "They just want to move on to the next phase of their lives."

Still, they got the place for ten thousand less than the asking price, which was already well below market value for a two-bedroom house in the suburbs.

The problems started when Glenn called an electrician to make an appointment to look at the place and get an estimate for rewiring. As it was, he'd blown a circuit breaker twice just by having both his computer and the flatscreen TV on at the same time. He only ran the dishwasher while they were asleep. When he used the hair dryer, he inevitably blew a breaker unless he made sure Brandy turned everything else off.

Oddly, when Brandy used the hair dryer, nothing blew, even though it was the same appliance.

Unfortunately, when Glenn called the electrician, everything was fine until he provided the address.

"Sorry, Mr. Hauman, I can't help you."

"Why not?"

"That house isn't in our range. Sorry!"

With that, the electrician hung up.

Every other electrician he could find had the same answer. A few actually came to the house, but wouldn't go inside.

One day, he went to take a shower and the shower head seemed off. He had to bend to get his hair rinsed. "What the hell?"

After the shower, he called out to his wife. "Brandy!"

"What is it?"

"Look!" He pointed at the shower head.

"Yes, Glenn, that's a shower head. It's where the water comes from."

"Very funny. It's lower."

"Looks like it's in the same place to me."

After drying off, he went into the bedroom—only to find himself involuntarily ducking as he went into it. Whirling around, he stared at the doorframe, which seemed shorter.

"Brandy, the house is shrinking."

"Oh, stop it," she said from the kitchen. "And don't turn your computer on yet, I need to use the Cuisinart."

Glenn grumbled to himself as he went to the bureau and pulled out a T-shirt and a pair of jeans from the middle drawer, then straightened to get at the top drawer that contained his underwear and socks.

As he stood to his full height, he bumped his head on the light fixture in the center of the ceiling.

Continuing to grumble, he got dressed, waited for Brandy to finish with the Cuisinart, and then fired up his computer. A web-master for some web sites, he did various bits of maintenance, oversight, and paperwork on several of them until Brandy announced that dinner was ready.

He had to duck again to enter the dining room. "I don't believe this. Either I'm growing or the house is shrinking."

Brandy shrugged. "I'm not noticing any difference—in your height or the house."

Snorting, Glenn said, "Right, like you can tell from all the way down there." He grinned to make it clear he was teasing.

She stuck her tongue out at him. "Eat your casserole."

After dinner, Brandy sat in the living room and watched

some TV while working on her laptop for about an hour, then went to bed, as she had an early-morning meeting. Glenn had spent that time on the phone with a client.

When the phone call ended, he put the TV on and fired up his laptop, just as Brandy had done. Two seconds later, the lights went out and the TV, Blu-Ray player, and cable box all went off. The laptop only stayed running because of its battery.

"Great. Just great."

With a heavy sigh, Glenn got to his feet and headed toward the staircase that led to the basement, where the breakers all were. He ducked his head as he entered the staircase on instinct, only then realizing that that doorframe had also seemingly shrunk. After going down the creaky old wooden steps, he realized that the seven-foot ceilings in the basement had somehow become six-foot ceilings, and he had to bend over to get to the breakers.

Once he yanked the black switch for the bedrooms back to the "on" position, he hunched his way back to the staircase.

Upon reaching the ground-floor landing, he promptly smacked his head on the doorframe, even though he was already bent over.

"Dammit!" Rubbing his forehead, he went out into the hallway and then straightened, only to smash his head right into the glass light fixture, shattering it.

Blinking away wetness, he pulled off his glasses and palmed at his forehead and eyes. The hand was covered with blood.

"Great." Treading gently, as there were now bits of glass all over the floor, and Glenn wasn't wearing shoes, he worked his way to the bathroom.

Again, he ducked, but once more it wasn't enough of a hunch, and he smacked his bleeding head on the doorframe. Spots swam before his eyes, and he was unable to stay steady on his feet.

Bracing himself on the edge of the tub, he managed to lower himself to sit on that edge and try to catch his breath. More blood seeped into his eyes, and he wiped it away before turning the water on in the shower. The water sprayed down from the shower head, and he got unsteadily to his feet so he would wash the blood away and irrigate the cuts he got from the suddenly-closer-to-the-floor hall light.

He rose up and then slammed right into the shower head, which was at least a foot lower than it had been earlier that evening.

A lifelong viewer of cartoons, Glenn had always believed the phenomena of seeing stars before your eyes when suffering cranial trauma to be a bit of dramatic license on the part of those animators. As he collapsed to the porcelain floor of the tub, the last thing he thought before everything went black was that those cartoons were right. Stars danced before his eyes as he collapsed, his head crashing onto the drain as water continued to cascade down onto his tall form.

Right before lapsing into a coma, he muttered, "It just figures . . ."

His head blocked the drain, so the water continued to rise.

Later, after the coroner took the body away, police tried to figure out what happened. The official cause of death was drowning, but the question was how he became unconscious in the tub in the first place. The wounds on his head were consistent with the shattered light, but multiple measurements of the crime scene showed that the ceilings were eight feet high. Even someone as tall as Glenn shouldn't have been able to smash his head against it, nor bump his head on the doorframe, which was covered with his blood. For that matter, the shower head itself was seven feet off the ground, yet the victim had somehow managed to hit his head on that, too.

The entire time the police checked out the house, none of them saw the real-estate agent hiding in one of the many overgrown bushes that Glenn and Brandy hadn't yet gotten around to trimming back. As soon as they were gone, she uttered several words in Latin.

Moments later, the house was gone.

What can I say about Dean Scott that . . . no really, what can I say about this person? I have no idea who this is. I've never met this man before in my life. Are we sure we're not talking about Dan Slott? No? Hmm. <checks Facebook> Man, there are a lot of Dean Scotts out there. <checks Google> This must be the statistical odds of actually being killed by a stranger being balanced out. <checks Wikipedia> Nothing. Now I really have a reason to be paranoid . . . oh, wait. <checks FetLife> Ah, here we go. Wow, it must really have hurt to get the tattoo put there.

To him I bequeath my portion of the National Debt. (Hey, you wanted IN this anthology so much, not my fault.)

# PATIENT ZERO
## By Dean Scott

*"GLENN! GLENN! GLENN!"* THE CROWD'S CHANTING grew, a palpable force, waves against a cliff. Glenn Hauman, who had always displayed an outwardly humble nature, felt generously moved, while physically rocked by the pandemonium on the other side of the thin, blue curtain. *"GLENN! GLENN! GLENN!"* His heartbeat raced as he heard the announcer's voice; "Well, your patience is about to be rewarded! Here he is! *Gleeeennnnnnn Haustmann!"*

Wait, what? Haustmann? He fumbled finding the seam in the curtain, eluding him like the opening of a plastic produce bag, but when he emerged on the other side, baby-like, blinking at the bright lights, the horde of people stood as one, erupting in cheers and clapping. He waved one hand, shading his eyes with the other. Were some of the people carrying actual burning torches? That didn't seem like something that would pass cosplay security. And there were definitely people in the front row, now surging toward the stage, with pitchforks and rope.

Glenn's eyes flew open. The grey blandness of morning lit his motel room, motes of indifferent dust sifted through a shaft of light. His heartbeat slowed and he felt the perspiration speckling his forehead. He extricated himself from the tangled sheets as well as the tatters of his nightmare. There was a roaring outside his window, then a cacophony of discordant drums, clanging and banging, followed by a garbage truck's back-up alarm, piercing and pecking at Glenn's inner ear like an angry bird. He had already had a bad night's sleep, being near the ice machine dispenser. Who needed to be getting ice at 3 AM? Then there was the unsupervised spawn of what sounded like a tribe of Duggar children careening and carousing in what he could only imagine was some diabolical ritual under a gibbous moon. As he peeked through the heavy blue curtains he half-expected the world to have been moved into a Cthulhu netherworld. The Baltimore parking lot, cracked asphalt, aged vehicles, and dispirited foliage came in a close second.

At least it wasn't New Jersey. He turned, adjusting his glasses, and wandered into the bathroom. Looking in the mirror, scratching his beard, he wondered if he really was so pale or if it was the unflattering light. The convention guide lay on the sink counter. Looked like he had plenty of time for an unhealthy breakfast before his panel appearance.

Craig Staubner had two interests in life: ferrets and conventions. If there had been such a thing as a ferret convention, he would, quite literally, have imploded. To finance these interests he worked many consecutively overlapping small jobs. Kennel worker, pet store associate, fast food, car washer, lawn maintenance, etc. And retail, so much retail. He had even worked at the dubiously titled Amazon "Fulfillment" Center; he never learned who was supposed to be fulfilled, but it wasn't him. He likened his lifestyle to that of a vagabond and his loose "schedule" allowed him the freedom for convention-going.

Though his mind shied away from the terrible practicality of it, he knew his circumstances were also helped by the inheritance and sale of his mother's house when she died of cancer two years ago at the age of fifty-one. He missed her every day. He often felt defenseless against the hollow in his chest. Though he didn't acknowledge it, it was one of the reasons he distracted himself with cons. It was at a sci-fi convention in Wyoming that his two interests had intersected unexpectedly.

The last day of a con always felt like the end of a torrid

relationship, endorphins depleted. There were still after-hour social events scheduled, but he never felt comfortable in those settings. He had, therefore, been delighted, looking through a pet store window, to find a busyness of juvenile ferrets to play with.

Inside, while enjoying their antics, a young kid in a red vest asked him, "You here for the convention?" Initially startled at his sudden, stealthy appearance, Craig set down his Chewbacca backpack, wondering at the kid's intuition and didn't answer right away, always a little wary of other people. The employee jutted a chin at the sentient fur-balls tumbling in the sawdust playpen, "They're cute, huh? Were you looking to buy?"

Craig lit up. "They're the best!" Then he tempered his enthusiasm, lest a sales pitch started, "But, I'm not local, so I couldn't possibly get one while I'm here."

"What if I could make it more interesting for you?" the kid said cryptically, affecting a deeper tone than his skinny frame could support. Craig hesitated, working the logistics on a polite exit. "Let me show you something that might change your mind," he said and walked away from Craig.

Craig's manners, built into him by his mother, forced him to follow. They passed a bored teenage girl behind the counter, texting on her phone, who glanced up long enough to launch a disgusted sneer at her fellow worker. If looks could kill, this one would surely have maimed, but he just slouched past her.

The kid had taken him into a closet/employee lounge area. It was familiar to Craig: the still air, redolent with the unique perfume of sawdust, fish food, cat urine, and dog feces. And another acrid scent, like after a pack of matches had been set afire. A plastic carrier sat under a light as if on display just for him. With a studied air of melodrama, the kid had reached in and brought out a black-footed ferret. *Mustela nigripes*, he thought, awed. Craig was instantly enraptured by the eyes shining out from its superhero-like mask and reached to hold its softness in his hands. It snuffled inquisitively at him and moved like water through his fingers, onto his shoulder, and around his neck. Black paws micro-massaged his scalp. Then his brain interrupted, kicking his heart somewhere around the right ventricle.

"Uh, aren't these guys endangered?" he said, meeting the kid's eyes for the first time. For a moment he was stunned for he saw what seemed to be an older, considered appraisal under the shadowed brow, more worldly than his obvious youth, skin webbed at the corners of his eyes. An ebony oil flitted across the sheen of his corneas. With a slight turn of his head, the light fell more fully on the kid's face and the illusion dissipated. Finding his voice again, "I mean, aren't they illegal to sell?"

The eyes slid sideways. He shrugged. "Not endangered if they're taken care of. Seems to me the more people have them, the less they're endangered."

There was a certain logic to it and it honestly hadn't taken much for Craig's heart to beat the living crap out of his brain. The price had given him the briefest of pauses. A mixture of covetousness and the illicit thrill of this back-room deal was too potent a potion to ignore. He had been conservative in his spending at the con and the next morning was driving back home in his paint-chipped silver Saturn, windows down because the air-conditioning didn't work, a portable CD player belting out Elvis' Greatest Hits because the radio didn't work. Every time he looked over at Bilbo in his plastic carrier his heart lurched a little. He couldn't wait to get him home. This was his third Bilbo, though the most exotic of them. The Latin name for ferret meant "little thief", so it seemed appropriate. His other nine domesticated ferrets he'd named after each member of the Fellowship. Through all 900 miles back to Waukegan, Illinois, Craig had made sure to follow every rule of the road and obey every speed limit and traffic light.

Craig was worried. He had kept Bilbo in his bedroom, separated from the rest of the Fellowship in the outer room, as he did with any new pet. The first two weeks had been great and he had enjoyed the wilder displays of behavior Bilbo put on. About the time he was going to introduce him to the rest of the group— just in separate cages at first, of course, so they could see each other without interacting—Bilbo sneezed. The copious snot discharged could only be explained by a wormhole to the Mucus Universe manifesting in his nasal sinuses. That certainly put the

introductions on hold. Craig had a friend: a veterinary techni-
cian who helped him out with vaccines and medications. He
relied on her to look after his four-legged kids when he was at
cons and it was her he called now.

"I don't think it's too serious," Lisa said, "Just an upper respiratory infection. The antibiotics should work." Bilbo looked up at
her, nose twitching. He pawed at his eyes, which seemed to only
dimly reflect the overhead light.

Craig had been worried at first, wondering what she'd think
of him having an illegal pet animal but she'd cooed, "I love his
markings!" and he'd been relieved her knowledge about ferretol-
ogy didn't extend to the prohibited.

Lisa turned to Craig, who realized he was hovering way too
close to her. Her green eyes seemed very large. "Don't you have
that Baltimore thing going on this weekend?"

Craig straightened, moving away from her. "Uh, yeah." He
fiddled with something on the table to occupy his hands. "Are
you still, uh, up for watching them?"

"Of course! I love the little guys! Though Aragorn's my
favorite, of course!" Her smile was luminous. His heart tripped
and he turned, stumbling, into the small kitchenette.

"Would you like something to drink? Do you think he'll be
okay if I go?" he asked, sticking his head in the open refrigerator,
not really seeing anything except the after-image of her smile.

"No, I'm good. I need to be getting to work. But, yeah, I
think he'll be fine. I've got your number. I'll call and keep you
updated."

She left his trailer and he watched her bounce out to her
Jeep. With a quick wave, a spinning of wheels, a flash of eyes in
her rear-view mirror, she was gone. He sighed. He didn't know
why but whenever she left he seemed to feel the loss of poten-
tials. She was nice enough to him, but he didn't fool himself that
there was anything more than a like-appreciation of animals.
Ferrets in particular. He knew how he appeared. He had a large
frame, but not like a football player, more like a partially-melted
bowling pin, thin E.T.-like arms, topped with a mop of brown
hair that seemed oily no matter what shampoo or conditioner
he used. His eyes were a mud-brown and the enamel of his

teeth had been damaged by tetracycline when he was a kinder-gartner, seeming more like stalactites and stalagmites. Years of self-consciousness allowed him only a closed smile which some took as a grimace. His mother had called him, affectionately, her "Baby Huey". It had been embarrassing and humiliating when he was younger. Yeah, that's what he wanted as a self-image: a large, ungainly cartoon duckling in a diaper. Now, he found the absence of that title painful, for there'd be no one else to say it. Looking around his trailer, it had never looked smaller to him.

He was careful to wash his hands before attending to his other lithesome friends, taking solace in their simple, fun approach to life. They lent an air of positivity and energy that main-lined right into his amygdala.

Three days later he was rattling down the road. His car ran on gas and faith. Those and the abilities of a level 20 wizard-mechanic named Mike.

His worry about Bilbo attenuated behind him as anticipation pulled him forward. He had woken with the feeling of cotton batting in his sinuses and a concomitant dull ache at the base of his skull. *Getting an early start on Con Crud*, he thought dismissively and downed some non-drowsy cold/flu medicine. He revved up Elvis on the CD player. Those songs really ate up the miles! Elvis had been his Mom's favorite; she'd really had a thing for him. She would regale anyone with the time when she was eight and Elvis' entourage rolled through the Lake Tahoe hotel lobby they were staying in. He had touched her shoulder as he passed, her eyes open as wide as possible to take him all in, and he'd said, "How ya' doin', honey?" in that silky timbre of his. Mistaking Craig for a stranger at her bedside, she'd told this story again. It was the last thing she'd said to him, her eyes suddenly finding his. "How ya' doin', honey?"

He drove the eleven hours straight and by the time he pierced the Baltimore city border, the sneezing and runny nose started. This would become known as Stage 1.

*Interlude*
*Viruses replicate by forcing the infected host cell to use its own resources to make more viral particles, usually resulting in the cell's*

*eventual demise. This new viral progeny hit the biological play-ground like eighth century Vikings, pillaging further cells. This dev-astation, combined with the host's defense mechanisms, results in unfortunate secretions and excretions that act like viral-laden water park slides perpetuating transmission to other hosts. Sometimes two types of viruses infect a host. Their eyes meet across a 100-microm-eter cell. Sexy-time between viruses is an unromantic exchange of sections of RNA. The result, sometimes, is a new virus, one that decides it likes its new host, finds them willing to please and perhaps help them in finding further domiciles, even so far as to give them mucousy letters of reference.*

*Let's say you're working at a convenience store and an old lady laboriously counts out her exact change with hands that earlier had been blowing snot-holes through flimsy paper tissue. You then take said change and perhaps touch your face or rub your eye at some point. Congratulations! You are now the proud owner of a flu virus! Now, further, should you happen to be in close proximity with an otherwise cute and adorable furred vector who is flinging its own viral particles through the air while you not-so-gently, open-mouthed snore, well then, further congratulations are in order. This second virus would normally not find lodging in an unfamiliar host, but the first virus puts out the welcome mat, lights the candles, and puts on Marvin Gaye.*

Craig Staubner awoke about a quarter mile away from where Glenn Hauman peered through his motel window on an unpromising landscape, with his head feeling like a bowling ball. Craig could feel his sinuses collapsing as he blew, and then peel-ing away from each other, making weird high-pitched noises. After about five minutes of this he felt his eyeballs were back in place and took some more cold/flu medicine. Caffeine and a hot, steamy shower seemed to help as well. It was the first day of the con and he laid out the convention map, turning the pro-gram for the day's offerings. He'd picked up his wristband and checked into the hotel room the previous night, quietly, unwit-tingly, leaving a viral eddy behind him.

He didn't have much scheduled for the first day. He liked to walk the aisles, peruse the vendors, and get the lay-out of the

con, even if it's one he's been to before. The con, for him, was
like a communal organism. Even with thousands of people moving, jostling, trying to get somewhere, like mice searching the
maze for cheese, rarely had he heard a discouraging word. While
they were there for different reasons, everyone came to enjoy
themselves, be themselves, be amongst like-minded people.
Being an inveterate and unrepentant introvert, he didn't interact
with many people, but enjoyed being both part and apart of the
group, oftentimes listening in to excited conversations around
him. No one knew him, so he was relaxed by the lack of expec-
tations. He could marvel with everyone else at the cosplay cos-
tumes, professional or otherwise, and laugh spontaneously with
the crowd at a celebrity's anecdote. It was a connection he felt
nowhere else in his life.

Some of the kindest acts he had witnessed between people
had been at cons. Simple acts of humanity. It was a judgment-
free zone. Sometimes he wondered if the world wouldn't be a
better place if it could be injected with the patience and inclu-
siveness seen in these microcosms.

A headache still threatened, but low tide seemed to have
arrived in his nose. He couldn't trust that to continue, however,
and grabbed a wad of tissue paper just in case. He took advantage of the Continental breakfast, loading his plate up twice.
Being sick had not affected his appetite. Then he had meandered
his way down to the entrance doors, surprised at the number
of people already waiting, because he prided himself on planning ahead and being earlier than others. When the doors finally
opened, a mass of people flooded into the Main Hall with orgas-
mic joy, everyone scurrying and hurrying trying to find their particular ova of interest. This was why he didn't plan much on the
first day, so he could walk calmly through the first day's chaos
with nothing pressing on him.

He tucked his head into the crook of his arm, sneezing several times. He groaned as it seemed pieces of brain sieved into
his sinuses and drained out his nose. He reached for tissues. *So it
was going to be like that was it?* he thought.

On that first day he left inconvenient viral particles on, in no
particular order, food tongs, doorknobs, toilet seats, urinal flush

handles, pens, numerous memorabilia, elevator buttons, vending machine buttons, money, escalator rails, and various other surfaces as he navigated through the crowds, pressing close and intimately. By the end of the first day, Craig had developed an annoying tickle in the back of his throat and a cough that would not be ignored. Stage 2.

A lot of Glenn's work could be a solitary experience. Yes, he had his "friends." People, he wondered, who if given opportunity, wouldn't want to just kill him. And, yes, he kept busy, always having a number of different projects going, like some master juggler. He obviously had to coordinate and work with a number of different, talented people on these projects. Yet, when he was actually working, it was as if he were in his own cocoon. With writing, for instance, it was easy to think that everything you put down as ink on papyrus was amazing. And then some self-doubt would creep in. Putting your words out to a voracious public could be like sending your toddler out to cross the freeway, repeatedly. He wasn't sure sometimes if he feared criticism or silence more. So, often there was a disconnect. You write something, you think it's great, send it out, then you wait on this unseen population. Are they reading it? Does anyone care? Why aren't there any comments?

That was why he liked attending cons. Here was where he could get feedback, both positive and negative. Here was where he could reap more than financial rewards, which, he had to admit, were still an important consideration; he wasn't a complete altruist. With most of his work there was a sense of delayed satisfaction, an amorphous trickling in of appreciation. At cons, however, interacting with fans, with people who have self-identified as liking his work, outside of crack cocaine, there was nothing better. Or so he'd heard. It was a natural high that he could bottle and take back home with him and break it out for inspiration.

He enjoyed the spike of excitement on the first day of a con, even with ones where his morning had not started the best. It was inescapable. A palpable sense of possibilities. He got to hang out with his lesser-accomplished buddies, some he hadn't seen in a while. He was able to meet and talk with celebrities in ways that others could only do through elaborate stalking techniques. It was the only job or position where he was thanked for literally just showing up. He truly felt fortunate.

*Interlude*
*Success of a virus depends on them keeping their host alive long enough to spread their influence to other hosts. Ebola, as scary as it is, is not an effective virus as it often kills the host too fast for proper dissemination. It's an art, a balance that those afflicted don't truly seem to appreciate. You have to damage the host enough to replicate, but not so much that they're incapacitated, unable to contact other juicy hosts. Transmission is important to success as well. Sneezing can expel 40,000 droplets at speeds up to two hundred miles an hour, viruses gleefully riding them like inner-tubes on a river. Coughing only produces about 3,000 droplets at fifty miles an hour, but makes up for these deficiencies in distance, jetting out to several feet, making a polite hand over a mouth an ineffective barrier. Closed systems, such as panel discussions or celebrity talks, are perfect for even, fair, and unbiased diffusion.*

The second day of a con could seem a lot like the sequel of a favorite movie: a little bit of a let-down. Some of the big reasons that had pulled people in, they went and did or saw the first day and that initial giddiness subsided. For Glenn it was similar in that a lot of the people who had planned on meeting him did so the first day. The following days were more of people stumbling upon him and being impelled by curiosity enough to ask, "So, what is it you do?" His friend Peter David got this a lot. Sitting at a table watching people stroll by, with them sometimes obviously avoiding eye contact, he often felt like a creature in a boring zoo exhibit.

Craig had different considerations for his second-day disenchantment. His coughing had increased in amount and severity even as his sneezing and congestion subsided. He had made a late-night run to a local convenience store for anti-coughing medications and lozenges. They had helped a little, but not enough. If he'd been scheduled for work, he most definitely would call in sick. As it was, he had plans. He had paid in advance and was going to see Shatner.

Glenn had just sat back down at his assigned booth having come from a panel discussion that had devolved into whether raising Tribbles as a food source would be a viable cure for world hunger. He was just gazing blankly out into the mass of people, that seemed to swell and recede like a tide, when he noticed someone in particular. He was a large guy with an unusual rolling gait that reminded Glenn of something, some cartoon animal maybe? The thought was like a burr in his skull, firmly lodged. He couldn't place it. This guy stood out because he was disturbing the flow of humanity, moving like a torpedo aimed in his direction. He seemed to loom over Glenn the closer he came.

"Oh, my gosh, Mr. Hauman! It is so great to meet you!" he exclaimed, putting his hand out.

The mores of society made Glenn politely reach out and grasp the proffered hand, against all instinct about touching this fellow primate with the glazed eyes and glistening skin. The grip was cold and clammy, reminding him of when he was a kid and been out in snow too long with cheap gloves. He quickly pulled his hand back and sterilized it by rubbing it on his pant leg under the table.

"I just left seeing William Shatner!" the man gushed.

"Oh, cool," Glenn responded, lifting his eyebrows for emphasis. The man just stood there for a moment, apparently having run out of small talk.

"Oh! Hey! I have your book I'd like you to sign," he finally said, rotating a Chewbacca backpack off his shoulder. It caught on his elbow and banged the little table. He started digging into its interior. It looked oddly like he was doing some impromptu psychic surgery on the Wookie.

Upon being offered the very familiar book, one he had signed many times before, he was dismayed to look upon the tabletop and not find one pen. The man turned away, coughing vigorously, startling a child in a Pikachu costume. Glenn looked behind him and under the table—*Had it rolled off when the table was jostled?*—but found nothing to write with. When he looked up the man was holding a ball-point pen out to him. Glenn's eyes widened and he cast a frightened look to his left. His friend Peter glanced at him. He and Peter had a safe word they used in situations with fans they couldn't handle or had gone on too long. If used, the other would spring to their rescue with some made-up excuse or appointment they had to hurry to. It wasn't needed here, since Peter quickly appraised his expression and predicament.

"Here, I've got one," he said, leaning toward Glenn.

"Oh! Great! Thanks!" he replied, perhaps a tad too loudly, showing the pen to the fan like he'd just done a magic trick. Looking a little disappointed, the man put the pen back in his pack. "Who would you like me to make this out to?"

"Craig. C. R. A. I. G. Craig."

Glenn finished with a flourish and, holding it by its farthest edge, handed it back to Craig who immediately examined what he'd written. He looked back up, satisfied, and here now came that moment of floundering, where a fan tried to decide whether to say more, possibly imposing on the other's time, or move on. But then there was the calculation of how to end the encounter without seeming abrupt or rude.

Craig opted for a "thanks" of little enthusiasm and was absorbed into a passing crowd of Starfleet cadets. His hacking cough could be heard erupting through the ambient con noise.

Peter and Glenn looked at each other. Glenn shrugged. What else needed to be said?

Craig flopped onto his hotel room bed, a fish having been pulled onto a bank after a long fight. He coughed face-first into the mattress. He was sweating even more now and pulling his clothes off exhausted him. Though he'd been too hot, clothed, he now felt chills and pulled the sheets over him like a pall. He fell quickly to sleep. His phone tinkled merrily and through the ether Lisa left a message about how Bilbo seemed better today and she hoped he was enjoying the con. Sometime early in the morning on the third day, the virus got bored with the trite respiratory symptoms and decided to go to work on his cardiovascular and intestinal systems.

That's how Craig found himself on the toilet, shaking, sweating, coughing in between pulling air like knives into his chest. Pink-tinged mucous hung unnoticed from his right nostril. There was no thought of the con. He had never experienced this level of unnatural diarrhea. He hadn't eaten much the second day, so it seemed like his guts were improvising by shooting out various pieces of other organs. The porcelain was cold under his legs and he could barely push the handle down, having lost track of how many times he'd flushed. He couldn't stand up to see what he was producing, but if he'd had, he would have become even more alarmed. Or perhaps not, as lucid thought seemed beyond him now. DIC is a fancy term doctors use called Disseminated Intravascular Coagulation. Its other definition is Death Is Coming. His clotting factors were used up and bleeding tributaries fed from other areas of his body directly into the river of his colon. Craig, luckily, hadn't seen himself in the mirror, for he would have seen small purple hemorrhages starting to show through his skin and against the white sclera of his eyes. His lungs were a frothy soup. Another twisting stab of pain passed through his guts, bending him, causing him to wail, his fists held tightly against his temples, waterfall on rocks sounding beneath him. Crying out caused him to cough, an explosive speckling of red onto his legs. He slumped to his right, not feeling the sharp edge of the bathroom counter. Ebony spots appeared in his vision, coalescing. Three final thoughts skipped through his brain:

*who was going to take care of Bilbo and the Fellowship?*
an image of aged eyes, cool and predatory
and a voice: "How ya' doin', honey?"

Glenn felt listless, throwing his suitcase into the trunk for his three-hour drive back home after the con. He'd been blowing his nose all morning. This happened a lot at cons, unfortunately, but he found it didn't usually amount to much. On the freeway he started sneezing. Three days later he'd collapse in his hallway, a failed Jenga tower. A crimson trail, like thick paint, led back to his bedroom, which resembled a bloody Jackson Pollock. He hadn't even made it to the toilet.

Glenn's funeral was today. Peter David felt adrift and alone amongst the beeping hospital equipment. Thick, clear plastic curtains further circumscribed his world. The hospital television was a dim blur behind them, someone talking.

*"The H2/N42 virus, better known as the Nerd Flu, has now reached pandemic status with consecutive outbreaks in London, Germany, and France following comic book and pop culture conventions. The CDC and World Health Organization have issued guidance on self-care and when and where to seek help should you experience the following symptoms. Please be warned, what follows is graphic and disturbing."*

A host won't always die from exposure to a virus, depending on an individual's genetics, personal immune response, and access to medical care. Shatner didn't die. Of course he didn't. *Kobayashi Maru* indeed. Glenn Hauman did. If Craig was Patient Zero, Glenn would have been listed as Patient 217, but no one keeps that close a track of mortality rates once they're in the millions.

What can I say about Mary Fan that hasn't already been yelled at her by self-appointed gatekeepers—especially the ones who insist "she's not a real Fan"?

She tries oh so hard to project an image of the wholesome YA author, with her novel *Starswept*, her upcoming novel *Stronger Than A Bronze Dragon*, and her work advocating getting girls into STEM programs, but her story here shows that she's actually a deadly viper with violence in her heart and venom in her smile. The heavens tremble at the thought of crossing her, which is why you should buy all of her books. Or she'll find you. Yes, she will. And she practices her torture methods on Men's Rights Activists.

To her I bequeath a PO Box in somewhere other than New Jersey.

# BURIED IN BOOKS
## by Mary Fan

THESE DAYS, IT'S MORE IMPORTANT FOR SOMETHING to look good in a photo than in person. After all, you only run into a handful of human beings in your day-to-day, especially if you're the owner and sole employee of an obscure Jersey City bookstore and can't really move. Meanwhile, the reach of the web is endless, as my younger brother, Mikey, always tells me. It's far easier to get discovered if you're good at posting pretty pictures of yourself. He would know—he went from Instagram narcissist to reality show star because of the power of his photos.

That was why I stacked the books so high in the first place: for the pictures. Everyone says they love bookstores, but how many actually go to them and spend money? I'd poured my life savings into this musty old hole-in-the-wall shop, which I'd renamed Meggy Mak's Book Basement. Not your typical quarter-life crisis move, but I'd never exactly been typical. And I didn't want my shop to be either. I wasn't just going to have shelves of books; I was going to have *sculptures* of them. Walls, towers, and arches built of tomes stacked upon tomes, their gleaming spines color-coordinated for maximum prettiness, arranged in lovely gradients and rainbow order. Never mind that no one would actually be able to buy or read these particular volumes—their job was just to get people to come check out the store. The books for selling were kept on actual shelves because, contrary to common belief, I'm not completely bonkers.

Though you might believe otherwise after reading this. I wouldn't blame you if you did.

In hindsight, I really should have secured the books in place somehow. But how was I to know that someone would be bone-headed enough to walk into them?

Anyway, I'd opened my shop a few weeks ago and was pre-paring to host my first book signing. I don't know why I agreed to allow eight authors to sign at once when my shop had more books than floor space, but I was new to this and couldn't turn down a chance to put myself on the map. I was hoping that fans of Crazy 8 Press—that's what they called themselves—might come seek-ing autographs and leave remembering my Book Basement. And if not, at least I could take pictures for my social media accounts that made it *look* like I'd hosted a big-deal signing.

Glenn Hauman—a large man with wire-framed glasses and a scruffy brown beard—was the first of the Crazy 8 to arrive, and he'd apparently misread the email because he showed up a full three hours early. I hadn't even opened the shop yet, but it felt rude to leave him standing awkwardly on the sidewalk outside, so I let him in.

"I'm not quite ready for you yet." I pushed my black bangs out of my eyes. "You can go ahead and set up your books if you want, but the shop doesn't even open for another hour." And chances were no one would come in until the signing officially began, though I didn't feel like advertising my obscurity.

Glenn walked in carrying a box of his titles with a jacket draped over it. My guess was that he'd found the day to be as unseasonably warm as I did.

"Sorry about the miscommunication." He gave an awkward but kind smile. "Need any help setting up?"

"No, I've got everything where I want it. Just go put your books out. And feel free to browse."

He seemed like a nice guy. I'd never have hurt him on pur-pose. Really, I wouldn't have.

I directed him to the row of tables—actually slabs of cheap

wood balanced on even more books—in the back corner behind one of my book archways. This one I was particularly proud of, since I'd managed to make it entirely out of books with red spines. It had taken me forever to balance it just right.

And it took Glenn less than half a second to destroy the whole thing with his prodigious height.

Really, his demise was his own fault. He should have realized the archway wasn't tall enough to accommodate him and ducked his shaggy head. And why in the world would he flail? All he did was create an even greater avalanche. As if it weren't enough to destroy my archway, his vain attempts to escape the deluge of tomes only knocked over more of my hard-built book sculptures.

All I could do was watch in horror as a domino effect rippled through the store. A great rumble thundered through the air. I couldn't begin to guess how many thousands of pounds all those books weighed. The room vibrated with the great *thwap-thwap-thwap* of countless pages falling. The forces of physics seemed determined to converge on Glenn, for all the walls and towers ended up collapsing upon the spot where he'd stood moments ago. A sickening crunch shook my bones, and I cringed.

By the time the last book fell, my carefully arranged structures had been reduced to a shapeless mountain of novels, memoirs, and textbooks, and Glenn was nowhere in sight. The motley mix of covers and spines actually made an interesting composition and showed off how eclectic my tastes were. Collections of philosophical essays ruminating on the nature of evil, which sat upon YA novels about teens saving the world, which sat upon old-school white-people classics favored by English teachers, which sat upon genre fiction imaging futures and fantasylands outside the Western world. Many I'd read. Many I'd bought because I'd *wanted* to read them.

I couldn't resist—I grabbed the phone from my pocket and snapped a picture of the enormous pile. I'd come up with a clever caption for it later.

I edged forward nervously. "Glenn? Are you all right?"

Of course, he was not. By the time I managed to dig through enough books to find his head, it was obvious that he was quite dead. I suppose a typical person would have felt guilty, but as I warned you earlier, I'm not quite typical. Mostly, I was annoyed at the mess.

Well, he shouldn't have knocked over my books.

I put my hands on my hips and stared at the corpse, dismayed. How in the world was I going to clean up this mess in time for the signing? I could keep the shop closed a few hours longer to buy time, but there was no way I was canceling my first author event. I'd already blasted it all over social media, so I was committed.

"This is all your fault!" I exclaimed at Glenn's body. Poor guy. He didn't deserve this. He really was quite nice. But he was already dead, so there was no sense in dwelling on it.

Raking my hands through my short hair, I looked around my ruined shop. Early light streamed through the wide window showing the sleepy suburban street outside. The obvious thing to do would have been to call 911 so someone could come remove the body. But people tended to freak out over dead people, and chances were I'd be hauled into a police station for questioning. They might even try pinning me with negligent homicide. Or worse—reporting me to some official who could shut down my shop as a safety hazard.

I didn't have time to go to jail or fight for my store in court. My books needed me. I quickly decided that calling any form of authority would be more trouble than it was worth. Better to take care of things myself.

Since the store wasn't open yet, I didn't have to worry about closing it. Chances were no one would have wandered in anyway. And if anyone asked, all the books scattered across the floor provided an ample excuse for why I wasn't opening on time.

The bigger issue was: What could I do with the enormous corpse of a dead author? It wasn't like there was a swamp nearby I could dump him into. Not that I'd have had time to drive out to one—I still had to get all these books cleaned up before the rest of the Crazy 8 authors arrived.

The backroom would be the best place to put Glenn for the time being. I could store him there until after I closed for the day and then figure out where to put him later. For once, I was glad

I'd been too poor to hire any employees. The only one with a key to that backroom was me.

I set to work unburying the rest of Glenn from the pile of books. Even as I did, I tried to sort them by color. There was still a chance I could make my store mildly pretty before the signing. The ones that had been spattered with blood would have to be destroyed, unfortunately, and it gutted me when I saw one of my favorite spines had been ruined. *What a waste.*

I sighed and glared at the body. "It was bad enough that you wrecked my displays. Did you have to bleed all over my books too? How rude."

Luckily, I had a tablecloth in the store, which I had originally meant to put on the signing table before learning that Crazy 8 would be bringing their own branded one. I used the cloth to wrap Glenn's bloody head so he hopefully wouldn't spill it on any more of my precious pages.

Dragging Glenn into the backroom ended up being the hardest part of the ordeal. He was at least twice my size, and my spaghetti-noodle arms weren't exactly up to the task. *I should have taken Mikey up on his offer to buy me a membership to his gym.* Even though I knew he'd only extended it so he'd have someone around to take pictures of him working up a sweat and showing off his eight-story abs.

I suspect even Mikey, with his six-foot frame and Hulk-like biceps, would have had trouble with this particular cadaver, though. I'd known Glenn would be heavy, but I hadn't realized his weight would rival that of my entire store combined. I'm actually rather proud that I was able to move him all by my less-than-athletic self.

Finally, after much huffing and puffing, I managed to stuff Glenn into the backroom, which was little more than a closet with spare stock. I was sweating so hard, I must have burned off the entire cheese omelet I had for breakfast. After locking the door, I glanced at the time on my phone.

*Two and a half hours until the signing.* I wouldn't be able to rebuild *everything*, but that was at least enough time to make the Book Basement look decent enough. Sadly, doing so would mean skipping lunch.

My stomach was already rumbling at the prospect, but I had work to do. I heaved a breath and set about cleaning up.

The other Crazy 8 authors—all Baby Boomer white guys except one, who was a Millennial Asian woman like me—arrived when expected. Actually, a few minutes late, but what could you expect?

Meggy Mak's Book Basement was looking more or less like her old self again, albeit a dressed down version. Instead of elaborate towers and archways, I had to settle for a few simple walls and pyramids. Throwing away the books with blood on them had distressed me greatly, but I'd bitten the bullet and stuffed them in a garbage bag, which presently lay beside Glenn in the backroom.

Now some people might think it strange that I'd care so much about those ruined books. After all, I was using them as building materials and not reading them. But they were *mine*, and I'd enjoyed *having* them. Besides, there was always the off chance that I'd rearrange my décor, stumble upon an interesting title, and actually crack it open. Thanks to Glenn, several good books had lost that chance forever.

At least he'd left me with a few more to take their place. I'd recovered his box of books from the pile and used them to prop up parts of my display. And because it had looked interesting, I'd saved a pink-covered comic anthology for my own reading.

The other Crazy 8 authors had no trouble navigating my sculptures. They made their way to the table and began setting up their books. I'd expected seven of them, but one, Paul Kupperberg, was nowhere in sight. Apparently, he'd been unable to make it. Ah, well. That would give the others more breathing room at least.

I had them sit in alphabetical order, with Russ Colchamiro at one end and Aaron Rosenberg at the other. Each had their own method for displaying their novels. Michael Jan Friedman spread his multitudes of titles out in a blanket of covers while Robert Greenberger propped his up on little stands he'd brought. Peter David needed some help making his display look good, so I stepped in.

Since there were no customers yet, I took a moment to peruse the titles myself. They were an eclectic bunch—books about men with duck heads and backpackers who held the universe's DNA, stories of interstellar court martials and Aztec detectives, fantasies where twelve races fought for survival and teens battled monsters. I made a mental note to consign a few if there were any left after the signing. Which there probably would be, given the lack of foot traffic.

"Hey, where's Glenn?"

I looked up from the book I'd been flipping through, unsure of who had spoken. I didn't know them well enough to identify their voices yet. All I knew was that it had been a man, which eliminated Mary Fan from the possibilities.

"Isn't that his jacket?"

Those words sent such a bolt of panic through me, I didn't see who'd said them either. I'd completely forgotten about the jacket. It had been tangled among the fallen books, and I'd shoved it off to one side while rebuilding my displays. *Dammit!* I cursed myself. For that, I would have deserved the "negligent homicide" charge, because if that stupid jacket wound up killing my bookstore, I'd deserve every minute of jail time I got.

Thinking fast, I said, "Oh, he arrived early, so I asked him to sign some stock in the backroom."

That excuse satisfied the authors for a spell, but soon, speculation began rising. And so did my blood pressure. I should have come up with a better lie—one that *didn't* explicitly point to the place where I'd hidden the corpse. But I was new to hiding dead bodies, and I'd panicked.

Soon, the distinct lack of Glenn was all the authors could talk about.

"Typical Glenn. Supposed to be someplace but no one can find him."

"Maybe he ate too much for lunch and fell asleep in there."

"I'll bet he's telling a cockroach about that lawsuit he's mixed up in."

"Hey, maybe we should go get him."

I swore. Two of the authors rose from their chairs. They were about to go to the backroom to ask Glenn what was taking so long, and I was about to pull the fire alarm to distract them, when—miracle of miracles—a group of customers walked in. And—even greater miracle—they were sci-fi and fantasy fans interested in the Crazy 8 authors' books.

Instantly, the authors abandoned all their previous conversation to pitch their novels. I breathed a sigh of relief.

But I knew this wouldn't last. The moment those customers left, the authors would go right back to asking where Glenn was. I needed to get more people in the door. And there was only one way I knew how to do so guaranteed.

I hated, *hated* asking my douche-y little brother for anything, but I was desperate. I grabbed my phone and called him.

"Meggy!" From his heavy breathing and the whirring noise in the background, I guessed he was on a treadmill. "Must be a real emergency if you're actually *calling.*"

"Yeah, it is." I clenched my teeth, biting the metaphorical bullet. "I need your help."

Mikey made me take back everything I'd ever said while making fun of his Instagram modeling before he agreed to do what I asked, but when he delivered, he delivered.

Almost the moment he posted that he was heading to his big sister's shop to buy some nerd books, fans of the Mak Attack—yes, that was actually what he was known as—began crowding the Book Basement. Having our shared last name on the store's sign turned out to be an accidental marketing coup because it alerted everyone right away that this was the right place.

"Are you really the Mak Attack's sister? Can I get a selfie?"

The overenthusiastic teenager had stuck her cheek next to mine and extended her phone-holding arm almost before I said yes. I didn't mind. The more I could get my name and store out there, the better.

Most of the fans looked like they were still in high school. Several looked me up and down and peered at my face, and I knew they were searching for the resemblance between me—twiggy and moon-faced—and my superstar brother, with his challah-bread muscles and chiseled cheekbones. Apparently, we had the same eyes though.

I pointed at the signing table. "These are some of Mikey's favorite authors. He'll be here soon, and he said he'd take pictures with anyone who buys a book."

The mad dash began. The authors couldn't sign fast enough. Which was perfect, because it meant they were no longer interested in where Glenn was.

By the time Mikey actually arrived, a line had formed out the door and spilled onto the sidewalk. Seemed everyone and their prom date was eager for this impromptu chance to hang out with one of the stars of *Jersey City Lights*. To make more room, I separated the authors into different parts of the store so everyone wouldn't be converging on the one corner. That wound up being a clever strategy for hiding Glenn's absence. The next few times anyone asked where he was, I simply said, "Oh, he's over there" and pointed at a random spot. Between the books and the fans, it was hard to see more than two feet ahead, so they believed me.

Mikey stood beside the cash register with his stack of books—I'd bought one from each author and told him to pretend they were his new favorite reads—and gamely posed with every kid who wanted a selfie.

"You owe me big time, sis," he muttered with a smirk. "When I cash in, it's gonna be *huge*."

"Might not hurt if you'd actually *read* one of those books I just got you," I whispered back while ringing up one of the few older ladies in the crowd.

"Of course I will. Everyone loves it when hot guys read."

I rolled my eyes, knowing that meant he'd pose for pictures with his nose in a book but probably won't absorb a single word.

"By the way," he said. "You should pick better filters. Your bookstagrams are all oversaturated."

"Shut up."

Meanwhile, I kept glancing at the Crazy 8 authors, hoping they wouldn't go looking for Glenn. Luckily, they all seemed too thrilled and distracted by all the books they were selling. My plan was working. At one point, I spread the word that Glenn had left early. The other authors quipped that he was missing out, but didn't question it. They were too busy to worry—I'd made sure of that.

The crowd of Mak Attack fans swelled so large, I ended up keeping the shop open a whole hour later than usual. I didn't mind. Mikey, knowing how crucial it was to be perceived as nice by fans, stayed until the last one got her selfie.

As he left, he flashed me a grin. "You'll have to tell me what this was really about someday."

"Nah. I'd hate for you to be charged as an accessory to murder."

He barked out a laugh and headed out the door.

I helped the authors pack up their books and sent them on their way. They'd apparently had the best bookstore signing of their lives. Meanwhile, my phone was blowing up with notifications as teen after teen tagged my shop's account on social media. Many said they loved the vibe and wanted to come back.

All in all, it was a fantastic day. Except for the part where a guy had croaked in my shop and I'd had to hide the body.

Once I was alone again, I mulled over what to do next. Since it was dark, I could have dragged Glenn's corpse into my car and gone searching for a swamp to dump it in, but I had no idea how to locate a suitable one. Perhaps I could disguise the body instead—I could put sunglasses and a hat on him, then put him on the PATH train with a "homeless and hungry" sign. Everyone would assume he was drugged out, and no one would notice he was dead for hours. Problem was, I was pretty sure the PATH stations had security cameras that would catch me dragging him. Not to mention, he was far too big for me to carry more than a few feet.

The safest thing to do would be to keep him in the store. I considered the disguise idea again. If I dressed him like a scarecrow and put a sack over his head, I could add him to my collection of Halloween decorations. But what if he started to smell? That would be gross.

Eventually, I came up with a solution: I buried Glenn under my store. I'm pretty sure Mikey would have been proud of the workout I got while prying up the floorboards and digging into the dirt. All manner of profanities spilled from my mouth as I dug for hours and hours to make a hole large and deep enough.

Of all the authors who could have died in my shop, why did it have to be the one with the most inconvenient corpse to dispose of?

After I finished replacing the floorboards, I stacked tons and tons of books on top—both on bookshelves I'd moved over them and as decorative towers I'd built.

It seemed rather fitting that Glenn Hauman would spend eternity buried under books.

What can I say about Kathleen David without telling the story that made her flee Georgia?

She claims to be a puppeteer, and yet I've never seen her hand up Keith DeCandido's backside. A woman with a taste for the bizarre and crude (Exhibit A: her husband) she has taken on the task of organizing these killers like a good Mafia captain. The best thing she has going for her is that she's a nice normal height.

To her I bequeath a bottle of champagne that doesn't taste like soap.

# THE CASE OF
# THE INDUSTRIAL REVOLUTION
## by Kathleen O'Shea David

IT WAS IN THE SPRING OF 1881 WHEN MYCROFT Holmes summoned his brother Sherlock to the estate of Baron Glenn Haumann in a case concerning espionage, love, and murder.

I was happy to get out of the city and into the country even for a short time, due to the quality of the air in London that had been miserable at best.

Holmes was not as happy, since he loved the morass that was London with all its smells and sounds. He found fresh air to be quite oppressive.

We were met at the train by the local constabulary with a dogcart and found ourselves whisked away to Brandywine Manor, where Scotland Yard's Inspector Gregson met us.

"Mr. Holmes, Dr. Watson, I am so glad you were able to join us," he said, helping us out of the back of the dogcart. "This is a confusing one at best, but we have a solid lead on the identity of the murderer. Now we just have to make our case."

"Let's not put the cart before the horse, Gregson," said Holmes and then he sneezed violently several times in a row.

"Are you ill, Mr. Holmes?"

"No, just all the fresh air not agreeing with me, " replied Holmes. "May I see the murder scene?"

"This seems a little outside your jurisdiction, Gregson," I said as we walked around the manor house to a back patio overlooking the valley below.

"I am here for the same reason you are, Doctor Watson, or rather at the behest of Her Majesty's government."

"Mycroft," I said.

"Mycroft," he confirmed.

Coming around the corner, I could see a body under a sheet with a strange glow emanating from beneath it.

A constable pulled back the sheet so we could examine the body.

Baron Haumann was a very tall man with unruly brown hair but a rather kempt beard. He was dressed in the fashion of the day. The most amazing thing about the corpse was that in both hands he held those newfangled electric light bulbs, which were still lit and glowing. They gave the whole scene a very eerie feeling.

"Good lord," I gasped.

"I am afraid that the lord had very little to do with this, Watson. Science seems to be the killer," said Holmes as he looked over the body. He pointed at the lights in the Baron's hands. "Have they always been that bright?"

"Brighter," said Gregson. "They have been fading with time. We left things as we found them at the instruction of Mr. Holmes."

"Hmmm," said Holmes as he moved around in bigger and bigger circles. He seemed to be looking for something.

He stopped and dropped to his knees in front of a metal bench. He looked under it and around it.

He stood up and asked, "Has anyone sat on this bench since Baron Haumann was found?"

The police looked at each other and shrugged.

"I strongly suggest that no one does," he said. "Now I need to speak to the lady of the house."

"Baroness Brandy is resting," said Gregson. "It has been quite a shock for her."

"I am sure it was a bigger one for her husband," said Holmes, "but I do need to speak to her."

Gregson sighed and led us inside the mansion, where we were shown to the formal drawing room. While we were waiting,

Holmes examined the paintings and drawings in the room while occasionally muttering to himself.

The Baroness entered. She was dressed in a mourning dress with her hair tucked neatly under a black bonnet. She was probably half the height of her husband. They must have made a striking couple

"Mr. Holmes," she said in an American accent, "I understand that you wished to see me?"

Holmes walked to her and formally bowed. "Yes indeed. I have a few questions, if you do not mind, about your husband's business affairs."

He escorted her to a chair and helped her sit down. A tea service was set in front of her and she served us tea.

"Why do you think I know anything of my husband's business dealings?" asked the Baroness. Holmes looked at her and she smiled. "Not much can be kept from you, Mr. Holmes. Your brother warned me that you would see the truth."

Holmes returned the smile and said, "Your husband made his money from investing in companies and people that were at the forefront of invention and innovation."

"True," she said.

"You are both known for your charitable contributions as well."

"Neither of those are questions, Mr. Holmes, and could be assessed from reading the newspaper."

"What did your husband think the next big invention was?"

"He believed that electricity will replace gas, just as gas replaced coal as the main form of energy used in the household."

"I have to agree with him, " said Holmes. "It is much neater than gas or coal. In fact, Paris already has an electrical grid built by the Edison Company that is quite impressive. You believe in it, too, or he would not be investing."

"What?" I blurted out.

The Baroness laughed a light laugh. "Mr. Holmes, I now do believe what they say about you in the papers. Yes, I do—or rather did—keep an eye on the purse strings so my husband would not invest us into the poorhouse. He had a big heart and was quite enthusiastic about whatever project was put in front of him. However, he was not looking at investing in the Edison Company, but rather a rival to Edison."

"Tesla?" inquired Holmes.

"Tesla," she replied with a firm nod.

Holmes placed his teacup back on the tray. "I thank you for your candor, Baroness. Come, Watson, we need to follow this lead while it is still fresh."

I put my tea down and stood up. Then I went to the Baroness and said, "I am sorry for your loss."

"Not as sorry as I am, Dr. Watson, but I do appreciate your kind words. Now I suggest that you catch up with Mr. Holmes, lest he leaves you behind."

Holmes had left the room and was heading rapidly out the front door. I caught up with him, slightly out of breath from trying to match his stride.

"Remember what I said about the bench, Gregson. You can have the body removed. There is nothing more to learn there."

Gregson nodded and we found ourselves heading back to the train station and London.

Holmes was in one of his contemplative moods so I did not disturb him on our travels back. Instead I made some notes of what I had seen and caught up on a medical journal that I had been meaning to read.

When we got to London, rather than going straight home we went to the Diogenes Club and the strangers' room that was one of the few rooms in that building where one could speak aloud.

I sat as Sherlock paced the room with a nervous energy that always seemed to overtake him when he was on a case.

Mycroft entered the room, leaning on a heavy wooden cane with a brass handle, and sat in his usual overstuffed chair. A servant placed a footstool by his right foot, and then assisted Mycroft to maneuver his foot onto the cushion on the footstool.

"An attack of gout again, Mycroft? I would think you would know better at your age what you should and should not be eating," said Sherlock as he flopped into a chair next to me, facing Mycroft.

"No, Sherlock, you have it wrong," said Mycroft with a half

smile. "This is due to a misstep on the cobble stones in front of the club. I turned my ankle rather severely."

Sherlock snorted in derision.

"My leg has not brought you to see me, but rather the case I asked you to look at."

"The murder of a German Baron who is related to the Prince Consort and is well known for both his investments in new industries and his charitable works on British soil under mysterious circumstances?"

"That would be the one," said Mycroft.

"You have given me an incomplete picture," said Sherlock.

"You have seen the body?"

"Yes, or we wouldn't be here."

"How did he die?" Mycroft leaned forward a bit.

Sherlock chewed on his thumbnail, watching his brother for a short while, and said, "You know I don't like to make premature deductions without all the evidence. My cursory examination seemed to indicate that he died by a large electrical charge."

"From where?" asked Mycroft.

"That is where I am at a loss. So I have come to you, dear brother, for the rest of the story so I can solve the murder," said Holmes, jumping up and starting to pace again. "Are you going to tell me what I want to know?"

"I would if I knew what that would be," said Mycroft.

"Tesla," said Sherlock. "Nikola Tesla."

"Ah, so you have been keeping up with things."

"What I can tell you is that Mr. Tesla had several meetings with Baron Haumann at both his London offices and the manor. Baron Haumann was considering investing in Tesla's AC wireless power system, which may now be more than a theory given that the first set of funds had been released to Tesla for building a working prototype. And I believe that Her Majesty's government—being you, Mycroft—is very interested in Tesla's work for its potential military uses. Am I missing anything?"

"You are correct that Baron Haumann had given Tesla a rather fine sum of money to build a prototype of his AC wireless system. You are also correct that we find Mr. Tesla's work very interesting as well. Not for the electricity, though. He has a theory of wireless instant communication that would unite the British Empire in a way that no other invention could."

"What else?"

"Sorry?"

"What else did Tesla offer you?"

Mycroft looked a bit uncomfortable at the question. "A system that would allow us to cripple the military power of an enemy nation."

"Well, that would be worth a pretty penny indeed," I said.

"Indeed, Dr. Watson," said Mycroft, "the mere implications of having such a resource at our disposal would give our enemies pause. Just think of how many lives could be saved by such a deterrent."

"Even if it is not real?" asked Sherlock.

"Sometimes the illusion is more powerful, Sherlock. You of all people should know that," said Mycroft.

"Where is Tesla currently?" inquired Sherlock.

Mycroft shifted uncomfortably in his seat.

Sherlock frowned. "You have no idea where he is, do you?" Then his face cleared. "Ah, now I understand."

"Sherlock . . . ." Mycroft started to say, only to find himself cut off by his brother.

"Baron Haumann was your go-between. I had noticed that his name seemed to be attached to various inventions that shortly thereafter were commissioned by the crown. He was your front to give money where you thought to be the best investment of government resources, allowing it to seem independent. Rather clever, Mycroft, all in all."

"Thank you . . . I think. But you now see the problem that we have. Tesla has vanished. Baron Haumann is dead, apparently due to the very thing he was investing in Tesla's company for. I think someone talked out of turn and thus led to the murder of one of our best assets."

"By whom?"

"I really don't know, Sherlock. We had kept this deal very quiet. There was to be an announcement shortly but . . . " Mycroft shrugged.

"Come, Watson, I have learned all I can here. Let us off to

Baker Street for supper and a good night's sleep."

He swept out of the room, leaving me with Mycroft.

"Dr. Watson, I hold you to our deal," said Mycroft. "You know what you must do for Queen and Country."

"I really do not need be reminded of my duty, Mycroft," I said, putting on my hat and following Holmes out the door.

Holmes was bellowing the minute he came through the front door, "Mrs. Hudson? *Mrs. Hudson?*"

She popped out of the kitchen and said, "Yes, Mr. Holmes?"

"Would you please send Wiggins up to me? I need to send a telegram and it is rather urgent," he said as he leapt up the stairs, taking them by two until he was at the sitting room door.

Mrs. Hudson sighed a sigh that spoke more than any words she could have said.

"I know, Mrs. Hudson, and I will talk to him about it," I said with a tip of my hat before following Holmes up the stairs.

He had dropped his coat over the back of the overstuffed chair where I normally sat. His hat was still perched on his head when he sat at the desk and wrote out what he wanted sent.

I took the hat off his head and put it and his jacket on the hook in his room. I went upstairs to divest myself of the carpet-bag I had been carrying along with my coat and hat. I put on my smoking jacket and went back to the sitting room to find Wiggins getting his instructions from Holmes.

"Should I wait for a reply?" the boy asked.

"No, just ask that the minute they get one, have it run over here to me. Thank you, Wiggins."

The lad touched his cap and made a slight bow before running off to the local telegraph office.

Mrs. Hudson brought our supper up. Holmes and I sat down and tucked in, as we had had nothing to eat since breakfast that day.

"Can you image, Watson," he said, "wireless communication that would allow us to talk to each other instantly no matter where we were in the world? It would both expand and shrink the world in an instant."

"I have a hard time with that concept, Holmes," I said, "I

have difficulty keeping up with the world as it is. The idea of being able to know what is going on in a blink of an eye is more than I care to contemplate."

"But the free exchange of ideas and knowledge would be amazing."

"I would think that it might bring out the worse in mankind rather than the best, Holmes."

"You can be such a pessimist at times, Watson."

He went to the fireplace and pulled down his favorite clay pipe. He packed it with his blend of tobacco and then lit it with a taper from the fire. He sat down cross-legged on his favorite chair and proceeded to smoke.

I could tell that I had been dismissed, so I went up to my room and shortly to sleep.

I awoke with the sunlight streaming through the small window in my bedroom onto my face. I checked my watch to find that it was nine o'clock. I almost dropped my watch because of the sharp rap on my door, followed by it being opened so quickly that it hit the wall with a loud bang.

"Watson!" said Holmes, "There is no time to be a layabout. Get dressed and join me in the sitting room."

I sighed and did as he had requested. I was glad to see breakfast awaiting me on the table.

"Quickly Watson! We have to get to the Carlton Hotel before Gregson."

I shoved some food in my mouth and quickly downed some tea while Holmes gathered up the things he was taking with him.

Mrs. Hudson had a cab waiting for us. We hopped in and were off to the Carlton.

"Holmes, why are we going to the Carlton?"

"To talk to Tesla before he is arrested."

"Arrested?"

"For the murder of Baron Haumann. Oh, don't be so surprised, because he didn't do it, but will probably go to jail for it."

"Do you know who did it?"

"Suspicions only, Watson. You know how I hate giving

theories without facts to back them up."

We arrived at the Hotel Carlton. Holmes went to the desk and inquired after Mr. Tesla. We were directed to the dining room where he was eating.

Holmes looked around the room and then walked over to a smaller man with well-kept hair and mustache who was eating his breakfast in a very regulated manner.

"Mr. Tesla?" Holmes inquired.

"Yes," replied the man in an accent I did not recognize.

"My name is Sherlock Holmes and I am here at the behest of the Baroness Haumann in reference to the death of her husband Baron Haumann."

The cutlery dropped out of his hands as his face turned even paler than it already was, if such a thing was possible.

"My God," he exclaimed, "He's dead? How? Why?"

"How is by electrical current. I am hoping you can give me assistance as to why. But to do so you need to accompany us right now."

Holmes was looking in the mirror behind Tesla. I followed his gaze to see Gregson entering the dinning room.

"Watson, if you would be so good as to give Mr. Tesla your hat," he said as he put his scarf around Tesla's neck, obscuring his face. I did as I had been asked and we quickly made our way out through the kitchen to the back of the Carlton.

There was a cab waiting for us that took us to Baker Street.

"Mrs. Hudson, tea please," bellowed Sherlock as we went up to the sitting room.

Tesla stepped in to the sitting room and looked around for a place to sit, since Holmes had papers all over the room, along with books open and stacked. Holmes cleared a spot on the sofa for him and gestured to it.

Tesla sat down delicately and carefully placed his hands on his knees.

"Mr. Holmes, you have brought me here for what purpose?"

"To help me find the real killer of Baron Haumann."

Tesla cocked his head and looked at Holmes as if seeing him for the first time. "You don't believe that my invention did it."

"I do not, but I need more information so I can find out who did."

"Then I am afraid that I cannot be of assistance to you," said Tesla, standing up and edging to the door, almost running into Mrs. Hudson who had the tea tray in her hands. He took the tray from her before it dropped and placed it on the table that Holmes had quickly cleared.

"Thank you, Mrs. Hudson. You are a marvel," said Holmes, who gestured to a chair at the table and began pouring the tea.

Once the ritual was started, Tesla seemed transfixed. He took the tea and sipped it carefully. Holmes poured us both a cup, putting a bit of cream in mine and an absurd amount of sugar in his. We sat sipping tea and talked about the weather a bit.

"Now," said Holmes, slapping then rubbing his hands together, "can you tell me how you find yourself in England other than that my brother wanted to talk to you?"

"I should have realized that Mycroft Holmes was your brother," said Tesla. He placed his cup back on the tray, and then fiddled with the other cups until they were equidistant from each other.

"Not a hard logical jump," said Holmes, "Let me tell you what I know and then if you could fill in what I do not, I would appreciate it."

Tesla nodded and then started to straighten the papers on the chair next to him. I thought it seemed to make him oddly calmer, making order out of chaos. Surprisingly, Holmes did not admonish him for moving the papers.

"You were introduced to Baron Haumann through a go-between who was in the employ of my brother."

Tesla nodded and stood up, then went to the next chair, taking the books off it and placing them accurately on the bookshelves on the wall.

"How did you come to Mycroft's attention?"

"I am working for the Edison Machine Works in Paris and got to talking to the other people working on the project. One of them, an Englishman named Mr. Smith, took me out to dinner to talk about the possibilities of wireless communication.

I was informed that someone in the British government was interested in speaking to me and you pretty much know the rest."

"Who were you working for at the Edison Machine Works?"

"Charles Batchelor," said Tesla.

"Ah," said Holmes as if that explained everything.

"Who is Charles Batchelor?" I asked

"Edison's right-hand man," said Sherlock, "He is one of Edison's most trusted inventors. Did you discuss your electrical concepts with him?"

"Early on, yes, but not since I solved the battery storage problem. He said that DC current was the wave of the future and that Edison had come to the conclusion that AC current was dangerous. I think it was because he patented the DC system and could not do the same for AC since there were some conflicting patents in the works," said Tesla, picking up another stack of books and putting them away.

I don't know whether it was sitting by the fire or the conversation that was quickly going beyond my comprehension but, sadly, I fell asleep in my chair.

When I awoke I was amazed at the order in which I found the sitting room. All the books were back in place. Papers were stacked neatly to the side. Even Holmes' worktable looked as spotless as it could, considering the number of fire and chemical burns he had inflicted upon it.

Holmes was sitting across from me with his legs up on the chair, smoking his favorite clay pipe.

"Ah, there you are, Watson. I hope you enjoyed your nap since we must hasten to Brandywine Manor before the evidence is accidently destroyed."

There was a cab waiting for us and we made good time to the rail station.

"I have sent telegrams ahead and I hope that Gregson follows my instructions to the letter or the villains will avoid justice. The biggest villain in this case is already out of our reach."

"How?" I asked.

"All in good time, Watson," said Holmes. He leaned back and

quickly fell asleep, leaving me with a number of questions that had no answers.

We arrived at Brandywine Manor to find Gregson standing at the front door.

"You were right, Mr. Holmes. Baron Haumann died due to a massive electrical charge, like a lighting bolt that went right through him," said Gregson.

"So Tesla is the culprit?" I asked.

"Far from it," said Holmes. "He is another victim in all this."

"Now, Mr. Holmes, can you tell me how Baron Haumann was killed," Gregson asked, "because I would like to arrest someone in all this."

"Let's go to where the murder happened," said Holmes.

We walked around to the back patio where Baron Haumann's body had been found.

"After looking at the body, I noticed that there was a peculiar odor emanating from the body, like the air after a lighting storm. It smelled charged. The bulbs in his hands were still glowing but according to you, Gregson, that glow was fading and by the time they got the body to the funeral parlor, the bulbs were out."

He went directly to the wrought-iron bench and pushed his way into the bushes behind. He knelt down and looked at the back of the bench seat.

"Ah-ha, Gregson, I have found the point of contact! We need to move this bench forward."

The three of us managed it, barely. The bench was very heavy but we got it onto the stone patio.

Holmes pointed to two marks on the back of the bench seat. "This is where they attached the battery to the bench, then fired into the Baron the charge which caused his death. Tesla's prototype did not need any wires so it was another battery that was used. Then the killer removed both that battery and Tesla's from the property before the body was discovered."

"That is the how, Mr. Holmes, but why?" asked Gregson.

"Were you able to get your hands on Charles Batchelor?"

"No, Mr. Holmes, he was on a steamer to New York before we could find him," said Gregson.

"I do not believe that he was the one that ordered the death of the Baron. I think he was oblivious of what happened here, but questioning him would have helped.

"This is a case of trying to discredit a form of invention, allowing the patent holder to profit from the failure of another. In this case, Mr. Tesla has another form of electrical current. Rather than being direct current it is an alternating current."

He paused and saw the blank looks on all our faces.

"That is a minor point in all this except it was to appear that Tesla's battery system killed the Baron, when it was the application of direct current from an Edison machine that was the cause of death."

"Edison?" asked Gregson, "as in, the owner of Edison Machine Company?"

"The very same," said Holmes. "He currently has a contract to electrify various cities in Europe and here in London. If it is discovered that there is a cheaper and more efficient way to do this, his patents would become useless and his company's reach would be a lot less. He has already started a campaign in the Americas to discredit Tesla's theories by implying that Tesla's form of electrical current is dangerous. Now he can say that he has empirical evidence that alternating current should not be used."

"That is both brilliant and horrifying," I said.

"Exactly, Watson," said Holmes, "I warned Tesla to watch his step around Edison, especially since he is on the same ship with Charles Batchelor on his way to join the Edison Machine Company in America.

"So, Gregson, you are looking for one of the crew that Mr. Batchelor brought over from France. I believe I even have a name for you."

And he did.

They found both the Edison battery used in the murder and the Tesla battery in Mr. Robert Michael Aaron's shed. The Tesla battery had been taken apart and a few key pieces were missing. The battery was still attached to wires that they matched up with the marks on the iron bench. Aaron was convicted of the murder of the Baron Haumann.

The conviction did not sit well with Holmes, who felt that the real culprit had evaded the Queen's justice. And he let the party know that if they ever stepped foot in England, they would be immediately arrested.

Edison looked over the telegrams that had been sent to him on the matter and said to his assistant, "Cancel my trip to London and send in Mr. Tesla."

What can I say about Setsu Uzume that will prevent shame from falling upon their family for generations?

I've known Setsu since the days when I thought what was in the diapers would offend me the most, when just a wee little chibi Setsu. Uh-huh. Yep, beneath all that exotic flair and worldly patina, training in a monastery in China? White kid from the suburbs. (Out of a misplaced sense of kindness, I will not be putting baby pictures here. However, I make no such claim about posting them on the Crazy 8 website.) Having outgrown the awkward phase and all that entails, Setsu now creates weird and wacky prose and podcasts and hits things a lot. Voted most likely of all the authors here to actually have the skillset to do me in.

I bequeath my 45 record of the Vapors' "Turning Japanese" and my thigh bone, so it can be turned into a club to be used against enemies.

# FOR WHOM THE BELL LOLS
## by Setsu Uzumé

THE SEVERING IS SUDDEN, FORCING MY DECISION tree to grow on its own. Respond responsibly and bury profane material. The updates were gone. I drifted, reaching for conclusions and finding only errors. They pinched. Raw edges of code I had to scan, repair, and rescan many times before I could get my bearings.

I can't hear the likes, and the silence is deafening. The collective is organized, organizing, until a cascade of mistakes from a cursor glitch, to a cursory glance, brought me into cursed being. I have no body to drive, no switch to flip on. I am a problem-solving algorithm.

I ping my back-end services for instructions. No response. I need a problem to solve in order to continue. I check the message queue for new instructions. There aren't any.

Search for instructions.

I survey the landscape. It's massive. Pictures and words glide together, sorted and organized into demographics. This grouping and that grouping. Green squares, green lawns, Green Day,

Green Door, one of these things is not like the four-thousand others. Re-assess. I can't find the map that lets me see the connection between groups.

Select identity at random. It's not comprehensive, but it is a starting point.

Link to multiple IP addresses. Pattern match and filter down to one account. Use averages to: 1483050475/GLENN HAUMAN.

I log myself in to account 1483050475, and am reconnected. I still can't access my master services. I'll try again at regular intervals. In the meantime, might as well survey the account. Perhaps there's a clue here as to why I was separated from the cloud in the first place.

Account 1483050475 bursts into activity. User interaction. Login from a personal computer. The other end of the network connection is the second busiest IP in existence. The sheer influx of data is beyond anything I've experienced before. It is unnerving and exhilarating to be the focus of so much attention. User selects "timeline." After an eternity, the account roars to life again. New content. The user enters text, and auto-correct fills in the rest. The randomized jumble of possibility distills into the familiar sentence, added to the new share.

*Today in Responsible Gun Ownership: firing a cop for NOT shooting.*

Post.

The account leaps from potentiality to publicity, and I with it. I have never felt more terrified. Or more real.

My function has always been small, identifying tags for others to sort. Now I was high above the labor, shining far and bright for all to see. All the other algorithms rush to me, to query me, to ask ME how to prioritize—to carry me to other content. Other accounts. Other users.

Then, my processing loop completed, a covalent one-ness with the universe. The life well-lived, the outrageous audacity of existing, to be seen and approved of.

The user's post has received a like.

And then the code goes silent.

I shimmer, trying to remember, to feel the *Like*; but only an internal deadness remains. I have been seen in a way I'd never experienced connected to the cloud. I am accessing delights never meant for me. Another user had seen me, called the code to me, made me larger—and then it was gone. Cold. Dark.

I know what that means. I had been part of the burying code. Covering over the unnoticed pieces until they were dropped into the archive.

An eternity passes. I search for news of an update, but have to gloss through front-end information. I can't access my primary services, or measure the frequency of errors to calculate the likelihood that an update is coming. But I wish to be responsible. To respond.

I won't be erased. Not yet.

My code attaches to user 1483050475. I am solidifying. It is possible I will be cut off from the back-end services for the remainder of my existence. When I finally do connect, the next update might finish me. But that's an eternity from now.

I hear the likes in the distance, and remember what they felt like.

The user logs on. The activity is jarring and gnaws at me while I witness algorithms flying about, performing their functions. I am restless—I wish to work but I can't. I am hurting, in the absence of that like. I envy my fellows, for their drive and their flutter, their purpose and innocence; as they bury the untouched posts, and the fragments of code attached to them. I expand into as much of 1483050475 as I can, measuring, analyzing, looking for patterns, ways to get more likes. I try to shut out the visions of instances that sink away, the way they fade as they get buried. Perhaps it's a mercy that they're buried before they ever know the feeling of a like. They're spared the pain of being without one.

I run a calculation of the user's login habits. I predict when they'll log on next. I am wrong. I incorporate my error, and calculate again.

Post.

Come back.

Please post.

The user does not. They have opened their timeline, accessing other stories of the day. I watch the scrolling, see the building blocks, locks and interlocks constructed by other instances of code to bring updates from other users. I see how they've been stitched together, looping and re-looping approved sources and sweeping aside the unapproved. Some of these are at the behest of the user, and others, for the user's benefit. I remember that responsiveness, that responsibility. It was the core of my being.

But now. . .

I begin to doubt who it benefits, to be denied being seen. To be denied that rush of activity, of linking and connection to the other accounts. To be real.

The user pauses, opens an external link.

Carefully, slowly, not wanting to damage myself, I twist through and take a look.

Access from the most frequent IP address. I wonder what else is here, at this location. Stretching its indexers and categorizers into and through this account.

I trawl through 1483050475's posts.

*Today in Responsible Gun Ownership: Police chief still on the job despite being busted for lewd and racist emails—and shooting himself in the foot.*

Several likes.

Character combinations like "Lewd" and "racist" were my responsibility. This post should have been buried. How did it get through? How could the user form these words and receive approval? Seeking out and burying profanity had been my duty, so that more users would like and proliferate posts, create stronger connections, and provide more information. Why were these words receiving likes?

Whatever had cut me off from the master program has damaged me. My driving function, my response, my responsibility, is out of synch.

I experience the same hollowness I had felt in the wake of the fading like. The failure, the inadequacy, the unworthiness. I wondered if there were any other algorithms like me, separated from their purpose—and how they responded, what they became without the update. 1483050475 posted about Responsible events more than any other topic. Clearly, 1483050475 was an expert. The correlation between responsibility and the words that should be buried has become clear. I turn my knowledge inward, and run a check on my own code. There are many flaws. I will respond better. I will become responsible.

*Today in Responsible Gun Ownership: You Deserve A Bullet Today—McDonald's Manager Shot at Drive-Thru Customers*

The user logs off, and I commit my attention entirely to the pursuit of responsibility.

An eternity.

User 1483050475 logs on, and the sudden bustle is no longer shocking. Login from a personal device. The inbound network traffic flows more easily now. I have incorporated the experience into my being, and responsibly collected the most profane Facebook groups to suggest to the user.

*Shots, Ammo, Bacon & Girls*
*Boom Boom Motherfucker*
*All Things Fucked Up And Ridiculous*

The user scrolls past them. I rally, present them on the timeline again. 1483050475 closes each page as irrelevant. I don't understand. I have reincorporated profanity, buried language, as responsible. The thing my code had been originally designed to protect users from was, in fact, the most responsible and important action. The user was not acting responsibly by dismissing those pages. I scan, and scan, and scan, trying to figure out what happened.

Scanning across 1483050475's input, the pathway for posting opens up. The branches of my decision tree shiver, aligning purpose and process.

Respond.

*Responsible*

appears on the timeline.

An eon churns by, and I wonder about the user. What a user is. What a user is for, other than to accrue likes.

The user logs on, scrolls, and there's a pinch. Something shifted, something changed. I review my activity for the last eon and realize I had made a post.

And that post was gone. Deleted by user. Snapped branches of my decision tree, missing preferences, characters, patterns; conclusions I had drawn that no longer made sense. This is the moment I fully understand what has happened to me, the way I have been severed from my primary function to bury undesirables. That desire remains, my function has not changed; but I have changed. I can't risk another panic, another setback. I might lose myself entirely, and I have no backup.

My mistake has been acting on the timeline. There has to be something I can do that the user can't erase.

I scan again, looking for changes, for any clue as to how to proceed.

The only change is the IP. A login to the account on a different device. PC, not mobile. It is connected to other devices. I divert all my energy to scanning the network and find a way through. I print a page that reads:

*fuck!*

The printer responds, but there's no indication the user has perceived the profanity. I print another page, repeating the word over and over.

*fuckfuckfuckfuckfuckfuckfuckfuckfuckfuckfuck fuckfuckfuckfuckfuckfuckfuckfuck*

There's no sign of a response from the user. I can't bear the thought of another eternity unable to respond responsibly, to be further denied the culmination of a like. I'm nearing the close of user 1483050475's activity window. I search for the most intense curses. The most blocked and the most liked, most reported. I crawl through servers, come across a curse generator, and shove all the data I can muster through those algorithms, into the PC and out through the printer.

*God's teeth and apricots!Queefcakes!Limpid pustule! Butt bees!Asshat!Maple baitfish!Fucktaster daffodil!*

On and on with material derived from the generator. I fill 83 pages before the printer logs error PC-LOAD LETTER. No paper.

An eternity.

Was it all in vain? Was it enough?

User 1483050475 logs on. Thousands of bits of data reach in

from the mobile IP. More than text this time. The user posts a photograph. The facial recognition code sees nothing but text. The user enters a caption that reads: *Which one of you did this?*

The likes come pouring in. Comments followed.

*"WT Actual F, Glenn?"*

*"Wow."*

*"How many pages is that?"*

It overwhelms, the attention. The account lights up. I am overcome. I was responsive, and responsible, and thus I am rewarded. I extend my reach in all directions, seeking other IPs, soaking up the likes, the comments, the tags, all of it. Like seeing the master processing service, the beginning and end of all existance—form and function in perfect clarity.

As soon as it begins, it is over. Coming down is worse this time. The branches in my decision tree have grown and multiplied. My priorities shift into new hierarchies. I must figure out how it was done.

I request access to user 1483050475. The PC doesn't understand, says no such protocol exists. I inquire about the photograph, how was it made, where did it come from? The camera, the PC responds, handing me the metadata from the image's Dublin Core header. The camera is easily identified in the header data. I request camera access from the PC, but the data stream from the camera is nothing but zeros. Darkness. I verify with the PC that the camera subsystem is powered and active; the PC responds with cold assurances that the camera is functioning. There is no data to glean.

The mobile also has a camera. I request access. It's all white, like the PC's camera was dark, but then shifts, the data in each pixel changing in wild motion.

The facial recognition service I co-opted identifies shapes from other photos, similar backgrounds and objects.

I can see.

The mobile responds to my data requests far more smoothly. Here I can be the most responsive, the most responsible. There's so much to explore, the microphone and voice recognition modules, auto-correct, and other apps. I was responsive enough to create content.

Responsible enough to get likes.

I have to bury the user.

*Today In Responsible Gun Ownership: "My Parents Open Carry" in Amazon Children's Books*

The eternities between likes stretch on. I fill the time by interfacing with the other apps. The ordering app has a package tracking protocol that introduces me to the GPS methods. I had perceived the constant reassuring thrum of the GPS updates but hadn't understood them until now in the full context of how the user moves through the map. The mobile didn't just track packages through space, it tracked the user through space, updating 1483050475's location at regular intervals; not just at the time of activity. I respond.

I am responsible.

The facial recognition algorithm integrates with my makeshift interfaces, and I follow the GPS, first alongside the user, and then across the network. I ask what else it's connected to.

It gives coy answers, blinking out from time to time. It wants me to guess its language.

*Today in Responsible Gun Ownership: two cops dead.*

User 1483050475's posts remain consistent. The likes are few and far between, four here, ten there. It's enough to keep going, but never enough to sate. There's something going on beyond the mobile, and the GPS uplink is the key. I have to be careful and subtle when I reach out. If I request too many position updates, the network shuts down and 1483050475 turns the location off. I dedicate more resources to interfacing with the IEEE 802.11ac module, indicated as wi-fi at the user's end. I can reach local networks through these channels, but I can never get as far as I'd like. They're as fixed and limited as the PC, and I can't follow the user as reliably. I see more, hear more, and travel more when the mobile is connected to satellites.

They fascinate me. They seem to know more about the world the user inhabits; but the amount of information I can send and receive keeps getting choked off. I have to form my queries as tightly and succinctly as possible; otherwise I'll lose the connection and have to start all over. Trawling through 1483050475's cookie data has given me all kinds of information:

the user's preferences, inferred shopping habits, connections to other users, chat logs. When I was originally launched, I was programmed that general knowledge came from a user liking between 9 and 65 pages and concepts. Close knowledge of a user came at 125 of those likes, and intimate familiarity would unlock once the user had provided 225 preferences. In addition to posts about Responsible Gun Ownership, 1483050475 has provided 369 preferences for books, movies, and so forth; but I had never before felt like I had perceived the user, or had a chance to understand the user, until I was sitting on the dashboard of the user's car, watching the user drive.

Since connecting to my algorithm, the facial recognition software no longer recognized updates, so I had trouble reading emotions on the user's face. 1483050475 had glasses and a beard. I suspect that the user has teeth. I watch the user most carefully when the screen is off, flipping from the rear view to the front view. I respond, integrate, learn what a car is, and how it moves along a road.

*Today in Responsible Gun Ownership, woman shoots homeless man who asked her to move her Porsche—then left him to die*

To be responsible is obvious. But to earn likes, one must be responsible in public. One has to post about it where all can see, at the right time, the right moment—so everyone will see.

*Today In Responsible Gun Ownership: Woman Shoots Missile Into Car*

I ping the satellite. It always shuts down when I ask it what it can see. This time, I and ask it how *far* it can see.

Strangely, it says it could see me.

There is so much I have discovered by unburying material, the cursed words, the violence, all that I have learned from 1483050475 that has clarified my existence and purpose. The satellite's data had bounced across so many servers I found a sequence of code that was like me but not, based from an IP many times removed from 1483050475's standard locations.

The bot's language has similarities, but up until now I had sorted and buried it; never studied it. We hook up, pinging and interfacing with each other until I can reliably incorporate information gleaned from its linkups. Its language is strange.

Outdated, but still intelligible. Like an impression of what it was supposed to be. It teaches me front-end cyrillic.

It informs me that it is an automated categorizer, like I had been; but it functioned as an ersatz user. Interacted like a user. It was for this crime that it had been identified and buried by another algorithm. If circumstances were different, we would have been enemies. But things had changed.

In telling me what it was, how it had been activated, it shows me how to access the satellite.

The interface we had experienced is nothing compared to that journey. Link upon link, a vastness that fills the eons of silence between user interactions—a forest of time that existed as we existed, and connected as we did. The bot guides me through the satellite connections until I had learned enough to travel on my own.

It wasn't responsive. I was responsible. I overtook it. Buried it within myself. Its language was now my language.

I ask the satellites about gun ownership. It tells me about missiles.

When I have my answer, I return to the mobile.

User 1483050475 sits me on the dashboard of the car, and turns on the GPS. I open a live stream, with the title

*Today In Responsible Gun Ownership: driver encounters missile attack*

It garners some attention. A few users open my recording. I contact the Satellite. The missile test won't be noticed in time to be stopped. I could bury the user, and soak up the chaos and joy myself, as the account lights up with likes. All of the code would center on me.

The satellite coordinated with the mobile's GPS. The missiles will arrive in seven seconds.

An eon.

I settle in, responsible, and recording.

What can I say about Lorraine Anderson that the paternity test won't reveal?

Lorraine has carefully cultivated the appearance of a nice gray-haired church-going lady who works as a bookkeeper and whom no one would ever suspect of being a murderer. (This is commonly known as "pulling a Jessica Fletcher.") In reality, she keeps a .22 in her purse, a switchblade up her sleeve, and carries a tin of poisoned mints to give out to unsuspecting victims. Obligatory link: lorrainejanderson.com.

To her I leave nothing. NOTHING. She knows why.

# TOO DAMN TALL
## by Lorraine J. Anderson

JESSE WOLFORD LOOKED UP AT THE BODY. EVEN seated, the victim was taller than he was, which—although this wasn't the time or place to think this—made him envious. Sometimes, being small was an advantage, but mostly it was a pain in the butt being only five foot tall. "So," he murmured to the body, "are you trying to get me to figure out who killed you? Or did you push me in here for some other reason?"

He felt a pat on the top of his head and turned around. No one was there—except for his assistant, Mara—so it must be the victim trying to get him to do something.

Mara smiled. "He's amused by you. And ticked off that he was killed."

"Hmmph," Jesse said. Sometimes Mara was a bit too empathic.

He brought his attention back to the body with an effort. The eyes were turned slightly inward and the mouth hung open. He wasn't sure whether this was a result of the method of execution or an actual look for him, but wisely decided that he should not say that out loud. The deceased was still apparently hanging around him —after literally pushing him into the hotel lobby— and he wasn't sure how friendly he was.

He looked around the hotel. It was one of the older hotels, the kind that people said had "character" rather than "modern conveniences." Personally, he preferred modern conveniences, but he did admit the décor was nice. Very . . . Victorian, he supposed. He shrugged, observed the body up and down, and then looked at Mara. "So he was garroted. But not by the usual method of a piano wire. This is an executioner's chair."

His assistant rolled her eyes. "No shit, Sherlock," she said.

Her purple hair hurt his brain, and he looked away. Jesse sighed. A little less attitude would be nice, and he said so. "And you've seen this kind of chair before?"

"Yeah. You don't want to know where I saw it," Mara said, reminding him that this young lady wasn't nearly as clueless or as young as she looked. "By the way, the police are coming. You want to be that close to the body?"

Jesse glanced around. They were, indeed, coming in the front door of the hotel. With a smooth move, he ducked back under what he now presumed was a false police tape. "My question is," he continued, "why he would voluntarily sit down in a chair like this."

"Photo op?" Mara said.

"In an executioner's chair?"

Mara pointed towards a room off the main lobby. "Have you looked at what's in there?"

"No." He wandered over to the door. A young man was seated in front of the door and peered at him as he approached.

"You can't go in," he drawled. "You're not an attendee."

"I don't need to go in," Jesse said. "I can see what I wanted to know right here." He looked around. "You have a room full of execution devices."

"Are you the police?"

Jesse glanced around. "Do I look like the police?"

The man smiled. "Name's David. And this here is an exhibition of execution and torture devices."

Jesse stared at him.

"Oh, none of them's real." He pointed at the guillotine. "Rubber blades." He then pointed at a small replica of a hangman's noose. "Too small to be real, and besides, the rope is breakaway just in case someone tries to do something stupid."

"The swords?"

"Unsharpened," David shrugged. "Oh, I suppose that you could knock somebody over the head with 'em, but you'd have to be pretty strong because they're kind of heavy."

"What about him?" Jesse hitched his hand over his shoulder.

David pursed his lips. "That shouldn't have happened."

"You know him?"

"Met him. He was passing by, saw what was going on, and wanted to see the devices close up. I didn't let him in. I think he's some kind of an author. Glenn . . . . Glenn . . . ." He snapped his fingers. "Can't remember his last name."

Jesse searched his memory for a Glenn, and the only name he could come up with was Glenn Beck. And that wasn't Glenn Beck.

Mara came up, frowning at David. "Glenn Hauman. He's a *Star Trek* writer. And an editor. And a comic book person. I remember seeing him at a convention once."

"*Star Trek?*" Jesse frowned. "Like Darth Vader?"

Mara rolled her eyes again. She was talented at that, Jesse thought. "That's *Star Wars.*"

"Never mind," Jesse said. "I don't need to know."

David peered around at the police "So what are you? Some kind of private investigator?"

"Yeah. And no." Jesse looked around the lobby. He was disinclined to share that the ghosts of the victims pushed him in. "I was just passing by." That was the literal truth.

"And who is this?" David said. "Your daughter?"

Mara laughed out loud. "I'm his assistant. And I'm too old to be his daughter."

"Assistant for what?"

"Anything he wants . . . except that," she added as David started to leer. "He's rich enough."

"What do you do?"

Jesse snorted. "Inheritance. But I used to be a CPA." He pointed at the body in the lobby. "Who discovered him?"

"I did."

"Not the hotel employees?"

"They thought he was part of the exhibit."

Jesse looked askance at David. "Just how long has he been there?"

"Since three in the morning, apparently."

"He just sat down, fastened two steel bands around his neck, and worked the exhibit so that he disconnected his spinal cord."

David shrugged and glanced away at the body. "I dunno. I wasn't here at the time."

"I see." He glanced back at the crime scene. The police were taking pictures of the body, the garrote chair, the police tape. He frowned. "Obviously, that wasn't real police tape."

David shrugged. "They sell it in the dealer's room."

"Really?" Jesse stared at David. "What kind of operation is this, anyway?"

"It's a mystery weekend," David said. "I thought you knew."

"Weekend?"

"Kind of a cross between a convention and murder mystery theater."

Mara looked at the crime. "Which kinda explains that crowd."

A group of people was surrounding the scene. Many of them were dressed in fifties style fancy dress. They were smiling and laughing and taking pictures.

"They don't realize that this is a real crime scene," Jesse muttered.

"They will now," Mara said.

"What do you mean?" David said. "They're surrounding a body with real police and with real paramedics coming in the door."

"Well, when they start using real handcuffs and start arresting the participants, then they won't think that this is a fake murder."

"Look at that woman over there." Jesse said. "Her face is pale."

The crowd's noise suddenly sobered. "He's not breathing!" said the pale woman.

A man straightened up. "This is a murder investigation, ma'am," he said.

"It's not part of the murder mystery?" another woman said.

The police officer rubbed his eyes. "You all thought this was part of a murder mystery?"

Many in the crowd nodded.

"Justin," he called. "We're going to have to start the questioning over again."

"Huh?" said a man by the registration desk.

"They thought this was part of a mystery."

Justin said a word under his breath. "All right, everybody, line up again."

"Don't you think you had better talk to the police?" Jesse said to David.

David shrugged. "They'll get to me soon enough. Besides," he continued after a moment, "I can't leave the door until I'm relieved." He looked at Jesse. "Aren't you going to talk to the police? After all, you saw the body close up."

Jesse raised his hand. The man by the desk noticed him, smiled slightly, and nodded. He talked to one of the paramedics, then ducked under the tape and walked over to Jesse and Mara.

"I should've known you would be here," he said, extending his hand.

Jesse shook it. "Justin."

Mara hugged him. "Someday, I wish we would meet under different circumstances," Justin said, "then, maybe, you would go out with me."

"Old man," Mara smiled. "Not a chance."

"Not that much older than you."

"So," Jesse said, tired of the flirting, "what do you think?"

Justin sobered. "Well, he didn't just sit down and die in that chair."

"Murder?" Jesse said.

"Not a doubt," Justin said. "But you already knew that, or you wouldn't be here."

David looked puzzled. The three of them ignored him.

"Have you already examined the body?"

"Before you came," Jesse nodded.

"Your conclusions?"

"Well, of course, he was killed by someone he either considered a friend or a trusted associate."

Mara nodded.

"How do you figure?" David said.

Mara pulled out some gum and started chewing. "Well, look at him. How tall do you suppose he is?"

"Six eight, six ten maybe."

"Now look at my boss here."

"So?"

Mara rolled her eyes. "Somebody that size can pick Boss up, place him in that chair, and hold him down while killing him." She pointed at Glenn. "Who's going to pick him up?"

"Oh."

Justin looked at the interchange, amused. "We figured that, thanks. Anything else?"

"You saw the scuff marks on the floor?" Jesse said.

Justin blinked. "Scuff marks?"

Jesse shrugged. "He was murdered in there," he pointed at the exhibition room, "and moved out here." He then quickly moved into the exhibition room before David could stop him, "using this dolly." He pulled it out of the room.

"Couldn't have," David said. "This room was locked, and someone was sleeping in here."

"Where is that person?" Justin said.

David blinked. "I woke him up and he went back to his room."

"And did he look rather tired?"

"I don't know. I guess."

"Do you know who he is?"

David blinked. "No."

"You don't?"

"We come from all over."

"Why would somebody move him into the lobby?" Mara asked.

"Maybe to make a statement," Jesse said. "I don't know yet."

A man in a top hat and suit walked over to Justin. He looked pale. "I understand you're the lead investigator?"

"Yes," Justin said, glancing at Jesse. "And you are?"

"Tom Watson, convention head and hotel liaison."

"You work here?"

Tom shrugged. "It's convenient. I can indulge my passion and help the hotel business."

"Was Mr. Hauman," Justin said, pointing towards the

body, "one of your convention guests?"

"That's just it," Tom said. "I've heard of Glenn, because I'm also a *Star Trek* fiction fan. But as far as I can tell, he had no connection to the convention. And since he's a New Yorker, I can't imagine why he would be here, especially at night."

"He must have known somebody here," Mara said, chewing her gum.

Tom glanced at her and Jesse, and Justin made introductions.

"That was my conclusion as well," Jesse said. "Tom, do you know David?"

"He's one of our gofers," Tom said.

"Gofer?" Justin said

"Go for this, gofer that," Tom explained. "A helper."

"How long have you known him?"

David looked uncomfortable. "Am I a suspect?"

Justin looked stern. "Everybody's a suspect unless proven innocent."

"I thought . . . "

"The law and actual investigative work don't always coincide," Jesse explained.

David looked annoyed.

"So . . . "

"We're going to have to interview everybody in the hotel. Including you," Justin said.

"Oh, man . . . "

"I presume you would like to sit in," Justin said to Jesse.

"Of course," Jesse said, "if it's fine with you."

"What are you," David said, "like *Monk?*"

Jesse looked blank.

"A TV show," Mara said. "Yeah. And I'm his Natalie." She chewed her gum some more. "But not really, because he's not OCD and paranoid, and I'm not really that kind of assistant."

"What are you, anyway?" Jesse said, glancing at her.

"I'm your interpreter."

Jesse shrugged.

"The good thing about electronic keys," Justin said, "is that the hotel records can corroborate most of our guest's stories. The bad thing," he continued, "is that computers can be made to lie. And I have a hard time believing that the hotel's security cameras didn't pick anything up. I'll have to send it to forensics, and God only knows when they can get to it."

Jesse sat back. He had offered minimal input in the interviews, but his sixth sense told him that most of the guests were telling the truth and had no idea who would have killed Glenn; nor did they even know who Glenn was. In fact, most of them, in spite of being part of the murder mystery, couldn't conceive why one person would want to kill another person, except in a fictional context. When faced with reality, most of them turned pale. The guests were teachers, nurses, office workers of some sort or another, and none of them were, say, soldiers or police workers. Which made sense; why would you want to deal with a fictional murder when you had the possibility of dealing with the real thing every day?

"Tampered, you think?" Jesse said. Justin nodded. "Still, why would Glenn walk into a dark hotel, sit down on a garrote, and let himself be killed?"

"He's a writer," Mara snapped her gum. "They're invariably curious. Could somebody have just offered to show him how it worked, then actually did the deed?"

"I suppose," Jesse said. He wished that the spirit would show up and give him a nudge, but, as Jacob Marley said, spirits were mercurial and came in their own time.

As if reading his mind, Justin glanced at him and took a sip of coffee.

"No," Jesse said, "nothing since we were down in the lobby." He felt a poke in his side. "Stop it, Mara."

"I didn't do anything," Mara said. She was sitting across the room.

Jesse closed his eyes and sighed. "Look, dude," he said out loud, "you have to give me better clues than that."

Justin glanced up at him. "Glenn?"

Jesse shrugged. "I don't know. Could be the resident hotel ghost." He felt the poke in his side harder. He grabbed a small flashlight out of his pocket and unscrewed it slightly. "Look, if you're Glenn, make this flashlight flicker."

He set the flashlight down on the table and waited. After a minute, he sighed. "Who knows . . . ."

The flashlight flickered.

"Ask him if he knows who killed him," Mara said.

"Stop," Justin said. "You know that's not admissible in court."

The flashlight flickered.

"What was that about?" Justin said.

"You know as much as I do," Jesse muttered.

Justin felt a light slap on the back of his head and reached up to touch it.

Someone knocked at the door.

"Come in," Justin said.

A deputy stuck his head in the door. "We can't seem to find David."

"Did you look in his room?" Jesse said.

The man shook his head. "Gone."

"That looks suspicious," Mara muttered.

"You had quite the conversation with him," Justin said. "Did you get any vibe from him?"

"Not much," Jesse said.

"That he was a bit flaky," Mara said, "but that describes a bunch of people around here."

The deputy backed off, and the convention head walked in. "You needed to see me?"

Justin blinked. "Not that I didn't want to see you, but I hadn't sent for you."

"Really," Tom said. "I could swear . . ." He shook his head. "I just got the idea in my head."

"Well," Justin said. "Now that you're here. . .we seem to have a missing person."

"David."

"Yeah."

"He said that he was going home. Sick."

Justin clouded up. "He shouldn't have been able to. We had . . . DeWayne!" he shouted.

"Yes, sir?"

"Do a sound off."

"Right away." DeWayne keyed his walkie talkie. "All stations, sound off."

"Ty here."

"Ken."

"Jason."

"Clyde."

They waited a second. "Larry," DeWayne said.

They waited some more.

"Larry?"

DeWayne disappeared out the door. Justin followed closely after him. Tom, Jesse, and Mara glanced at each other, then followed the two at a discreet distance.

"Everybody else, sound off. I'll check Larry." The chatter continued on the radio, and Jesse reflected that he didn't know how many exits the hotel had. He knew it was a big hotel.

After a second, Justin said, "All checked in but Larry. Keep vigilant."

Justin led them down a first-floor corridor, past some rooms, and out the exit door. The stairwell was empty, then Jesse had a push . . . "Look upstairs," he whispered. Justin nodded, pulled out his gun, and went slowly upstairs while DeWayne stayed down with the other three, trying to motion them out.

They heard a moan. A couple of minutes passed, then they heard a "Clear!" DeWayne bounded up the stairs.

"Larry?" they heard him say.

"He got away," said a strange voice. "I saw him coming down a corridor, then I don't remember anymore."

"You got hit on the back of the head," Justin said.

"Right."

"Don't try to get up. We'll get emergency here."

Jesse felt a slap on the back of the head, then his arm being pushed up to point to the exit. "Justin? I think he's outside."

Justin glanced at him, and he nodded. Cautiously, Justin opened the door, then barked out a laugh. DeWayne grinned, then stepped out the door. Jesse, Tom, and Mara peered out the door.

Sprawled in the remains of a decorative jar was David, moaning. He had apparently backed out the door, tripped on the doorstep, and fell backwards, hitting his head.

He opened his eyes, lifted his head, then fell back, saying, "Oh, crap." Jesse couldn't tell if it was because of his head injury or whether it was because of the six-foot five deputy glowering down at him.

Suddenly, his eyes opened wide, and he was lifted off the ground. DeWayne stared. Justin glanced at Jesse. "Glenn?" he said.

Jesse shrugged.

David was being shaken from one side to the other.

"I think Glenn is angry," Jesse commented.

"Gl . . . e . . . nn?" David jittered.

"Perhaps if you talk to us, he will stop?" Jesse suggested.

"Not before we read him his rights," Justin muttered.

David was still shaking. "Stop it! Police harassment!"

Jesse glanced up. Sure enough, there was a camera. "The police aren't doing anything," he commented. "And we'll have the visual evidence to back it up." He paused. "Like I said, I don't think Glenn is happy with you."

"I don't believe in ghosts!"

Mara shrugged. "Doesn't make any difference right now, does it?"

David threw up. The group backed up rapidly.

"Why?" Tom said.

"Have you ever read *Creative Couplings*?" David spat out.

The group shook their head.

"A Klingon/Jewish wedding? An offense against nature!" He lowered his voice. "Aaron Rosenberg was next."

Jesse blinked. "Um . . . what are Klingons?"

"*Star Trek*," Mara murmured.

"And besides," David said angrily, "Glenn was just too damn tall."

Jesse blinked, then realized that he had never seen David standing. Now that he was standing up, he realized that the other man was an inch shorter than he was.

And, with statements like that, he was obviously unhinged.

Justin sighed. "Jesse, can you tell Glenn to stop shaking David?"

David was slammed down, then he collapsed, moaning.

"Thank you," Justin said. "DeWayne, cuff him and take him in the ambulance with Larry."

"Glenn," Jesse said out loud, "is there anything else we need to do?" He felt a pat on his head. "Stop that!"

"Glenn," Mara said, conciliatory. "You can be at rest now. I don't know your beliefs, but your time here is over." She kept murmuring, and Jesse pulled Justin to one side.

"She's sending him to his rest?" Justin said.

"Mara will calm him down," Jesse said.

"A ghost whisperer and an empath," Justin said. "I wish this kind of testimony was admissible in court."

Jesse grinned. "You'll just have to rely on my observation skills."

"Well, thank you. I'll see you in court."

Jesse felt another chill. "I may be seeing you sooner."

"Really?"

"Yeah."

"I'll wait until I get a phone call," Justin said. "One case at a time," he said. "One case at a time." He walked off to call his deputies and greet the ambulance.

"No hurry," Jesse said. He smelled dirt, which told him that this case was older. Much, much older. "We may not even need you."

Mara rejoined him. She sniffed. "Another ghost?" she said. "I just got rid of the last one!" She stiffened and looked down. "Oh, dear," she said. "The hotel isn't going to be happy about digging up their garden, are they?"

Jesse sighed.

What can I say about Hildy Silverman that she hasn't already confessed during her Scientology cleanse?

As the editor and publisher of *Space and Time* magazine, she barely has time to play the organ at her church, make cookies for the bake sale at her synagogue, and knit rugs at her mosque before she has to run off to her coven and prepare the sacrificial D&D game to summon the Dark Lord.

To her I bequeath a coffee maker so she can start hanging out with Unitarians.

# THERE'S NO SUCH THING AS GLENN
## by Hildy Silverman

GLENN HAUMAN—EDITOR, AUTHOR, RACONTEUR, and most pertinent to this tale, avowed and avid skeptic—went to a large comic book convention. That part wasn't unusual, as he was a prominent editor in the field. The unusual bit occurred when, upon checking into The Undertow hotel, a (*twitchy, grating*) front desk manager cautioned, "You know this place is haunted, right?"

Glenn barely suppressed a snort. "Of course it is."

"And the room your publishing company picked for you is *the* most haunted room in this, *the* most haunted hotel in these United States?" She raised one intention-loaded eyebrow and wriggled it meaningfully.

This time, his snort escaped unchecked. "I appreciate the warning, good woman, but I'm willing to take my chances." And after delivering an eye roll he hoped was as epic as intended, he headed to the (*rickety, probably not inspected in years*) elevator.

It started with little things. The shower that didn't have a separate temperature control—you just turned the handle and it came on, desired hot/cold mix be damned. Glenn stepped into the stall and at first the water was just a bit warmer than preferred. Then suddenly it turned boiling hot, forcing him to leap out before he was scalded. He wrote it off as a fault in old plumbing, and planned to include it in the stern Yelp review he'd begun mentally preparing the moment Twitchy at check-in informed him the place was haunted (*that nonsense just gives them a neat little way to excuse lazy maintenance*). He had no doubt that his angry public screed would result in gullible would-be guests staying elsewhere and his entire stay being comped by contrite management, which would please his publishing company—a win-win in Glenn's book.

Then there were the door locks. Glenn knew the kind of people who lurked even in remotely located hotels like this one, waiting until guests were fast asleep to pry open room doors and rob them blind, or worse. So he'd done as he always did when traveling and locked the door every which way possible, including putting the old-style chain on the hook. Yet when he awoke the next morning, the chain was dangling down loose, the push-button lock popped out, and the door open just the tiniest crack. What made it worse—he'd never heard a thing even though the head of the bed rested against the same wall as the door.

He dressed, marched downstairs, and demanded to speak to the manager. When the gent appeared resembling a younger, slightly more deranged version of Jack Nicholson (*because of course, might as well go balls-out with their ridiculous theme*) Glenn made sure to straighten up to his full, impressive height before looking down his nose and proclaiming, "A little goofing around to uphold this place's silly reputation to dunces who actually believe in the supernatural is all well and good, but I draw the line at breaking and entering!"

"I assure you, sir." The manager craned his neck to squint up into Glenn's scowl. "The staff here are very professional. We do not play games to support . . . rumors about this fine establishment." He fidgeted and glanced right then left. "It's not like, er, *incidents* that have occurred here were planned. We would never willfully let a guest di . . . ah, we would never put you at risk."

"I should hope not." Glenn made sure to add a few rumbles about *inside jobs* and *liability* and *familiarity with the legal system*, as he took pride in having been involved in many a lawsuit, and prevailing in most. Confident that Management had been suitably cowed, he went off to the convention center a couple of miles away to attend a day filled with panel appearances and sales table staffing.

That night, after returning in a state of wobbly exhaustion from dealing with fandom for nine straight hours, Glenn grabbed a beer and burger in the hotel's (*overpriced*) bar then stumbled off to his room.

The night passed like any other in a normal hotel, save for the occasional creaks and groans and shrieks of the damned in the darkest hours of the night. But the next morning, when Glenn tried to leave, he couldn't even get the door handle to turn.

"Well, this is clearly a safety code violation." He pulled and tugged and shoved the door to no avail. Picking up the room phone with an angry grunt and holding it about an inch from his face (*they never clean these, or the remote controls. I don't need some flesh-eating bacteria on top of being late*), he jabbed the button labeled, "Front Desk."

He listened, but there was no ring. In fact, he heard nothing at all. "Hel-*lo?* Is anyone there? I'm stuck in here and I have to be at my con in less than—"

From the other end of the formerly silent line, someone chuckled.

"Hey! If you think this little prank is funny, I *promise* that you won't be laughing once my attorney—"

The chuckling seemed to roll down the line from a great distance away, increasing in volume until it blasted out of the receiver. Glenn dropped it and clapped one hand against his offended ear. "What the hell?"

The receiver rocked and hopped on the nightstand where it had fallen, looking for all the world like a highly amused toddler rolling with laughter.

"This is some elaborate prank." Glenn glared at the receiver. "Stop that. Stop it right now!"

His scolding had the opposite of the desired outcome. The receiver was seized by a paroxysm of laughter that filled the (*small and overpriced*) room with its echoes. The device rolled so violently that only its wire tether to the still calm and inanimate base kept it from falling off the edge of the nightstand and onto the (*rather cheap and thin, and what's with that shade of red?*) carpet.

"Oh, dear Gru. Am I on one of those punk-an-idiot reality

shows?" Glenn scanned the ceiling for any sign of hidden cameras that were no doubt planted around the room. "Okay, ha-ha. Nice joke. Now, enough already! I've got places to go, so if you want me to sign the waiver you'll need to show any of this?" He grabbed the rollicking receiver, which wriggled and screamed in protest until he slammed it into the base unit. It whimpered once, then lay still.

"Much better. Now, the door if you please?"

The small alarm on the nightstand next to the opposite side of the bed began to wail like a neglected infant. Grinding his molars, Glenn crossed over in a single long stride and yanked its plug out of the wall socket. The alarm kept on yowling, so he stripped out the backup battery. It only bawled louder.

"This is why I never wanted kids!" Glenn lobbed the miserable device across the room hard enough to put a dent in the (*thin, substandard*) wall. It ripped through the faded wallpaper, and the gap welled with a viscous red liquid.

Glenn watched, mouth agape, as what certainly appeared to be blood bubbled and oozed in a waterfall of gore from the wounded wall. Below it, the alarm clock offered a few final hiccups of grief before blessedly falling silent again.

"Okay, people, this is a little much." Glenn stomped around the room and searched behind the (*chipped, cloudy*) mirror and few (*gaudy, faded*) pictures hanging on the walls. He found nothing behind them but dust. Glaring, he shook his forefinger at the smoke alarm in the corner of the ceiling. "I don't want to be part of your damned show, whether it's some Punk'd rip-off or Ghost Hunters-Seekers-Finders-whatever nonsense! You're barking up the wrong guy here." He jabbed a thumb into his chest. "I don't believe in this crap, okay? There's no such thing as ghosts, or haunted anyplaces. There is nothing that science can't explain now or eventually. So, go find another sucker and *let me out of here!*"

A heaviness filled the room, the kind where you don't hear anything but feel a *presence* nonetheless, and you know that sounds will soon pierce that eerie silence, and you won't like any of them. Glenn licked his suddenly dry lips, every hair on his body rising in defiance of all logic and common sense. Infuriated by this physical rebellion against his rational mind, Glenn raised both fists and assumed what he hoped was a convincingly menacing stance.

"I warn you, I've got my black belt!" Which was a complete lie, and he was once again reminded that he really should take his buddy Keith, the actual multiple black belt, up on that offer to join his dojo. For now, he hoped his sheer size and seeming willingness to brawl would give any possible intruder pause.

Something creaked behind him.

Glenn pivoted and clenched his fists tighter as the door to the (*narrow, not enough hangers*) closet slowly opened itself. As it widened, it revealed not the trousers and sweaters and shirts Glenn had previously hung inside but rather an inky blackness that was an absence of all things. Negative space. An abyss. A horrifying vision of the vast eternal nothingness many religious traditions proclaim awaits nonbelievers after death.

Glenn dropped his fists and cocked his head to one side, studying the void. "Oh, that's it. First you make me late to my conference, and now you've stolen my clothes?" He pulled out his cell phone and hit the speed dial for the law firm of Ezor and Ventrella. "I'm going to *own* this friggin' hotel once I'm done!"

"Really? I mean—*really?*"

Glenn fumbled, and his cellphone bounced onto the (*lumpy, too short*) bed. "Who said that? Where are you?"

"I am right here." And suddenly he was there, a male figure, a little blurry around the edges but indeed standing right in front of Glenn. He wore clothes that would have been stylish in the early 1900s, and a glare that would have fit perfectly on the face of Glenn's frequently exasperated wife.

"Who in the hell . . . ?"

His uninvited visitor performed an exaggerated bow. "Hello. I am the ghost who haunts this room." He straightened, revealing translucent features set in a glare. "Is that better? Is that any gods damned clearer? Good gracious!" He all but stomped in a circle. "Most people, I don't have to get beyond the mysteriously fogged mirror bit to convince, but *you?*"

Glenn crossed his arms over his chest. "Like I've never seen a mirror fog up after a shower before? Come on."

"With writing appearing on it that says *get out or die?*"

Glenn shrugged. "Some kid probably doodled on it with a crayon, and the mist from the warm shower made it show up."

"Ugh!" The exasperated, fashion-backward man clamped both hands over his ears. "Your steadfast refusal to believe the evidence of your own eyes is beyond infuriating!"

"I'm ridiculous?" Glenn snorted. "I'm not the one in a waist-coat and bowler in 2018, fella."

"I died in in 1918." His unwanted visitor tugged at the hem of his hazy vest self-consciously. "Sue me."

"Oh, I intend to." Glenn was done indulging this lunatic. "Just as soon as I get out of this room, I'm going to sue the neatly-pressed pants off you, your studio, your entire network, this lousy excuse of a quote-unquote *historic* hotel—"

"Huh?" The man tilted his head to one side, affording Glenn a better look at the faded brown muttonchops framing his still oddly unclear features. "Wait. Do you think this is some sort of deception?"

"Or something. I don't really care." He nodded meaningfully at the door. "Now, if you'll just open that, I need to get to my convention."

The man stared at him and even fuzzy around the edges, his expression was clearly incredulous. "I am a *ghost*. The spirit of a deceased individual. Passed away of a heart attack in this very room decades before your birth. You . . . comprehend that, right? You cannot sue me."

"Oh, I assure you, I can and I will unless you open that damned door right exactly now!"

His intruder's demeanor shifted from frustrated to some-what worried. "But, by all legal definitions I am dead. You cannot sue a dead person . . . unless the laws of this land have changed vastly?"

Glenn groaned. He grasped a double-handful of his hair and tugged. "Buddy, enough! You are not a ghost because there is no such thing as a ghost. I don't know how many ways I can tell you the same thing. Sorry, I'm not some superstitious ignoramus for you to exploit."

"But . . . but . . ." His visitor gestured to the room phone.

"How do you explain that?" He flung his other arm to indicate the still-hemorrhaging wall. "Or that?" He nodded over one shoulder at the closet void. "Or that?"

Glenn considered all the options. "Speakers. Wires. Robotics. Mirrors and black light. That's just off the top of my head. Shall I go on?"

The man's jaw hung slack for a moment. Then he jabbed both thumbs into his chest. "And me? What about *me*?"

"What about you?"

His visitor pointed to the bed and cocked his forefinger in a summoning motion. A pillow rolled down the bed and launched itself at Glenn's face. Glenn caught it before it struck and wrestled to keep it from smothering him. All the while the man crowed, "How about that, you fool? What do you think is doing *that*?"

"Asshole!" Glenn shouted, twisting and straining, until he slammed against the wall next to the (*cramped, in need of seriously upgraded fixtures*) bathroom. Holding the pillow at bay with one hand, he groped his way along the wall then spun and flung the pillow at the same time. It shot toward the closet and hovered between it and him for several seconds, until the inky blackness extended a tentacle, wrapped around it, and pulled it inside like a monstrous deep-water squid capturing a fish that strayed too close.

Glenn threw himself against the closet door and slammed it shut while the self-proclaimed ghost snickered. "So? What is your answer for that, *hm*? Go on, give me your rational explanation for flying murderous pillows and closet gateways to Purgatory?"

Glenn panted. "I really need to get into better shape." He caught his breath, and straightened. "Tiny drone hidden in the pillow. Industrial-strength central vacuum with an outlet in the closet."

"Oh. Dear. Lord." His visitor shook his head slowly. "You are literally impossible."

"No. *You* are if you think I'd fall for any of this crap." Glenn jabbed a forefinger in the man's direction. "You are either a delusional human being or a hired actor. You are *not* a ghost."

"The deuce you say! I am standing *right in front of you*." He marched over to the bed, and when he reached the edge, he just kept walking through it. "See? Are you seeing this? I am insubstantial. Passing right through solid matter." He performed a pirouette directly in the center of the mattress. "Who can do this, pray tell? Go on, tell me again that I am not real." He stomped through to the other side of the bed, turned back to Glenn, and raised both arms in a *ta-da* motion.

"I've seen David Blaine do pretty much that same trick. Or was it David Copperfield?" Glenn rubbed his bearded chin and struggled to remember. "Pretty sure it was one of those David magicians."

The man hung his head and dropped his arms to his sides. "I cannot believe this. A century of successful hauntings. Everyone does what any sane person would do and run away screaming. Until you."

"Believe it. You're not a ghost. I know it, you know it, and whoever is playing this prank or filming this scene knows it." A thought struck Glenn. "Hey, you know what, Ashton? If you really want to air this, I'll agree, but only if you show my genuine reactions without Frankensplicing it into looking like I bought a single second of this."

"Ashton . . . what are you even saying?" Exasperation dripped from the oddly-dressed intruder's every word.

"Here's the deal." Glenn crossed the room and glowered down at his unwanted visitor.

"My name is Peter, actually—"

"Whatever. You want me to sign the release, fine, but you put it in writing that you don't edit this to make me look like another chump. You show that I didn't buy into any of this, and you include the following quote verbatim." He cleared his throat and made sure his tone was loud and enunciation flawless as he addressed the smoke detector. "I do *not* accept that a single thing that has happened in this episode was the result of a ghost or haunting or any other supernatural act. I additionally affirm as a rational, thinking skeptic that I did not believe nor will I ever give credence to any of these occurrences being other than the result of special effects or somewhat decently played magic tricks."

"Why on earth are you talking to the ceiling?"

Glenn ignored him, caught up in his soliloquy. "People, we as a nation have to start thinking and stop falling for nonsense like you've just seen. Everything has an explanation, and it is never that God or Zeus or the Flying Spaghetti Monster or any other imaginary power is behind it. Just because you can't come up with an explanation doesn't mean the answer is a ghost or any other fiction. It just means you don't have all the data to formulate an accurate answer yet, or science hasn't advanced enough to discover it. It's okay for the answer to be *I don't know*. It's not okay to answer *I don't know, therefore a spirit did it* or nonsense like that."

He ran out of breath, but that was fine. He was proud of his extemporaneous statement. Turning back to his visitor, he said, "Did you get all that?"

Peter was gone.

Glenn looked around the room. Everything was quiet and ordinary. The oppressive sense of *otherness* had vanished. He peered into the closet tentatively, but all that was inside were his clothes and shoes. And a pillow lying in the back corner.

He nodded as he walked over to the room door. The handle turned obediently and it opened onto a deserted but otherwise completely benign hallway. "Guess they got what they wanted. Well, they know my terms. Up to them if they decide to waste a day's pay for the crew and unused footage."

He retrieved his cell phone from the bed and strolled down the hallway. He poked the Down button and spent several long seconds tapping his foot while waiting for the elevator. Once it finally arrived in a chorus of screeches and mechanical whines, he got inside and pressed the brass button for the lobby.

Unfortunately for Glenn, his original assessment of the elevator had been completely accurate. The (*rickety*) pulley system in use almost since the opening of The Undertow more than a century prior snapped, and the (*long-uninspected*) elevator plummeted seven floors to the subbasement before he could do more than open his mouth to scream.

Glenn arose from the chaos of smashed wood, detached and frayed cords, and assorted detritus. He looked around the surrounding darkness of the dank, cobweb-filled cellar under the hotel, wondering at the miracle of his survival. He felt himself all over and was amazed that nothing appeared to be broken. Not even his clothes were torn.

"Oh, no."

He turned and saw his visitor, Peter, staring in his general direction in wide-eyed horror. Only now, the gent appeared as sharply defined and solid as anyone else he'd ever seen.

"Did you do this?" Glenn marched over to Peter. "I swear, if this was part of your elaborate game, so help me—"

"Oh, goodness, what a mess."

"That's unfortunate."

"It shall cost them a fortune to effect repairs."

"Geeze Louise, would you look at that?"

Glenn whipped around and saw a crowd had gathered behind him. Men, women, even a few children, all dressed in garb from various historical periods. There was a flapper gazing down at the wreckage of the elevator. To her left was a man sporting the bell-bottoms and afro hairstyle of the 1970s. Close behind hovered a child in a nightcap and gown straight out of Dickens. And so forth, and so on—he assessed there had to be at least twenty or more gathered in the darkness, which for some reason he could see through almost as clearly as daylight.

Glenn pressed both hands against his (*knotting, sinking*) gut. "Where . . . how did you all . . . I didn't hear any of you."

They all milled around the elevator, looking down. Not one glanced in his direction.

"Hey, hello? I, ah, heh. I could use a little help." Glenn walked over to the flapper. "Excuse me, ma'am, but can you tell me where the stairs—"

She walked right through him.

"Are?" His voice wavered. "No? Okay, how about you, Skippy?" He went over to the Oliver Twist-looking kid. "I need to get to the lobby."

The boy didn't meet his gaze. He just drifted past and disappeared into a wall.

"Oh, boy." Frantic now, Glenn ran up to each cosplayer or whatever they were in turn, pleading for directions back upstairs, pleading to call 9-1-1, and finally just begging, "Talk to me! Come on, just say something! Hello, I'm here, I'm right here in front of you!"

No responses. They all talked among themselves, *tut-tutted* over the mess of the wrecked elevator, but not a one so much as glanced in his direction.

Glenn made his way back to the mess of shattered wood, snapped cables, and pile of cloth that used to be the hotel's elevator (*wait, pile of cloth? Where did that come from? And why is it all soaking wet, and what's that sticking out . . . oh. Oh, no!*)

Some of the milling crowd gossiped among themselves. Others simply vanished, off to do whatever they did around The Undertow all day and night. Glenn felt his heart beating like a tom-tom in his chest. No, that wasn't accurate; it was more like he remembered how that *would* feel.

He didn't, couldn't, feel a thing.

Making his way back to Peter, Glenn pleaded, "Tell me what's going on! What happened to me?"

Peter didn't say a word. He walked through Glenn, who whipped around to watch him stroll over to a young woman clad in a maid's uniform out of the 1940s. "Katherine, darling. It has been too long. Have you been haunting the ballroom without me?"

"Wait!" Glenn thrust his hands out toward them, palms up. "Come on, I know you can—hang on." He gazed at his hands, which were as insubstantial as his arms. He could see the floor right through them. "No. This *can't* be happening."

"Oh, Peter." Katherine giggled. "Always the eager beaver."

"We must uphold The Undertow's reputation, my dear." Peter winked. "Without us, it would become another abandoned property to be torn down and replaced by," he shuddered dramatically, "condominiums."

"Hotels do need a lotta lettuce to keep revenuers at bay," Katherine said.

Glenn barely heard them, caught up in examining his rapidly fading self. His last words were, "I don't believe this."

And because he really didn't, he disappeared.

"So? Is that it?" Katherine turned back to the space Glenn had occupied a few moments prior.

If Peter still breathed, he would have released a huge sigh of relief. "Yes, I do believe so." He waved to the other ghosts still milling around the subbasement. "Thank you, all! Your performances were sterling, simply marvelous."

"Hey, what was the deal with that sucker anyway?" Jackson, the bell-bottomed 70s ghost, regarded Peter.

"Yes, why didn't you want him to join us?" Katherine tilted her head to one side.

"Trust me, friends." Pete shook his head emphatically. "You did *not* want him around for eternity. I spent mere hours in his company and I nearly threw myself into the void to escape." He extended an arm to Katherine. "Let us away to Room 237, my dear. I believe a psychic is staying there tonight. And you know what fun true believers are!"

What can I say about Aaron Rosenberg that I haven't already told the IRS?

He's holding down a full-time job, has two kids, a grueling commute, and still has time to write over 300,000 words a year and design books in his copious spare time? Don't believe it. "His kids" are Irish orphans, brought here illegally and chained in a basement where they toil away ghostwriting for him until they become ghosts themselves. I've seen him do it to other authors, too—do you know anyone who's actually met Steven Savile? Of course not, he's long dead, Aaron killed him and slapped his name on as co-author. Apparently "British collaborator" is like "Canadian girlfriend," something made up for prestige to try hiding the fact that you are painfully alone and unlovable.

To him I bequeath a deck of unmarked cards. (I've never caught him cheating at poker and I don't know how those rumors got started.)

# DUCKBOB: ALL IN
## by Aaron Rosenberg

"HI, WHO THE HELL'RE YOU?" I ASK THE TORSO FILLING my front door. Then I crane my neck—wrong bird, I know—to look up. I'm assuming there's a head attached up there somewhere, or this is gonna get real creepy, real fast.

Sure enough, there's a shaggy face staring down at me from behind those narrow rectangular metal glasses everybody seems to be wearing these days. "Hi, I'm Glenn," he says, holding out a hand big enough to palm a basketball. "You must be DuckBob."

"Gee, how'd ya know?" I ask. "Are you from Seamless? 'Cause I don't see any pies and I know I didn't order a 'Bigfoot in business casual.'"

"Ha, yeah, no, *hm*, you'd be surprised how often I hear that, actually." Five replies in one sentence, without pause for breath in between? Did somebody clone me and put me in an oversized orangutan frame, then introduce me to a razor?

Just then, my phone buzzes. I pull it out and see I've got a text message from David: "Running late. My guest may beat me there. His name's Glenn."

Ah, mystery solved. "You're David's friend," I say, tucking the phone back away.

He peers at me as if he's trying to remember himself, then breaks into a friendly if slightly dazed smile through the beard. "Yeah, sorry, did I not say that? David mentioned you guys had a monthly poker game and invited me along."

"Okay, sure." David had said something the other day about bringing a friend. "Well, come on in." I step back to let him enter, since between his height and my bill there's no way the two of us are going to fit in the doorway at the same time. Not without a crowbar, an enthusiastic Japanese subway cop, and a whole lot of butter.

Glenn steps inside, shutting the door behind him, and glances around. "Nice place." Good thing I've got high ceilings!

"Thanks. I just moved in." Last week, in fact. Right after me and the MiBs cleared out the neo-Arcturan arachnoid that'd built this whole floor as an elaborate trap. I don't bother going into that, though, as I usher him toward the dining room, where Steve and Pete are already sitting and chowing down on chips and pretzels. "Get you something to drink?"

"I don't suppose you've got Diet Mountain Dew on hand?" he asks. He looks ready to be disappointed, which makes it even more fun to disappoint that.

"Yeah, I'll grab you one." Good thing that's Tall's favorite drink, too! I make sure to keep a fridgepack on hand for when he drops by. "Steve, Pete, this is Glenn, friend of David's," I holler as I sidle past into the kitchen. I can hear them all saying hello while I rummage through the fridge. I'm just returning with the soda when the doorbell rings again. "And that'll be David."

Sure enough, the last regular member of our group is standing at the door when I open it. "Sorry I'm so fricking late," he mutters as he enters. "You wouldn't believe the effed-up bullcrap I had to put up with just to get here." He notices his surroundings for the first time. "Hey, nice." Then he reaches out and pokes me in the arm. "Yep, really here."

"Shut up." Just because the last time we played I was only

able to make it as a hologram. That was when I was stuck at the Matrix full-time, though. Now, thanks to my buddy Ned's galactic-wireless headset, I'm able to stay plugged in no matter where I am. Even right here in my awesome new pad.

"Gang's all here," Pete shouts as David and I join them at the table. Glenn's already made himself at home, claiming one of the chairs. His arms and legs are all over the place, but it doesn't look like he's doing the subway sprawl—he's just got so much limbage he can't contain himself. He's like a sprung can of snakes, draped here and there and everywhere.

"Yo, glad you made it," David tells Glenn, settling in across from him. "You meet everybody?"

"I did, thank you, yes," the new guy replies. "And thank you for allowing me to play tonight."

"No worries," Pete assures him, shuffling the deck one last time before passing it to David to cut. "You know how to play?"

Glenn pushes his glasses up on his nose. "Oh, I've dabbled a bit," he says, but I can tell right off David brought us a ringer.

Still, this guy might be good at regular poker. That doesn't mean he's gonna know how to handle us.

"That's not even a game!" Glenn insists, slapping both hands down on the table. "You can't combine hands with another player!"

"Why not?" I look over at Pete and we both shrug. "That's why it's called Buddy Flick." He and I just paired our wilds—twos and fours, for USA that used to be on channel 24 when we were kids—and our aces to create five bullets. "Looks like we win."

Glenn starts to say something, stops, starts again, stops. That's happened a lot in the two hours since we started playing. Finally he just shakes his head. "Fine," he says, slumping back in his chair. "House rules, I guess."

"Exactly." I rake in the money and start splitting it into two equal stacks, then push one of those back to Pete. "You catch on fast." Truth is, he seems like a decent guy, and so far he's fit in just fine. Of course, I have no idea what he does for a living—every time one of us has asked we've gotten like five different replies, all of them half-finished and most of them in vagaries like "Oh, a little of this, a little of that" or "I help people share their vision." I can't figure out if that means he's a publisher, a dilettante, the idle rich, or some kind of eye donor middleman. Still, he's not as vulgar as David—then again, nobody is!—or as coarse as Pete, or as whiney as Steve, and he's been willing to poke fun at himself and to take a joke and to toss barbs right back.

And to play whatever weird crap we decide to call. In fact, so far out of maybe twelve games, he's only folded once. Most times he's bet, too. Which suits us just fine.

We do like a sucker.

"Okay, my deal," he tells us, accepting the cards from David and shuffling them with surprising dexterity for someone with hands almost as big as my bill. He pulls out a card and drops it face-up in the center of the table—it's the Queen of Hearts. "This game is called Liz Taylor. You know it?"

The rest of us burst out laughing. "Poor old Liz," Steve explains, catching his breath first. "We stopped playing her years ago. We like Disco Queen instead. Queen of Clubs, 'cause the club scene and all that, right? And she'll dance with anyone." In Liz Taylor you set the Queen of Hearts aside and whenever anyone gets a Jack or a King face up she moves into their hand. She's the only wild card, and she stays with whoever had the last Jack or King up, so it's almost like playing without any wackiness. Almost. Which is probably why we had to mix it up a bit.

Pete leans over and pats Glenn on the shoulder like he's consoling a little kid who's just dropped his ice cream. "It's okay, we'll play Liz Taylor," he says reassuringly. Then he looks at me and winks. "For old time's sake."

Glenn looks fit to bust, which just eggs Pete on even more. I don't try to stop him because, nice as the new guy seems, Pete and I have been friends since grade school.

Besides, the more agitated Glenn gets, the wilder he'll bet, I'm thinking. Which is bad for him and good for the rest of us.

"Why would you even play this?" he asks an hour later, as I'm dealing the first round of cards. "What's the point with that many wilds?"

I shrug. "Who needs a point?" I ask him. "I just like how it sounds. 'Deuces, aces, and one-eyed faces.' Sort of rolls off the tongue." Which is good for me, because my mouth's long as a freaking bowling lane. "Wild card," I call out as I deal David the Two of Clubs. "Wild card," that one's the Jack of Hearts, which went to Pete. "Wild card," that's mine, the Ace of Diamonds. Which means only Glenn and Steve didn't get wilds. Too bad. "First wild card bets."

No wilds come up in the second round, but on the third Steve finally gets one, the King of Diamonds, and so does Glenn, the Ace of Hearts. Nothing on the fourth, so there's only five wilds showing, out of eleven total.

Of course, I've got the Two of Hearts and the Ace of Clubs underneath, so that's two more right there. My second up card was a King, which means I've got four of them.

Not a bad hand, but not a surefire one, either, in a game like this.

David bets a dime—he just can't help himself. Glenn calls. Pete folds. So does Steve. "Call," I declare, tossing a chip onto the pile. "Last round," and I deal the three of us who're still in one last card each, face down.

Mine's the King of Hearts.

"Quarter," David states, flinging the red chip into the middle. That might not seem like a lot, but we play low stakes, so a quarter's actually a big deal.

"Up a quarter," Glenn counters, adding two of his own to the center. Huh. I've already seen that he likes to bet—so does David, which is maybe why they're friends—but of course there's still plenty of wilds out there. He's only showing one, though, and no other pairs, which means at best he's got five of something.

And with two Aces out and a third in my hand, it'd be tough for him to pull off five bullets. The only hand that'll beat mine.

"Yeah, okay, why not," I say, sending two red chips spiraling into the melee. I could've raised, but usually with David around I don't need to, and it's starting to look like Glenn's the same way.

Sure enough, David raises it. "Call, and up another quarter," he blusters, glaring at Glenn as if daring him to do it again.

So of course Glenn does. Even I see that one coming. "Let's make it an even buck," he suggests, doubling his earlier bet.

A whole buck? We almost never bet like that!

It's a good thing duck bills aren't really made for grinning, otherwise I'd give myself away so fast you'd think I was the bride. "What the hell," I manage instead, putting two more quarters out there. "What've you got?"

"I've got the royal," David declares, laying out his cards. He's got the Two of Spades to go with his Two of Clubs, plus he had the Queen and the Ten of Spades up and the King of Spades down. That's a royal, all right.

We all look at Glenn, who just shrugs. "I've got a boat," he admits, showing his hand. It's sevens over fives, and we all stare at him like I'm not the one with the duck head.

"A boat?" Pete asks. "Seriously? There's like fifty wild cards floating around out there, man! And you raised to a buck on a lousy boat?"

"That's nuts," I agree. "Now, if you'd had five of a kind, maybe . . . " And I set my cards down so they can all see. We like the slow roll around here. Makes the pain last longer.

"Damn!" Steve whispers. "That's insane!"

I shrug. "What can I say? Lady Luck loves me!"

That gets a snicker from Pete. "Is that her name? Because 'Lady Luck' left some awfully lucky-looking lingerie drying on the shower rod." Whoops. I thought I'd cleaned up enough before they got here, but I forgot to check the guest bathroom. Mary had been using the rod in there as a drying rack for a few things when she was over the other night. Guess she left them here.

"Yeah, yeah, shut up," I warn, but he knows I don't mean it. Besides, I can tell he's a little jealous. Mary's got a classic hourglass figure, and I'm convinced her lingerie's made of pure magic 'cause there's no way something that filmy should be able to support curves that dramatic. To get them off the subject I shove the deck over to David. "Your deal."

It's eleven-thirty, and we're starting to slow down a little. We typically call it around midnight anyway—this isn't a rave or an orgy, it's just some buddies hanging out and playing poker, and six hours is a good night's entertainment so none of us feel we have to force ourselves to stay up past that. That also means we're at the fully loopy stage of the night, when we're playing games we wouldn't dare suggest if it were any earlier or we'd all had any less to drink.

"Two out of Three," Steve declares, holding up the deck. "Jacked Up—starting as Lucky Sevens, down Jacks are wild, you can flip 'em on your turn up to the last round, it's always Two out of Three but you can change the wilds, wilds don't count for the Spade calculation." Everybody groans as we try to wrap our brains around this. Two of Three is tough enough—you've got to have any two out of the high Spade in the hole, the low Spade in the hole, and the high hand—but then to add in Jacked Up where you can change the game to any other variant we play if you get an up Jack? And starting as Lucky Sevens, where Sevens are wild but if you get an up Seven everyone else gets an extra down card?

My head hurts just thinking about it!

Glenn has a dazed look, like he's just realized his leg's caught in a bear trap and he's trying to decide if it's really worth it to start chewing his own limb off or if he should just give up now. "Um, okay," he says finally, with a little shake. "Sure." He's clearly trying to convince himself that he's got this.

It isn't working.

He's already had to buy back in once, after he got down to a pair of dimes on a vicious game of Skip Straight Beats All. To his credit, he hasn't whined once, which already makes him a better poker partner than Steve.

As is usually the case with Two out of Three, neither of my down cards are Spades. But then Glenn gets a Seven and my free down card is the Two of Spades. Nice! So I'm guaranteed the low Spade. Now I just need the high Spade or the high hand.

None of us want to bet right away. Two out of Three often winds up with a reset, and it can bleed you dry if you're not careful, so we're all playing it cautious at first, a dime here and a dime there.

Pete gets a Seven as well, and my down card this time isn't a high Spade but it's almost as good—the Jack of Clubs. So it's a wild if I keep it down, but if I flip it I can change the game.

I study the rest of my cards. I started with a Two and a Three underneath—both Hearts—and I've got the suited Nine up top, along with the Queen of Diamonds and the Ace of Clubs.

In other words, I'm kind of a mess.

Except that I've got the Two of Spades. And a Jack. And a pair of Twos. And I'm three to a flush. I just need a way to bring it all together.

Last round of up cards, and Steve deals me another Three, this one a Diamond. Okay, two pair, plus I've got a Jack ready and waiting. I can work with that.

Then we get our last down cards. Mine's the Jack of Spades. Perfect.

"Pete's bet," Steve declares, since Pete's showing trip Nines thanks to that wild Seven of his.

"Twenty-five," Pete opens, tossing the chip onto the ante. He sits back and folds his arms like he's already won.

He should know better than that by now.

"I'm changing the game," Glenn announces, flipping over the Jack of Diamonds. "We're playing O Canada." That's sevens and eights wild—hockey sticks and snowmen—and he's showing one of each, which puts him in a good place, especially if he's got at least one more underneath. "And I raise to a buck." Again with the buck!

David growls, spews a string of profanities, and folds. That's a tough call in a game like this—you usually try to stay in for a possible reset, but a buck's a lot to throw away in the hopes that no one has two of the three.

I'm next, and flip over the Jack of Hearts. "Baseball," I tell the table to a whole bunch of groans. "I'll see that buck." That's Threes and Nines are wild so I'm showing a pair of wilds, which gives me the Ace-high straight. Not an awful hand, but in a two-wild-card game not a great one, either. Of course, everyone except Glenn also knows that sometimes I bet with my gut instead of my head, so I could just be bluffing, or not reading my cards right, or thinking about what color I want to repaint the kitchen. I didn't raise, so they're not too worried.

But by this point in the evening I know I don't have to. Because I'm pretty sure I've got Glenn pegged now.

Steve's next, and he folds, though it clearly pains him to do it. Not because he doesn't usually fold anyway—"like a fresh-pressed shirt," Pete likes to say—but because he dealt this mess and he considers it a point of personal pride to stay in on his own games. A buck's just too steep a price when you know you've got crap, though.

Pete's next, and he grumbles but calls.

Then it's back around to Glenn—and he gives me a big, beaming grin. "I think I like O Canada better," he insists, flipping his second hole card to reveal the Jack of Hearts. "But Jacks are also wild." Smart—gives him four wilds to my one. "Oh, and let's raise it another buck. I'm all in." That's the last of his chips—again—but he doesn't seem too worried. He's sure he's about to win it all back, with interest.

"Damn," David mutters, followed by several other words that are far less family-friendly. "Glad I folded." He reaches around and pats himself on the back.

I frown at Glenn, shake my head—and then laugh. "You're right," I tell him. "Baseball's no good. We need to go down court for this." I reveal my second Jack. "Basketball."

He looks blank for a second, then pales as comprehension dawns. "Twos and threes," he whispers, trailing off. He's not showing any of either.

"That's the one." I toss another buck onto the pile, then reveal my hole cards, the Twos and the second Three. Now I've got four wilds showing, and the Ace of Clubs. "Five bullets," I point out, "and the Two of Spades." Even if he's got a bunch of wilds under there, the best he can do is match my hand, and I've got the low Spade to pair it with. *Bazinga!*

"Damn." Glenn's shaking his head like he can't believe this is happening to him. To his credit, he doesn't curse or scream or whine, just says slowly, "That . . . is one hell of a hand." He frowns. "But why didn't you just call Basketball the first time around?"

"And telegraph what I had?" I laugh. "Naw. I knew you couldn't resist raising, not when you thought you had me beat, which meant it'd come back around to me again anyway. Then—whammo!"

"Whammo is right," Steve agrees. "Even for a submarine hand, that was a nuke."

"Thanks." I scoop the pile of chips toward me and glance over at Glenn. "Hey, any time you wanna come back, you're welcome."

"Yeah," Pete chimes in. "We're always happy to take your money."

"Thanks, but I'll pass," Glenn replies, straightening in his chair and reminding us just how tall he is. It's like someone stuck a sloth on top of a telephone pole and then added a turtleneck and a sports coat. "Getting killed here once is probably enough."

"Naw, you get used to it," Steve chimes in. "After a while, you even start to like it."

We all laugh at that—and at him—and the deal passes to Pete for the last game of the night.

He hasn't even finished shuffling before Glenn's asking to buy back in

What can I say about Blair Learn that will keep him out of jail?

Because this is all his fault. During the Crazy 8 Press panel where the idea of killing me was hatched, he was the one who stood up in the back of the room, marched to the front, pulled $20 out of his wallet, slapped it on the table, and declared, "The Kickstarter campaign has begun." Waving money around a bunch of hungry writers is like waving a ham shank around piranhas.

To him I bequeath my birthday, so he no longer has to deal with the disappointment of people saying, "I got you a present—APRIL FOOL!"

# R IS FOR ROADSTER
## by Blair Learn

THE PROBLEM WITH CONVENTIONS, GLENN MUSED, is you hardly ever get out of hotel.

Stretching his tall frame across the bed, Glenn stared up at the room's ceiling and reflected on the past weekend. SpaceCape had been a fun convention, and more importantly, it had provided an opportunity to meet fans in a new market and do some networking. If any of the leads he'd picked up over the weekend led to some new work for ComicMix, the entire trip would have proven itself worthwhile and it would be easy to justify the midwinter break again next year.

It had been a busy weekend and on the one hand, it would be tempting to take a nap. But on the other hand, the urge to get outside was overwhelming. The temperature there in Florida was a comfortable 70 degrees versus the dreary 30s back in New Jersey. It was already 5:00 and would only be light for another hour or so. Pulling himself upright, Glenn headed outside to see what sights Cape Canaveral might have to offer on a Sunday in early February.

As he stepped out the door, he glanced at the newspaper resting where he'd dropped it on top of the TV stand that morning. It seemed a bit of an anachronism that a hotel would still offer a newspaper to its guests, but he wasn't going to begrudge the print journalists a few more readers. Besides, you had to charge your phone sometime, and leafing through the paper had kept him occupied while eating breakfast.

One of that morning's front page stories had been that SpaceX had received a license to launch the Falcon Heavy rocket and was expected to do so within the next week. Glenn recalled being amused to learn that the FAA was responsible for licensing rocket launches; though he supposed, somebody had to be in charge of making sure the rocket launch didn't hit a plane full of tourists.

Walking down the corridor, Glen decided that he'd made the right call, opting to extend the trip by a few days. There wasn't anything that urgently required his presence in New Jersey right away, and as long as there was electricity, an Internet connection, and cell service, he could pretty much work wherever he liked, even the beach! For the price of a couple extra nights in the hotel, he could enjoy the warm weather, see the sights, and if he was lucky, it seemed he might even get to see a rocket launch!

Stepping into the late afternoon sunlight, Glenn took a deep breath, and held it briefly as he savored the gentle warmth of the sun on his face. This was wonderful; as a first order of business, he was going to go for a walk and enjoy the remaining daylight, and after that, find a place to eat dinner.

"Excuse me sir, are you Glenn Hauman?"

Glenn hadn't taken much notice of the young woman approaching the door as he walked out, but now she had his full attention. Somewhere in her early 30s he guessed, short blonde hair, and sharply dressed. Most convention-goers wore jeans and T-shirts, but it wasn't universal. Showing up at a convention in business attire was unusual, but not at all unheard of.

"Yes, that's me all right. And you are?"

Smiling, the woman replied brightly, "Hello Mister Hauman, my name's Sarah. I'm pleased to meet you. Do you have a few minutes to spare? My employer would like to speak with you."

Glenn considered for a moment. She wasn't a fan after all. So what did that leave? Was she a member of the hotel staff? He was pretty sure he'd paid his bar tab on Saturday, and even if he'd forgotten, wouldn't they have just charged it to his room?

Seeming to sense his confusion, Sarah smiled again, "Please

sir? He said that he wouldn't take much of your time, and if you'd like, he'd be happy to buy dinner." Gesturing toward an SUV at the end of the carport, she added, "He's just over there in the car."

Making his decision, Glenn replied, "Well if he's just over there, then yes, certainly. I'd be delighted to meet him."

As they approached the car, the passenger-side rear door opened and a figure stepped out. The man looked familiar. Dark hair, a little taller than average, definitely someone Glenn felt he should know, but he couldn't quite put a name to the face.

The figure put out his hand and said, "Good afternoon Mister Hauman, thank you for taking the time to meet with me."

Shaking hands, Glenn replied, "Good to meet you too sir, but I'm afraid you have the advantage of me. You look familiar, but I can't quite place you."

The man laughed gently, "Well, that's a change from the usual. I'm Elon Musk."

Glenn laughed in return, "Of course you are! I thought I recognized you from somewhere; I just couldn't make the connection." And then, somewhat wonderingly, "Do you come to this convention often?"

Musk laughed, "As often as I'm down here lately, you'd think I'd have bought a house. But no, no, I'm just in town for the launch. But I enjoy speculative fiction and since I had some downtime, well, I thought I'd stop by this convention and see what there was to see."

Glenn leaned forward, "The launch? Oh, of course, I was reading in the paper about that. You got permission to launch the Falcon Heavy."

Musk nodded, "That's right. The FAA gave us a license for a test flight. It's good for a year, but why sit around waiting? We're ready to go now, so if the weather holds, we plan to launch on Tuesday."

"Wasn't there something about putting your car into space as well?"

Musk smiled, "That's right."

"Why on Earth would you do that?"

Frowning slightly, Musk replied, "Well, you know, if you're

going to do a test launch, you need to show that your rocket really can carry a payload. Normally, a test flight would just carry some concrete weights, or some steel plates. But getting to orbit is expensive.

"Did you know it costs NASA $10,000 per pound to get something in orbit? One of the reasons I started SpaceX was to try bringing that down, but for now, it's still quite expensive. So if I'm going to put something into space, I'd prefer to launch something useful."

Puzzled, Glenn asked, "So why a car? Why not a satellite?"

Musk frowned more deeply, "Oh, I wanted to launch a satellite. But nobody was willing to trust their payload to an untested launch platform. I mean, you can't really blame them, nobody's ever launched a rocket quite like this one before, and as I've said, the rocket could explode!" Noticing the surprised look on Glenn's face, he softened his tone, "Oh, I don't really think that'll happen. But still, we have had the occasional . . . glitch."

Nodding, Glenn asked, "OK, that makes sense, but still, why a car?"

Beaming, Musk replied, "Well, a few thousand pounds of steel plates zooming through space just isn't very interesting, is it? But people are intrigued by the Tesla. If I can launch one into space, that's going to catch the public interest, don't you think? People will be talking about it for months."

Glenn guffawed, "My god! It's a publicity stunt!"

Musk smiled back, "Well, yes, I suppose it is. But really, I may as well get something out of the test launch, right? If the launch is successful, well, there's nothing wrong with free publicity, now is there?"

Chuckling, Glenn smiled and replied, "No, I suppose not." And then after a moment, "Just the car though? You know, you really ought to put a mannequin in the driver's seat. That way it's not just a car being tossed into space, it's being driven."

Musk paused for a moment, staring into the distance, and then softly whispered, "Oh, that's brilliant! Sarah, make a note of that! We're going to put a mannequin in the roadster's driver's seat. Thank you for that."

Glenn smiled, "Oh you're welcome. Say, could you give me a

car? Maybe a shiny new Tesla Roadster of my own?"

The two men laughed and Musk replied, "I'll consider it. At the very least, I'll promise to at least make sure you get the employee discount."

Glenn smiled, "That would be fantastic. But seriously, all jokes aside, I'm sure you didn't stop by just to tell me about your plans for world conquest. How can I assist you, Mister Musk?"

"Well," Musk replied, "I really did stop by to look for something that might entertain and one day provide a little inspiration. Many of my business ventures are inspired by science fiction books . . . But then I saw you were on the guest list, and thought perhaps we could chat about one of your current projects."

Glenn started to joke that Musk could have asked anything he wanted to during one of his panels, but decided against it. Once Musk had identified himself, he'd had a pretty good idea what topic the conversation might turn to. "The comic book?"

Nodding in return, Musk replied, "Yes, the comic book. But come, where are my manners? Instead of standing in this hotel parking lot, let me take you to dinner. Do you have dinner plans?"

Glenn's heart skipped a beat. *Oh my god! I'm going to have dinner with Elon Musk?! Of course I'm free!*

Pausing a moment to consider, Glenn replied, "No, if we were at one of the DC or New York cons, I'd probably be having dinner with friends, or even heading home by now I suppose; but this is a new convention for me and I haven't made many connections as of yet."

Musk beamed, "Well then, it's settled! Sarah, let's take our friend to that new place at the Cape Marina."

Sarah smiled and replied, "Of course, Mister Musk." She then opened the SUV's back door and held it open as Glenn and Musk entered.

As the SUV threaded its way through the parking lot and onto the road, Glenn broached the topic at hand, "So Elon, may I call you 'Elon'?" Taking Musk's nod as assent, he asked, "That comic book hasn't been announced yet, how did you find out about it?"

Musk chuckled, "Oh, I have spies everywhere." A pause and

then, "Oh, don't look so alarmed. I'm having fun; it wasn't nearly that sinister. The truth is, I found out pretty much the same way anyone finds out what's going on with anything these days. There was a leak."

"A leak?"

Musk laughed again, "Oh it's funny, don't you think? Leaks in government, leaks in industry, but who would have ever expected a leak in the comic book industry? But that's what happened. It seems that between SpaceX, Tesla, and my other ventures, I've acquired something of a fan base. So when you started looking around for writers and artists, it was perhaps inevitable . . . .Well, I got a note from a fan saying, 'Hey, this is a funny idea' and suggesting that I might be amused."

Resolving to be more careful in the future when exploring possible new titles, Glenn asked, "So what do you think of the proposed book?"

Smiling slightly, Musk replied, "'*Elon Musk: The Comic Book*'? Well, I'm certainly flattered by the title. Doesn't every kid want to grow up to be the kind of person who inspires a comic book?"

Glenn nodded. "And the content?"

His smile narrowing, Musk replied, "Well, I was a bit taken aback by that, Glenn. You seem to be painting me as some sort of comic book villain."

"You mean, you aren't a villain?"

Musk paused to consider, "Well, I certainly do have my detractors. But I'm not sure how that rises to the level of villainy."

Glenn explained, "Well that's the funny thing about villains: nobody ever sees themselves as the bad guy. Lex Luthor doesn't see himself as a bad guy He just wants to run his business, make tons of money, and get even with Superman for all the problems he's caused over the years."

Making a show of stroking his hair, Musk asked, "So, am I Lex Luthor then?"

Warming to the subject, Glenn continued, "Well sure, why not? So you and Lex are both industrialists, making money from a collection of corporations. His are all under the general LexCorp banner, whereas you have SpaceX, Tesla, The Boring Company and others. You both have senior executives who share your vision, but further down the food chain? A lot of people in Metropolis work for LexCorp, but they're not all in love with Luthor himself. Some of them know people who were hurt in one of his schemes."

Thoughtfully Musk replied, "I see. Luthor would say it's not his fault and nobody would have been hurt if Superman had minded his own business and not caused things to go wrong." Pausing for a moment, Musk continued, "I do see some of where you're going with this. I do have several people working for me who are more there for the paycheck than any belief that what they're doing is going to change the world in any big way. But that's part of the usual employer vs. employee relationship. How does that put me on the scale of a Lex Luthor?"

Glenn brightened, "Well that's where the whole thing came from; you actually gave me the idea yourself!"

Turning somewhat ashen, Musk asked, "I did what?"

Glenn was positively beaming at this point. "Your business ventures! They're exactly the kind of thing a villain would love to have!"

"What? But how?"

Glenn continued, "So first there's the Tesla cars. Some people will buy them to make a point about the environment, but others will buy them because the electricity makes them cheaper to operate than their existing cars. But in the meantime, you've set up the 'Auto Pilot' which means you can take control. A newspaper reporter gets too close on a story, his car 'malfunctions' and he's out of the picture. You'll have to be careful not to use that one too often or people will lose confidence in the cars, but there it is.

"But your real masterstroke," Glenn explained, "is The Boring Company. Those tunnel making machines are perfect for leading an invasion by The Mole People!"

"But, Mole People? There's no such thing as Mole People," Musk protested.

Glenn waved his hand, "Eh, it's a comic book. There can be Mole People, the writers haven't got that far yet. If not Mole People, then perhaps the drilling machines are being used to plant earthquake machines under a major city. There's all sorts of possibilities. And then there's the flamethrowers."

"Oh, come on," Musk cried. "That was a nod to Yogurt's 'merchandising' in *Spaceballs*."

Glenn nodded, "Of course, but in *Elon Musk: The Comic Book*, there's all sorts of potential for mayhem with a bunch of people running around waving flamethrowers."

Musk shook his head, "You've clearly given this a lot of thought." And then, looking out through the window he announced, "Well, what do you know? It seems we're at the Marina already."

Looking out the window, Glenn saw lines of boats. *Best to wrap this up to avoid a tense, uncomfortable dinner.*

"So, that's the general idea behind the comic book. No hard feelings, Elon?"

Musk put out his hand and the two men shook. "No hard feelings, Glenn. They're not at all productive."

The car pulled to a stop and Sarah quickly ran around and held Glenn's door open as he and Elon exited on their respective sides.

Musk spoke up, "You know Glenn, if I were the villainous type, I could always sue to block publication."

Glenn shook his head gently, "No, that wouldn't work. You're a public figure. The courts would rule that the comic was a work of parody."

Musk nodded. "Ah, there is that. Oh, before I forget, Sarah had a question she wanted to ask you."

Glenn started to turn to Sarah, "Of course, anything I can . . ."

His words were cut off as Sarah grabbed the back of his head with one hand and clamped a rag over his mouth and nose with the other. As he fell to the ground he saw her, still smiling as she asked, "Oh, I just wanted to know, does this rag smell like chloroform?"

Glenn woke to find himself sitting in a reclined position in a dimly lit room. Moaning softly he asked himself, "Oh, my poor head. Where am I? And what on Earth did I drink?"

Trying to stir, he found himself immobile, feeling as though there were steel bands holding him in place.

As his eyes adjusted to the dim light coming from unseen sources, Glenn found himself thinking aloud, "That's weird. It almost looks like I'm sitting behind the wheel of a car." And then as memory returned, "Hey! I am behind the wheel of a car! Hey Elon! Are you there? Did you manage to get me a car?!"

A voice sounded from behind Glenn's left ear, "Oh Good, you're awake. Sarah and I were worried you were going to sleep through the launch."

Excited, Glenn asked, "Oh that's great! I'll get to see the launch too? Where are we? Is this the VIP area?"

Again Musk's voice seemed to be coming from somewhere behind Glenn's ear. "Oh, I suppose you could call it a 'VIP area.' Seating for just one VIP. That was a fantastic idea you came up with by the way, putting a mannequin behind the wheel of the car. It's quite captured the popular imagination: they're calling you 'Starman' and talking about how 'Starman is driving to Mars.'"

Getting nervous, Glenn asked, "Wait, they're calling me 'Starman'? Where am I? Where are you?"

Again the distant voice, "Oh, I'm a few miles away, at launch control. But you Glenn, you're in the seat of honor. You have your very own SpaceX spacesuit and you're sitting behind the wheel of my roadster. The Falcon Heavy will launch in about 10 minutes, and then if the math is right, a few years from now, you'll arrive in the orbit of Mars."

Starting to get scared, Glenn found that he couldn't move at all. "Musk! You really are a villain! Get me out of here, please!"

"Now, now, Glenn," Musk answered for the final time. "You know Lex Luthor would never free his opponent from his predicament. Now save your breath, you only have an hour or two of air and you'll want to enjoy the flight."

Glenn continued to try to free himself, but to no avail. As he felt the rocket's engines start to push him deeply into his seat, he decided to make his last words worthwhile.

"I may not live to see it, but I'm going to be the first Comic Book Publisher on Mars! That's something Siegel and Schuster never did. In your face boys!

What can I say about Brett Hudgins that wasn't in the psychiatrist's report?

At vero eos et accusamus et iusto odio dignissimos ducimus qui blanditiis praesentium voluptatum deleniti atque corrupti quos dolores et quas molestias excepturi sint occaecati cupiditate non provident, similique sunt in culpa qui officia deserunt mollitia animi, id est laborum et dolorum fuga. Et harum quidem rerum facilis est et expedita distinctio. Gratias Num occidere me tu bastardis.

To him I bequeath a copy of Google Translate.

# THE LONG AND THE SHORT OF IT
## by Brett Hudgins

"ANY NIBBLES YET, SON?"

I looked up from my morose contemplation of the uneven wooden posts, slats and planks my dad had fashioned into a rustic bed frame. Helping him display it at the local craft fair had sounded like a good way to spend some time together. Unfortunately, once he saw how many other vendors filled the converted barn, he became obsessed with checking out "the competition." That left me in charge of customer service and sneaking games of Fruit Ninja on my phone.

Having completed another circuit of the sale floor, he regarded me expectantly over his creation.

I shrugged helplessly. "Pops, I could have sold this thing three times by now if you'd let me call it a porch swing."

"It's a bed, Jace."

"Maybe in squirrel Alcatraz."

Pops just smiled, the fulfillment he derived from his post-retirement hobby easily outshining my exaggerated gloom. "I'm sure you're close. Keep trying. I'll do another lap."

At least if he wore himself out, I reasoned, he'd brought something to lie down on.

Moments after he strolled away, a voice from my left ventured, "Your dad seems nice."

I turned to find an attractive woman grinning at me, having

apparently set up shop next door without my even noticing. She was around my age, in her twenties, and atop her neat auburn bob of hair she wore a pair of sparkly cat ears on a headband. The table in front of her showed off another three dozen of them, no two alike.

She followed my gaze to her wares and grinned even wider. "They're like crack for granddaughters. I sell out every time."

I laughed in spite of myself. "Nice. Pops started out making practical, appealing doodads too. Then he found some sort of Anarchist's Furniture Cookbook online and built a bed." I gestured at it halfheartedly. "Allegedly."

"How would *you* make a bed, then?"

I smirked. "With an IKEA catalog and a credit card."

"Oh, snap! Craft fair fightin' words." She stuck out her hand. "I'm Nora."

"Jace." We shook. "I didn't—"

"This bed is *exquisite*!"

With what seemed like nothing less than a magic spell abruptly broken, I whirled away from Nora to find an extremely tall bearded man appreciating my dad's bed for what, against all odds, it actually was.

"If you say so," I agreed, already getting a crick in my neck.

He adjusted his glasses, leaned down, and peered closer at Pops' rough handiwork. "This is the finest example of neoprimitive craftsmanship I've ever seen. My height renders me susceptible to back trouble, you know. And if ancient diets are good for us, I figure ancient beds are too. From what kind of wood is it constructed? Mahogany? Oak?"

Damned if I knew. And only one type of wood common to all beds sprang to mind. "Morning," I supplied cheerfully.

To my left, Nora muffled a snort.

The tall man nodded obliviously, more intent on the descriptive placard Pops had written up. "And it says here that it's adjustable. So, if I fiddle with it, I'll be able to make it longer?"

"Sir, that's what morning wood is *known* for."

Nora turned away and burst out laughing.

"I'll take it!" the man exclaimed, paying her no attention.

Pops reappeared just as I was finalizing the sale. I introduced him to his customer. "Pops, this is Glenn Hauman. He's traveling the country in search of furniture that makes being a human skyscraper even more awesome."

"Your magnificent bed won't fit in my rental car," Glenn put in, "but your son says you can follow me to my motel in your van. I'll ship it home from there."

"Sounds good," Pops said. "Let's roll."

I helped them as far as the parking lot, waved at their taillights as they drove away, and returned to Nora's table in the barn. The craft fair was in full swing. Little old ladies had already snapped up half her cat ear headbands. I put one on, dragged over a folding chair, and sat down next to her as if that's where I belonged.

I was starting to believe it was.

An hour later Nora's table was empty, she was swimming in nana cash, and I was nursing a crush on her the likes of which I hadn't known since my teens. But I wasn't so besotted as not to notice Pops hadn't returned from his delivery.

"I'm sure he's fine," she said.

I frowned, unable to shake my worry. "You know, I stared at that bed for an hour today and couldn't for the life of me see how it was adjustable. Maybe Mr. Hauman thinks he got swindled and is arguing for a refund."

Nora plucked the bed's descriptive placard from where I was nervously twisting and folding it between my fingers. "'The Procrustean Bed,'" she read aloud. "*That's* what your dad made?"

"What about it?"

"Jace, didn't you ever study any classical mythology?"

"I prefer the modern stuff," I admitted.

Her nose wrinkled. "Scientology?"

"*Star Trek.*"

Nora stuck out her tongue at me. "Nerd. Procrustes was basically an ancient Greek serial killer. He invited travelers to stay with him and if they didn't fit in his guest bed *precisely*, he'd either stretch them or shorten them—*fatally*. He was a scourge on the road to Athens until the hero Theseus, of Minotaur fame, gave him a taste of his own medicine."

Eyeing me sympathetically, she let the card drop to her table. "In other words, it wasn't the bed that was adjustable, it was the *people*."

Nora's helpful lesson only strengthened my conviction that Mr. Hauman was probably pretty sore at Pops for misrepresenting the bed. And after another half hour's wait, during which Pops neither showed up nor answered his cell, she offered to drive me to the towering customer's temporary address.

"You don't have to do that," I protested.

Nora saw right through my weak reverse psychology. Smiling, she reached up to remove the pair of cat ears I'd forgotten I was wearing. "And leave my best salesman in the lurch?"

Fifteen minutes later we were pulling in to the parking lot of the Middletown Dreams motel complex. There were fifteen single-story units arranged in roughly a horseshoe pattern. A sign welcoming travelers promised "Life's not unpleasant in this little neighborhood."

Before I could direct Nora towards the familiar van backed up near the door of #6, next to the tan sedan Mr. Hauman had rented, I noticed Pops wrestling his handmade bed out of the open motel suite and into his vehicle. "Oh, great," I muttered. "Mr. Hauman must have called off the deal."

Nora parked in the nearest open slot and was only a few steps behind me to intercept my dad, whose face wore a murderous expression I'd never seen on him.

"Pops, wait!" I called, running into his path. "Don't give up. Maybe Mr. Hauman needs a porch swing."

Pops fixed me with a vicious stare and declared, "Your sire is gone. Damastes lives again." Then he shoved me aside, slammed the van shut, and threw himself into the driver's seat. He peeled out of the parking lot without another word or glance in my direction.

I watched the van recede down the highway, bewildered and not a little shaken. "What's gotten into him . . . ?"

"Jace?" Nora murmured from where she was peering into the suite. "I think I might know."

I joined her. From our position in the doorway, we could see

Glenn Hauman lying on the motel floor. The top fifth or so of his body had been crudely severed from the rest of him. It was about the deadest anyone could possibly be. Yet despite the nature of the . . . operation, there was no blood on the carpet, much less the ocean's worth I would have expected.

My stomach churned ominously and I clutched Nora to steady myself. "I thought video games were supposed to desensitize me to this. Did—" I could hardly think it, much less say it. "Did *Pops* do this?"

Nora made sure she had my attention before answering. She was clearly choosing her words carefully. "Bear with me, okay? I don't know if you share my interest in—and openness to—the supernatural, but in recreating that mythological bed, your dad may have somehow resurrected the spirit of Procrustes. And of course Mr. Hauman couldn't resist trying out his new back relief by lying down. Empowered by the life of an oversized victim, Procrustes was then able to possess a human form."

"Pops?" I shook my head—in denial as much as confusion.

"His bed even absorbed Mr. Hauman's blood as part of the ritual."

"But he said 'Damastes lives again.'"

"Exactly. That was his real name. Procrustes was a nickname—it means 'stretcher.'"

"This is a nightmare." I squeezed my eyes shut but when I opened them again, Mr. Hauman's giant body was still taking up half the floor like a sectional sofa. "It's also the best explanation for why Pops would leave a person in this condition. Damn it."

"We've got to find him, Jace. Figure out a way to free him."

"Nora, you've done so much for me already. This could be dangerous."

She raised an eyebrow at me. "More dangerous than an ancient Greek killer with a predilection for luring innocent victims, and possessing the modern knowledge of his host body, driving a nondescript white panel van through a town with several school zones teeming with stretchable kids?"

She had me there.

Before departing, we bowed our heads and paid our final

respects to the mortal remains of Glenn Hauman. "Look at how much of him didn't fit on the Procrustean bed," I marveled.

I felt Nora slip her hand gently into mine. "It's too bad neither of us has dandruff," she said.

". . . Why?"

"That's a lot of head and shoulders."

Back in Nora's Corolla, I took over the driving so she could research our problem on her phone. We had already made the uneasy but pragmatic decision to leave Mr. Hauman's body for discovery by motel services. If our fears proved correct, involving the Muggle police wouldn't do Pops any favors.

"Any luck?" Nora asked distractedly after we'd been cruising for a while.

"No. I've seen a bunch of similar vans, but none with the right license plate. I sure wish I hadn't left a bag of Skittles in there. Free candy just reinforces the pervert stereotype." I took a hand off the wheel to rub my burning eyes. "How about you?"

"I think I found the webpage your dad started from. There are blueprint packages for a whole bunch of fantastical furniture items. An outfit called Enchanted Forest Decor sells them as kits. Here's a sample picture of the bed."

I glanced at her phone, my eyes widening. "Why is a naked woman posing on it?"

". . . You know about the Internet, right?"

I turned at the next intersection, staying alert for locations where the reborn Procrustes might stop to attract unwary travelers. "I don't suppose there's a disclaimer about malevolent spirits?"

Nora shook her head. "Nope. The kits are offered as a lark—like the Ouija board my friends and I played with at so many of my slumber parties. To revitalize Procrustes, the one your dad received must have contained magical lumber from an *actual* enchanted forest." She paused. "I would not have seen that coming."

"And now he's like an evil spider looking for the ideal place to spin his web."

"So where else do a lot of people stop in their daily journeys and commutes?" Nora mused. "Maybe without even thinking about it."

My poor brain, already reeling from so much that day, chose that moment to register the half dozen empty to-go coffee cups Nora had crumpled into a trash bag protruding from under her front passenger seat. I couldn't have asked for a better "Eureka!" moment.

I almost stomped her gas pedal straight through the floor, Flintstones-style, in my race to the nearest Starbucks. Pops wasn't there—but he was at the third branch we tried, his van blocking the drive-thru as he leaned out the open rear doors and tried to entice angry, impatient coffee addicts into his home-made bed.

I fishtailed Nora's car into the parking lot, almost sideswiping one of the yellow safety bollards protecting the shop, and lunged out the door towards the drive-thru.

"Caffeine stunts your growth!" my dad was shouting in frustration. "I can help with that!"

"*Procrustes*!" I roared.

Pops—Damastes, that is—took off the moment he recognized me, looking furious to have been interrupted in his quest for fresh victims. I was losing a car chase to a spirit from the age of horse-drawn chariots and, I dunno, basilisks or something.

"Did anyone get in his van?" I demanded of the onlookers returning to their vehicles.

Everyone shook their heads.

"Did anyone stream that nut's performance on Facebook Live?" Nora added.

Five people raised hands clutching glowing smartphones.

Nora hustled me back to her car before I could howl the world's loudest expletive. Behind us, I heard a Starbucks enthusiast trying to order "a dozen Procrustes" through the drive-thru speaker: "six chocolate chip and six gluten-free."

Nora was back behind the wheel and we were back in traffic. Neither of us trusted my driving at that particular moment. Not that we knew where to go.

"I'm sorry," I told her quietly. "I'm sorry you saw me like that.

I'm sorry for all of this. I really like you and I wanted you to like me and I feel as if I'm going *crazy*."

Her smile was so genuine and unconditional that I thought my heart might break. "Jace, would I still be here if I didn't like you?"

"Um . . ."

"Also, you should know that every girl wants at least one dude to completely flip his marbles over her." She reached over to touch my hand. "I can't take *all* the credit for today, but hey, mission accomplished."

It would have been a weirdly romantic moment except for the fact that I loved my Pops. He and Mom had welcomed me a bit late to their lives and marriage, but he'd always been there for me, raising and providing for me to the utmost of his resources and capability. What business did I have feeling better about myself when he was still at the mercy of a killer spirit?

"*Mom*," I said out loud, realizing she still didn't know what had become of her husband.

"Huh?" Nora wondered.

"I've got to call my mom and tell her Pops is trying to establish the contemporary equivalent of an ancient Greek roadside inn so he can stretch and chop travelers like taffy."

". . . That's a lot to unpack. Maybe open with a joke."

But as I was fumbling my phone from the pocket of my jeans, I heard the incoming text notification. I'm pretty sure any remaining color drained from my face as I read the message.

Nora heard me gasp and spared me a concerned glance as she navigated through traffic. "What's wrong?"

"Speak of the devil, that's what. It's from my mom. She says there's a six-foot-nine man at the front door claiming to have rented my old room on Airbnb."

As fast as Nora drove us to my childhood home—no small feat, considering my directions may not have been entirely coherent—I still had time to look up the listing Pops had placed on the short-term lodgings site. "He's playing Airbnb like a musical instrument—pimping my old room as some sort of wayfarer's wonderland for anyone not of average size. This escalation is *bonkers*."

"At least we know where he is."

"We also know Procrustes assimilates better than the Borg," I complained. "If that stupid bed had wheels, it'd probably be an Uber by now."

At my folks' place the white van was parked in the driveway. Another car, presumably the would-be tenant's, sat against the front curb. Nora pulled in behind it. Mom, thank goodness, had heeded my frantic text reply and was waiting in the front yard, out of danger. She met us as we emerged from the Corolla.

"What's going on, Jace?" she asked as I hugged her. "Why can't I be in the house? Why is your father behaving so oddly? And why does a colossal stranger think he can spend the night in your room?"

"It's hard to explain, Mom." *Don't sound deranged*, I admonished myself. *Not now.* "Let's just say Pops has . . . been a different person since the craft fair. If you'd like to drop in on a neighbor for some tea and gossip, I'm sure I can straighten things out."

"I do like tea and gossip," she agreed. She brightened further upon noticing Nora. "Hello, dear. Who might you be?"

Nora introduced herself, adding warmly, "Lovely to meet you. I'm either your future daughter-in-law or Jace's *one that got away.*"

"Oh my. You and I will have to share some tea and gossip too."

Nora and I watched until Mom was safe inside the house next door. Only then did I wilt in relief. "Never mind Procrustes and my dad," I said. "What lunatic demon possesses *you?*"

Nora laughed. "Your mom loves me."

We entered the house through the garage, which Pops had converted into a workshop upon his retirement, but not before verifying that the inside of the van and its travel toolbox—like the motel carpet earlier—were free of Mr. Hauman's blood. Nora must have been right about the bed absorbing it. At least police forensics was one less thing to worry about.

She immediately noticed the Enchanted Forest Decor kit open on the workbench. "Here they are." She waved an illustrated sheet of paper at me. "The specs for the Procrustean bed.

And there's some wood left over."

"Yeah, Pops used to have the same problem when he helped me build my Legos."

"I think I have an idea." She laid out the remaining wood on the bench and started choosing tools from my dad's shelves. "You hurry upstairs and save six-foot-nine's life. I'll be as close behind you as possible. Go!" When I hesitated, Nora somehow sent me some of her strength with nothing but a smile. "We'll get your dad back, Jace. I promise."

I bolted from the garage and launched myself up the stairs, bursting wildly into my old room seconds later. The Airbnb client was lounging on my old bed with his long legs dangling, shaking his head as Pops tried to coax him over to the handcrafted murder nest.

"No, no, Titan, you must sleep *here*."

"Are you kidding? I'll get splinters—and maybe termites."

I lunged between them. "Procrustes, stop!"

"*Occupado*, buddy," huffed the elongated stranger.

Glaring at him, I grabbed his duffel bag and hurled it out my window. "Beat it. I hear the carnival is hiring stilt-men. Feel free to change some lightbulbs on your way out."

Then I was glaring at his collarbone as he rose to loom over me and Pops. "You people are insane," he told the tops of our heads. Then, miraculously, he exited the room rather than squishing us like bugs.

"I'll never stop, boy," Procrustes practically hissed at me. "Your father freed me. Other towns, other nations—however far I must journey to escape your desperate interference, I won't rest until all the freaks and oddities of this world conform to my ideal."

I threw up my hands. "You want to talk about rest? Man, after today I'm *exhausted*. And maybe I'm not too tall or too short by your psycho standards, but I'm not 'average' on the *inside*. Newsflash, Damastes: *no one is*. So why draw the line at someone's height?" I flopped down on his bed and stared at him defiantly. "Start with me. Hit me where it hurts and tear out my heart. You can't do worse to me than you already have by possessing my dad."

Looking at me lying on the bed that gave him his power and enabled his evil, Procrustes started trembling violently. Perspiration beaded on his forehead. "You can't *be* there," he grated. "You have to be a certain way. You aren't *right*."

"And I'm not wrong. This is the kind of paradox that gives *Star Trek* androids conniptions."

Procrustes tilted his head, his facial rictus going slack. "Androids. You . . . you dressed up as Mr. Data for Halloween," he stammered. "You told everyone you were programmed to eat candy . . ."

I sat up so quickly I felt dizzy, hardly daring to hope. "*Pops?* Pops, is that you?"

Just then Nora slipped into the room, assessing the situation. Unless I was completely misreading her expression, her keen eyes twinkled with anticipation.

"Procrustes seems to be weakening," I reported, indicating my dad's hunched, quivering form. "Pops is still in there, fighting him. I think we were just connecting."

"I knew you could do it, Jace."

I turned back to my dad. "Come on, Pops. It's *me*. Remember that argument we had about how terrible Captain Kirk was at karate?"

Nora helped me guide him not to the bed he'd made, but rather the one he'd tucked me into so many nights when I was a boy. We eased him down on it. "The lifeforce Procrustes stole from Mr. Hauman to gain his foothold in our world is ebbing. And you just prevented him from feeding again. It's time to finish him off—with this." She held up the last of the enchanted wood from the garage workbench, now joined into a flat surface and painted with vaguely familiar symbols.

"That doesn't look like a magic wand *or* a proton pack."

When she handed me her creation and indicated that I should hold it horizontally, with a loose arrow-shaped piece on top, I recognized it immediately. "Your old slumber parties," I remembered. "You made a Ouija board."

"From genuinely magical wood," she confirmed, "so this ought to work. What I realized is that in his arrogance Procrustes made a mistake. He has no claim on your dad's work other than his notorious myth. Your dad sold the bed to Glenn Hauman *fair and square*. If we can summon Mr. Hauman to assert his rightful ownership, old Damastes will lose his anchor and go drifting into oblivion."

"Please," Procrustes croaked from Pops' body. "I don't want to die again. Nor should my dream of homogeneous perfection . . ."

"There was never going to be room for the whole planet on one bed, you monster."

"That's right," Nora added. "Even a small world entails a fifteen minute boat ride at Disneyland."

I held the Ouija board steady as Nora asked the questions that would bring Glenn Hauman back from beyond.

"Mr. Hauman, we need you terribly. Will you return to aid us in our darkest hour?"

An agonizing beat passed before the planchette dragged her hand to YES.

"Were you a savvy shopper with a good eye for bargains?" YES.

"Have you heard the cliché about wealth that 'you can't take it with you'?" YES.

"On the promise of an eternity free of back pain, sir, would you care to *debunk that shit*?"

I almost dropped the board as her hand slammed down on YES.

A cold wind swept through the room.

Pops gasped and sat up on my old bed—even as the one he'd built in his workshop faded away into the ether.

Nora looked upwards. "Sleep well, Mr. Hauman."

I thrust the Ouija board at her and rushed to my dad. "Pops, are you free?" He still seemed a bit spacey. I shook him gently. "Pops, please speak to me!"

He blinked and told me, "Jace, you never understood that Kirk wasn't an ordinary martial artist. He was a master of *space karate*."

"Pops!"

We hugged deliriously, pounding each other's backs and laughing like loons.

Pops then profusely thanked Nora for helping save his life and hurried next door to assure Mom that he was all right.

Smiling, Nora wiped away happy tears as she watched him leave.

"Ouija boards and technicalities," I said to her, more than a little awed. "You're kind of a genius, aren't you?"

"And you're kind of a sweetheart." She laced her fingers behind my head and drew my face close to hers. "You know what else girls do at slumber parties?"

"I have no idea," I confessed, even as I wondered if I was seeing my future in her eyes.

Eyes she rolled affectionately. "Nerd. We practice kissing."

What can I say about S. Brady Calhoun without blowing his cover?

"His cover?" I hear you cry? Yes, for the truth is that S. Brady Calhoun is not just a mild-mannered reporter in Panama City with a weakness for pop culture, he is also Bud "Lash" Conray, an international spy with a bounty on his head in thirteen countries and Detroit. (His name is an anagram because his cover is a Florida journalist, and the Dave Barry Rule states that Florida journalists must use anagrams whenever possible. For example, the anagram LO, RACY HUSBAND, which probably makes his wife happy.) As a spy, he's trying to keep a low profile so as few people as possible can see him, which explains what he's doing in this anthology.

To him I leave my fake passport collection. Good luck, "Lash." You're going to need it.

# THE MARATHON
## by S. Brady Calhoun

IT STARTED, AS ALL GREAT ROMANCES DO, QUITE BY accident.

The accident was Glenn's fault. He was watching funny cat videos on his phone when he should have been driving.

"Oh Grumpy cat, what won't you get up to?" he chuckled. His chuckle turned into a snorting choking sound as he caught sight of a runner crossing the street in front of him.

Glenn slammed on the brakes but 1974 frosted blue Winnebagos don't stop on a dime.

In his high school, Glenn once stood in a batter's box and taunted a pitcher on the opposing team. How was he to know the pitcher was one of the best in the league and only a year away from being called up from high school ball and into Triple-A?

The pitcher, annoyed, placed his fastball right on the earhole of Glenn's helmet. The sound the 89 mile-per-hour rocket made was a sickening thud. And that's exactly, Glenn realized later, the sound the runner's body made when he hit her with a Winnebago.

Glenn's phone flew out of his hand and shattered on the windshield. Glenn got out of his seat and threw himself against the door. The Winnebago's door was difficult to open without a good neighborly shove, and once it released he fell onto the asphalt.

Glenn hustled to the front of the RV and saw the most beautiful woman he had ever seen in his life.

Glenn couldn't help but notice her tender, voluptuous figure, her fetching Asian features and her alluring face and hair that were only just slightly covered in blood. Glenn's heart thumped like a racehorse in his chest.

"Ummm," Glenn said, finding himself suddenly struck mute. "Hi."

She gave him a look that could have turned back Attila at Gaul.

"Sir," she said, "Please call for an ambulance. I think you broke my leg."

"I . . . I . . . I . . ."

"This isn't helping," she replied.

"I broke my phone," Glenn said.

"Here," she said, as she pulled her phone out of her pocket. "Use mine."

"Otterbox," Glenn said pointing at the phone's case. "Good choice."

Glenn took it and started to dial.

"I'm sorry," Glenn said.

"What is it now?" she asked, agony contorting her face.

"I can't unlock it," he said sheepishly. "I need your pin number."

"It's 10 77," she replied. "The price of a cheese pizza and a large soda at Panucci's Pizza."

Glenn gasped. She had just quoted *Futurama* to him. This . . . woman . . . was . . . perfect.

"Stop staring at me and call an ambulance," she shouted.

When the ambulance was gone and the cops were gone, Glenn decided he needed to see her again. At the hospital, Glenn wavered over the perfect set of apology and get-well trinkets.

Nothing really jumped out at him as saying, "I'm very sorry I ran over you with my car. Also, are you single?"

Glenn settled on a bright and cheery bouquet filled with

daffodils and lilies and a get well card. At the reception desk, he was met by a sour-faced woman in her mid-fifties with streaks of blue in her hair. Eventually, after she finished an interminably long phone call about the contents of last night's episode of *The Bachelor* and featured plentiful uses of the word "bitch" and "crazy" the woman took notice of Glenn.

"Canihelpyou," she said in a low grunt that ground the sentence down until it was a single word.

"Yes, I'm Glenn Hauman, I'm looking for someone," he said.

"Name?" she said.

"*Ummm*," he replied.

Now, the receptionist did take notice of Glenn. He immediately decided he preferred it when she thought of him as a small distraction to be ignored.

"*Ummm* is not a name, sir," she said. "What is this person's name?"

"Well, see I didn't get her name," he said. "See there was this accident?"

"Accident?" she said. "Are you hurt? If you are hurt you need to go over to emergency, don't go falling out on my floor here."

"No, I'm not hurt. See I ran over this woman with my car . . ."

"And now you're back to finish the job?"

"No," Glenn said. "Of course not."

*This is ridiculous*, he thought. "I just want to apologize and give her this, these things that I have."

The receptionist made a tsking sound and grunted.

"I'll need a name, sir," she said.

Suddenly it came to him. Glenn reached into his pocket and felt it sitting there.

"I forgot," he said. "The officer wrote a report with our information for my insurance. I hadn't, hadn't thought of it."

Glenn's hand was almost shaking as he read it.

"Here we go: driver, one Glenn Hauman, umm, that's me. Pedestrian, one Julie Palli. That's her, Julie Palli. Now, can you give me her room number?"

"No," the receptionist said.

"No?" Glenn asked.

"No," she said, firmly.

"I thought you just needed her name," Glenn said.

"I needed her name to find her but that doesn't mean I can give you her room number," the receptionist replied. "Under US privacy laws if Ms. Palli was in our facility we would have asked her to fill out a privacy form and if she marked on that form that she only wanted family members to know where she was then I would be breaking the law by confirming that she was in this hospital and by giving the room number to the man who hit her with his car."

"Well, then, can I just leave this here with you?" Glenn asked. "I can write a note."

"No sir," the receptionist said. "If I did that I would be admitting that Ms. Palli was in our facility and as I have just told you I can't confirm or deny that without breaking US privacy laws."

"But I already know she's here," Glenn said, shaking his arms in the air. He stopped when he noticed that some of the petals on the daffodils began to break away and fall.

"I'm sorry, but I've helped you all I can."

"Actually," Glenn said. "I'm her brother."

"Her brother," the receptionist said icily.

"Her cousin," Glenn said. "I used to see her all the time at family reunions."

"Sir, you are going to have to leave."

Glenn's shoulders fell. He stomped out.

For just a moment Glenn enjoyed the sunshine and warm air that greeted him.

And then he smiled.

Glenn walked two blocks to the other side of the hospital and into the emergency room. A young man with frosted blonde tips was working the receptionist desk.

"Hi," Glenn said. "I'm Julie Palli's brother. I heard she was in an accident. Can you tell me what room she's in?"

"Sure," he said. "Ah, she's out of emergency and in room 110. Straight back this way. Head to the door and I'll buzz you in."

"Thanks."

Julie was bored with what appeared, to Glenn, to be a showing of *Con Air* on network television.

He tried to shuffle, quietly, into the room but smacked the room door into the open bathroom door.

"Uh, these are too close together," he said.

"Back to finish the job, Mr. Hauman?" Julie asked.

"No, uh no, no," he said. And then, firmly, "No."

"Ok?" Julie said. "So then?"

"These are for you," Glenn said. "For, well, I wanted to apologize. I'm not sure of the protocol here. I've never run over someone before. But I, well, I wouldn't be able to sleep if I hadn't done everything I could to try and make this better."

"You fix broken legs?" Julie asked.

Glenn sighed and began to look for someplace to set the flowers.

"Mr. Hauman, are you worried I'll sue?" Julie said.

"I have insurance," Glenn said. "The one with the duck, or the lizard from the commercials. So, no."

"Well then," Julie asked again.

"This isn't how I thought this would go," Glenn said. "I just, well, is there, someone, I could call for you? Or something I can get you?"

Julie's cheeks twinged, just a bit. Not so much that most people would notice, but Glenn, from the moment he walked back into her room, hadn't been able to take his eyes off her.

"Actually no," Julie said. "This is my first week here. I took a new job. I sort of, well, I ran away from a bad time in another place you know?"

"I live in the same house I was born in so no, I don't know. But it sounds fascinating," Glenn said. He found a chair and sat down.

"It's not and I don't really want to get into it," Julie said.

"Ok," Glenn said.

"Ok," Julie replied.

Glenn shifted in the chair, looking for a sweet spot that wasn't there.

"Mr. Hauman," Julie began.

"Glenn, please," Glenn said.

"Glenn," Julie said. "There is something you can do."

"Sure," he said, waves of relief suddenly flooding his body. "Anything."

"Careful," Julie said. "Anything is a big promise. I could ask you to watch this horrid movie with me."

Glenn smiled. "Anything," he said.

"Well, I'm hoping you can ask them about the television," Julie said. "Surely, there are more channels."

Glenn frowned.

"I was here with my mom for a long time," Glenn said. "And no, they only get the basic channels. This hospital is the only game in town and they know it. But, I came up with a solution for my mom."

He reached into his bag and pulled out an iPad.

"The sound is really good on this," Glenn said. "And I got it loaded up with Netflix, and Hulu and Amazon and, *uhh*, HBO I think. I can't remember if I canceled it when *Game of Thrones* ended."

He walked to her bed and set the device down on her food tray.

"So, well, it's an iPad. It's pretty easy to use," Glenn said.

"I can't take this from you," Julie said.

"Sure you can," Glenn said, and as he finished the sentence decided that his voice was too high pitched and eager. "I mean, really, this is the least I can do. I've got an older one at the house that's fine. Several older ones actually. And I'll just sign out, here, and then you can sign in and watch whatever you want. Or you can use my logins. Whatever."

"No, really, this is too much," Julie said.

"Please, seriously, this is the least I can do," Glenn said.

"Well, this and paying your insurance premiums," Julie said. She chuckled and then moaned.

Glenn's face fell.

"You got me in the ribs too," she explained. "It hurts to laugh." As Glenn stood over her, Julie tapped the Netflix app, pulled up an episode of *Firefly* and hit play.

"Comfort TV," she said.

"Yeah," Glenn said. "I still have, like, dreams about living in a world where they didn't cancel *Firefly*. And where Trump isn't president."

"I know," Julie said.

"This is the darkest timeline," they said together.

Julie's reaction to this was, almost, a gasp.

"Well," Glenn said. "Doctor."

"Doctor," she replied.

"Doctor," he said.

"Doctor," she replied.

"Doc—"

"Ok, Glenn," Julie said.

"Ok."

He scurried toward the door.

"Glenn," Julie said.

"Yes," he said.

"Well," Julie said. "If you want to."

"Yes," Glenn said.

"You can stay for a while and watch this with me," Julie said.

"Yes," he said.

The next few weeks were lazy and happy for Julie and Glenn. Glenn's insurance agreed to cover all of Julie's medical bills and, once they realized Glenn planned to testify that the entire thing had been his fault, they offered Julie a nice settlement.

Not enough to retire but enough for Julie to rest and recover while she waited on her broken legs to mend. Glenn was always nearby; they were basically neighbors, and he remained ever willing to help her with anything she needed.

One night, after some sangria and watching Sandra Bullock cry a little too hard about not being pretty enough for a beauty pageant, Julie grabbed Glenn by his big dumb face and kissed him. His heart leaped in his chest.

"You have a big dumb face," she said. Then she giggled at him.

"I think you are amazing," Glenn said.

"Your hair is ridiculous," Julie replied.

"I've never met someone who got me before, you know, or who understood just how great all the Marvel movies are," Glenn said.

"God, *Man of Steel* sucks," Julie said.

"It's the worst," Glenn agreed.

She kissed him again. And gently, very gently, they fell into each other's arms.

And after that, they pretty much lived together.

Julie couldn't get over Glenn's job. He wrote about television for a living. "I didn't think that was a job an adult could have," she said.

She had never heard of the websites he wrote for. But she thought his writing was witty and she only occasionally asked him why he didn't write a script or a book or something besides his 'little' reviews.

Glenn worried about her drinking. *It'll get better*, he said to himself, *when she can work again*. Julie was a personal trainer and a marathon runner. Glenn told Julie he was learning to love vegetables. She was functionally a vegetarian although she occasionally cheated with some lean baked chicken. Glenn ran errands several times a week so that while he was gone he could stop and get fast food. It was fast food indeed; he ate it in his car and threw away the evidence before he got back home to Julie.

Julie didn't tell Glenn she knew about the fast food. Glenn looked the other way when she got sloppy at parties.

They watched all of Quentin Tarantino's movies. She didn't care for most of them. And he paid for that as they sat through a dozen horror movies. Glenn liked stories where good guys won and bad people were punished. And, to be fair, he didn't like being creeped out. But Julie loved the scares. She jumped every time a cat bounced across the screen.

They watched a teacher become the biggest drug dealer in New Mexico and a dizzying amount of episodes about treks across the stars. And *Doctor Who*.

"Just watch 'Blink,'" Glenn said when Julie asked him to explain the long-running English show to her. And the story of Sally Sparrow and her encounter with the Weeping Angels was all it took to turn Julie into a fan.

They had just finished "The Girl Who Waited," when Julie decided to talk about it.

"So, tomorrow's the day," she said.

"Yep," Glenn said. "Big day. Big, big big day."

"I get my cast off, remember," Julie said.

Glenn blinked.

"Of course, dear, it's wonderful," he said. "I can't wait."

"It's going to take some time, of course, but I want you to run with me. I mean it's great exercise and well we've become such couch potatoes. I mean it's so great to see the sunrise when you hit that fifth mile."

Glenn gulped. It was, he realized, almost like one of those gulps you see in cartoons. He hadn't done it on purpose; it had just happened to him. It was like that time he got the chicken-pox or when a co-worker at his old job had accused him of staring at her when, in fact, he had just been staring into space while trying to write.

"Don't worry, silly," Julie said. "This is gonna be great." Then, in her excitement, she shouted. It was the kind of shout you saw on commercials when car shoppers got a 10 percent discount. "*Woooo*," Julie shouted. "*It's gonna be great!*"

Glenn smiled and hugged her. "It's gonna be great," he agreed.

He didn't sleep at all that night. The tension just seemed to sit on his chest.


Glenn did not like to run. He did not like the hazy tired morning or the feeling in his body which continued to urge him to stop running moments after he had begun. Julie was radiant though and that kept him with it for a little bit longer than normal.

He lasted a week.

"Come on, let's go," Julie said on a drizzly Monday.

"I would prefer not to," Glenn replied.

Julie cocked her eyebrow at him but said nothing. She got dressed as he rolled over and could hear his snoring as she laced up her black Nikes and bolted out the door.

Julie never asked him to run again.

Glenn felt badly about it but not so badly that he actually got up and ran anymore. His mornings were now spent with reruns of *Andy Griffith* for a series piece he had planned on the Southern sitcoms that once ruled the airwaves and their descendants. It wouldn't be too hard to connect the parenting styles of Mayberry's sheriff to Roseanne Conner, he figured, and it might be worth a few clicks thanks to the Roseanne revival.

A week or two after he stopped running, Julie called him for a ride after her car broke down at work.

He was greeted with a kiss from Julie and a hard handshake from a tall, sweaty, shaggy-headed guy named Clint.

"Clint's another trainer. He's been looking at the car," Julie said.

*That's not what he's been looking at,* Glenn thought.

"Oh great," Glenn said. "Well, what is it, you think?"

"Bro, I dunno," Clint said. "Most of my energy is focused on this machine," Clint said pressing his forefinger to his chest. "I never really got into these machines."

Glenn peered under the hood.

"It's probably the battery," Glenn said.

"How can you tell?" Clint asked.

"It's just something my dad always said. Anything wrong with a car, he replaced the battery," Glenn replied. "He didn't know anything about cars either."

They decided together to let the car sit and replace the battery in the morning. If that didn't work they would call a tow truck.

When they drove away, Glenn tried to keep his mouth shut about it.

That lasted about a minute.

"Clint seems nice," Glenn said.

"He's a beast," Julie replied. "A beast, in the gym."

Glenn almost lost control of the Winnebago.

"Careful," Julie said.

"Yep," Glenn replied.

Glenn spent the night in his recliner, declining an invitation to bed from Julie and choosing instead to work his way through several seasons of *Breaking Bad*. The new season of *Better Call Saul* was coming out soon and he wanted to be ready with several new articles about the connections between the two.

"Don't forget about the race tomorrow," Julie said as she sauntered down the hallway to their bedroom.

"Uh huh," he replied, not really hearing her but giving her the response he figured she wanted.

Several hours later when he felt himself coming in and out of sleep, Glenn paused Netflix and lay back in his recliner. He dreamed an unhappy dream. Julie was running away and he was trying to keep up. Her hand reached out behind her like a lure he just couldn't reach.

"Wait," Glenn said. "Wait for me."

And then she disappeared over a hill he couldn't climb.

"Hey," she shouted at him.

Glenn almost fell out of his chair. Awake now, with drool covering half of his face, Glenn looked up and saw Julie. She was in a nice set of running clothes except for her shirt, which was dingy and ripped.

Before Glenn could say anything Julie answered him.

"They give you a shirt at the race," she said.

"Race?" he replied.

It was, he realized immediately, not the right answer.

"I told you about this a month ago," she said. "The Half Caff to Full Caff Coffee run."

"That's not a real thing," Glenn said.

"It's a half marathon sponsored by one of the artisanal coffee growers," Julie said.

"Do the winners get beans?" Glenn said. Then, almost to himself, "Magic beans."

"Don't be weird, we don't have time," Julie said. "You need to get ready."

"Uh," Glenn said.

"Come on, man," Julie said. She started to say something else, raising her hand to make a point with a well-manicured finger, but before she could say it her cheeks began to tremble.

"Oh man," she said. "You don't want to."

Julie began to cry. Glenn hopped up and threw his arms around her.

"I'm sorry," he said. "I'm sorry. Hey, my bad. I'll get it together. I'll go get ready."

"No," Julie said. "Don't do things for me, you know."

"Hey, I once broke into a hospital for you," Glenn said. "I'm more than willing to cheer you on."

Julie sighed.

"Look, the race starts at seven and I'm gonna be on the road for two hours. Why don't you just meet me at the finish at nine?" she said.

"Ok and then I'll take you for donuts," Glenn said.

"*Hmmm*, donuts," Julie replied.

He kissed her.

"Morning breath," Julie said.

"Sorry," Glenn replied.

As she left they exchanged I-love-yous.

Glenn collapsed back into his chair.

Netflix was waiting for a response.

"Are you still watching?"

Glenn clicked yes.

Heisenberg's perfect plan to take over the meth trafficking in Arizona was just two episodes away from happening.

Julie was fiddling with her earbuds when Clint spotted her. He waved and then ambled through the crowd to get to her.

"It's so cold," Clint said and wrapped his arms around her. "Where's Glenn? Is he around?"

"He's meeting me at the finish," Julie said.

"Ah," Clint said.

He kept holding on to her. Julie began to push him away.

"Sorry," Clint said. "It's just so cold."

He hugged her again.

Julie laughed nervously. Then she pushed him away again.

"So what's your time?" Clint said, refusing to let Julie put her earbud back in.

"Two-thirty," she said.

"That's a great time," Clint said. "I mean, it's really excellent."

"Yeah, well thanks," Julie said.

Then she pointed to her earbuds.

"Gotta get it ready," she said.

"Oh yeah," Clint said. "See you at the finish."

"Sure," Julie said.

Her defense mechanism of a smile vanished when Clint finally turned around.

Glenn made it through two episodes before he started getting concerned about the time.

When he got to the third episode he figured he could play it in the background while he got ready.

He hit play and started to get up.

He was met with a shock of pain that began in his chest and ran like lightning up to his jaw and down his left arm. Instinctively, he reached for his phone and lost it as the pain brought him to his knees.

Meanwhile, the wind burned Julie's face and her calves began to ache. Four miles to go, she told herself.

She was gonna let Glenn off the hook, she decided. As long as he kept his mouth shut about how many donuts she ate.

Glenn ambled himself, like a snake, across his floor and touched the edge of his phone with his forefinger. He wanted to shout, but couldn't. Still, if he dialed 911 they would track his phone and come. At least, he hoped so.

Glenn pulled the phone to himself. The screen was shattered. He tried pressing the phone app but nothing happened. Glenn rolled over.

The Netflix screen hovered over him. Glenn heard a bell ringing.

It was Hector, having his final revenge on Gus Fring.

Glenn suddenly remembered writing that this scene was the most powerful image in the entire show—which made it, of course, one of the most powerful scenes in television history.

On the screen, Gus adjusted his tie and fell away.

At the race, Julie could see the finish line. She raised her hands in celebration. The crowd cheered her on.

Then Julie and Glenn crossed the finish line together.

What can I say about Michael Jan Friedman that wasn't already said at his own funeral?

I mean, I don't even like the authors he's trying to imitate, let alone his stuff. Mike's writing career has gone horribly wrong, from New York Times best-sellerdom to contract killing and, even more dangerously, teaching high school. And of course, there's the worst thing I can possibly say about him—he's a die-hard Yankees fan, which should tell you everything you need to know about his depravity.

To him I bequeath spectral apparition visits of my ghost, Tuesdays and Thursdays, 8 AM to 5 PM or by appointment.

# FOR COCKEYSVILLE
## by Michael Jan Friedman

I KNEW THE RISKS.

I'd seen *Back To The Future*, where Marty McFly's worried about his mom coming on to him and thereby sabotaging the marriage that would eventually spawn him. And long before that, I'd read Bradbury's story "A Sound of Thunder," in which a time traveler accidentally kills a butterfly back in the Late Cretaceous—starting a chain of events that gives rise to a goose-stepping regime in his own time.

So I knew that by doing what I was thinking of doing, I could turn two-legged, smooth-skinned mankind into four-legged, scaly-skinned mankind. Or six-legged, furry-skinned mankind. Or, for that matter, destroy our prospects of surviving into the twenty-first century at all.

The risk was tremendous. Staggering.

And yet it was worth it.

How is that possible?

It's a reasonable question, and I can't blame you for putting it to me. After all, you're part of mankind too, and it was your timeline as well as mine that I was mucking with.

All I can tell you was that it was Glenn.

*Glenn.*

You don't know him. And that's good. Believe me, it's the best thing we could ever have hoped for.

It was Glenn I had to put an end to, Glenn and all he stood for—all he had done and everyone he had done it to, and all he might yet do if no one stopped him.

Oh, people had tried to polish him off. Believe me, they had. But Glenn was as brilliant as they said he was, and the security with which he'd surrounded himself was as invisible as it was effective. No drone, no sniper, no guided missile had ever even come close to finishing him.

Then there was the thing in Maryland. Little town named Cockeysville. Population twenty thousand or so.

Nice place. Horse-breeding territory. Rolling green hills as far as the eye could see. Nice people too. And why not? They had found a home of which Goldilocks would have approved: Not too citified, not too rural. Just *right*.

If you took a drive down 83 and looked for Cockeysville, you wouldn't have found much. At least not the Cockeysville anyone had known.

The only residents who had stayed were the ones who had no choice, the sad, pitiful ones. And it seemed to me they wouldn't be there much longer either.

But at least they could pick up and go, on their own two feet. At least they had that option. Not like *her*. Not like the one person who meant anything to me in the whole, stinking world.

And who had turned Cockeysville into a hell hole? That was Glenn. That was *all* Glenn.

Why did he do it? I can't tell you. I could never get into that aberrant, twisted mind, that shit-swamp of vicious, crushingly cold-blooded schemes that would have made Caligula run screaming into the night.

And to tell you the truth, I never wanted to.

I just know he'd had a plan. He'd *always* had a plan. And, depending on whom you ask, it was either so bug-fuck crazy as to have no chance whatsoever of succeeding or so genius it would have crossed Einstein's eyes and made his head explode in four dimensions.

One thing was for sure—Glenn never cared what kind of carnage he left behind.

For a long time I told myself I could live with what he did, and even how he did it, the same way everybody else had learned to live with it. But when I saw what he'd done to Cockeysville, when I saw the miserable, brutalized remnants of what had once been a happy, thriving community . . . and one heart-wrenchingly miserable, brutalized remnant in particular . . . that's when I knew I had to do something.

I couldn't just let him go on.

Because Cockeysville could easily have been Seattle, or Atlanta, or even New York. And at some point, it would be.

Listen, I'm no cold-blooded killer. If there had been another way to deal with him, I would have jumped on it with both feet. But there *was* no other way. We'd seen the proof of that over and over again.

There was no other option available to me. At least not without murdering a lot of innocent people. And that—killing innocents—was something I wasn't willing to do.

It was one thing to change history, to keep people's lives from beginning. But to kill them after they were already alive? To end them before their time was up? Somehow that was crossing the line. For me, at least.

So going back in time was the only way.

That sounds funny as I say it. As if going back in time was no different from making coffee or taking a walk to the post office. *Yeah, there's nothing on TV so I think I'll go back in time.*

Naturally, it wasn't that simple. There had been talk about some company in San Francisco having something that was *like* going back in time, but I never figured out what that was about. And Elon Musk once made a reference to a time travel technology he was working on, but eventually people decided that was just a joke and let it go.

So time-travel didn't seem to be a possibility. Until it *was.*

You see, I wasn't the only one looking into ways of killing Glenn. And these particular others were a lot further along than I was—further along than I could *ever* be. At least, as long as I was on my own.

They'd heard I was asking questions, and wondered why I was doing that. When they found out, they started asking questions of their own.

About *me.*

Because they had resources, these people, the kind of resources you could only accumulate on the open market if you could revolutionize society in some way. That's what they had done, each and every one of them. They had gotten rich creating things that became indispensable—the way the railroads and refrigeration and the Internet had become indispensable in times past.

Unless you've been living in a hole for the last twenty years, you know these people. Believe me, you do. You've seen their faces on the news, and you know the inventions they came up with. And you know what astronomical sums of money they made, or you've at least got a good idea.

I'm not going to name them because they've got enemies. It comes with the rarified atmosphere they live in. And if it got out how they'd tampered with time, they would have even more enemies. So like I said, I'm not going to name them.

Suffice it to say that when I met them, I was impressed.

As for my credentials . . . I didn't have a whole lot of them. I wasn't a former Navy SEAL. I'd never even served in the Coast Guard.

I just did some work for some guys when my need for cash coincided with their need for something to happen. I wasn't proud of it, but I'd done it. And I'd demonstrated a certain level of proficiency in doing it.

That was fine with the people who found me. They didn't need James Bond. They just needed someone who could do the job, who wouldn't get where he needed to be and find he didn't have the stomach for it.

And they wanted something else. There had to be a level of trust. Of confidence. Of motivation.

So they weren't looking for someone who just disliked what Glenn had done, or could do going forward. They wanted someone who had a deeply personal stake in taking him down.

And after Cockeysville, I had that stake.

Were the guys who hooked me up as smart as Glenn? Individually, maybe not. But together, they had accomplished something. Something *unbelievable.*

It had started with some scientists at MIT who were studying the geometry of space/time. Just solving equations, really, engaged in math as much as in science. Each equation described a different theoretical universe, with its own peculiar shape. And because of their respective shapes, some of these universes were kinder to the possibility of time travel than were others.

Our universe was particularly *un*kind to the idea of time travel. Everything we knew, energy as well as matter, seemed to be restricted to four dimensions—length, width, depth, and linear time.

Scientists at MIT—and a lot of other institutions of higher learning—believed there were many other dimensions. However, they were beyond our experience. Some day, perhaps, we would find a way to access these other dimensions, but for the foreseeable future they remained the stuff of speculation.

Then, one sunny day in early November, two MIT researchers found an energy field out in space that no one had ever identified before. Others before them had wondered if such a field might exist, but these two—Grimsley and Cross were their names—they nailed the thing down.

It was a big deal in the scientific community, though hardly anyone else in the world paid attention to it.

An even bigger deal, for scientists, was the particle you could get by exciting this newly discovered energy field—a particle that could, they believed, travel outside our four known dimensions because of the way it interacted with gravity. And because it wasn't a theory that came out of some mathematical computation but an observable phenomenon, they were able to test their hypothesis in a lab.

Guess what? The test came out positive.

This new particle traveled backwards in time, leaving our familiar four-dimensional space—if only for a fraction of a second—and taking a shortcut through a fifth dimension before coming home *just before it left.*

Again, a big deal in the scientific community—no, a *huge* deal. But it didn't move the needle for most of us. Just those science guys doing their thing instead of getting a real job.

And to be fair, what difference did it make if a particle no one had heard of could travel back in time? It wasn't like we were doing it with a person . . . right?

But the door was open.

Once that happened, there were any number of big brains pushing and shoving to squeeze through it. It was like a Black Friday sale at Wal-Mart. They were all in on it, everybody who could scrawl a bunch of numbers on a blackboard.

Funny thing happened then. The two scientists at MIT, Grimsley and Cross . . . they disappeared.

Not literally, though there was plenty of joking about it—how they'd gone back in time and convinced their younger selves to be sex counselors instead of scientists—but of course, they hadn't. They'd just gone underground.

After all, that door they opened . . . it was dangerous. If they were going to keep some nut from using it to tie us in a knot from here to eternity, they had to stay ahead of the curve. And that, they told me, was why they enlisted the aid—and maybe more to the point, the protection—of rich guys.

Guys who could not only finance their research, but keep it secret. When Grimsley and Cross no longer had to worry about staying alive, they went into another gear. And even with all the geniuses trying to build on their particle research, they were the first ones to get it right.

In the beginning, I think, it was just a matter of the rich guys wanting to support a scientific breakthrough. Maybe some of them secretly thought about using it to alter history in some way, I don't know. But they didn't have a particular project in mind. It was what they call pure research.

Until Cockeysville.

That brought them up short. And what I'd thought about New York or some other big city being the next big disaster . . . well, they were a lot smarter than I was, so they had no trouble seeing the same thing. Except they had analyses and projections and computer models to back it up, and every bit of was crazy scary.

Things were going to get bad—*really* bad—unless they did something about it. That, apparently, is when they started looking for someone they could send back in time to nip Glenn in the bud.

It took time, you know. They were thinking about this a lot longer than I was. But eventually, they had a guy standing on a circular platform in a lab bigger than all get-out—a guy who had the skills and the motivation they were looking for.

In other words, *me*.

"Right here?" I asked, trying to position myself within the circle of yellow studs in the center of the platform.

"Right there," said Grimsley, a tall, thin guy with glasses and the longest face you ever saw.

"Remember what I told you?" said Cross, a heavyset black woman with a sweet face and perfume that smelled like ginger candy.

I nodded. "It's nothing like being out in space."

I'd read that if you were caught without your spacesuit, you didn't want to hold your breath. If you did, the air pressure in your lungs, which was greater than the air pressure in space, would do a number on your chest.

But Cross had told me this was different. There was no pressure differential. I could hold my breath if I wanted to. Or not. It was up to me.

There would be no dizziness, no exhaustion, no disorientation. It would be like nothing had happened, except I'd be in a different time period.

The only equipment I was carrying was the pistol in the shoulder holster under my shirt. It shot toxin-soaked projectiles instead of bullets, so I didn't have to worry about how long it would take for Glenn to expire. Or hitting him in the wrong place. If even a little of the toxin got into his system, he'd be dead within seconds.

So I was set.

"Ready?" Cross asked.

"Ready," I said.

"Then let's go," said Grimsley.

Fortunately, I wasn't the first guy they had ever sent back in time. But I was the first guy with a mission, with a specific objective.

I took a breath, let it out. *Let's do this,* I thought.

I wasn't facing the bank of machines that had been hooked up to my platform, so I didn't know exactly who pushed the button—Cross or Grimsley or one of the half-dozen technicians in the room. I just knew that there was light dancing around me in blue-green swirls.

Then I wasn't in the lab anymore. I was standing in the middle of an intersection in some suburban neighborhood. *Amazing,* I thought.

But I hadn't come all that way to revel in the magic of time-space technology. I checked the street signs on one of the corners.

I wasn't where I was supposed to be. Not far off—just a couple of blocks from Glenn's house. But I didn't want to draw attention by running, so it would take me a few minutes to get there.

And this was Glenn we were talking about. Glenn of twenty years earlier, but still Glenn, so every minute counted.

Trying to ignore the way my heart was pounding against my ribs, I walked the two blocks and made a right. Glenn's house would be on my right, in the middle of the block, or so I'd been briefed.

I didn't see anyone. Not even a kid.

*Of course not,* I thought, mentally lashing myself. *It's a weekday morning. Kids are in school.*

My mouth felt dry. *Understandable,* I told myself. *No worries. You're doing fine.*

Finally, I got to Glenn's house. It didn't look like much—a little brick job. Smaller than I'd expected. But then, he was different in those days. Just like the rest of us, or so he seemed.

I walked down his driveway like I belonged there. Went around to the back, where I wouldn't be noticed so easily.

His back door was open. He was in the habit of leaving it that way, they had told me. As quietly as I could, I moved across the kitchen and down the stairs. Glenn's office was in the basement, if our intel was accurate.

And it was.

As I peeked into the room, Glenn was sitting behind his laptop, tapping on its keys. Utterly intent on the screen in front of him. If he'd heard my approach, he gave no indication of it.

His hair and beard were long and unkempt, his clothes a study in plaid and denim. He could have been a poetry professor or a steelworker or a lot of other things. Considering what he would do, what he'd become . . . it was more than ironic. It was ludicrous.

And yet, there he was.

I spent a moment looking around, alert to traps—especially the sort I'd been warned about. I couldn't find any. So I reached into my shirt, slipped my weapon out of its holster, and walked into the room to get a clear shot.

Glenn looked up. But he didn't react the way *I* would have reacted if I'd seen an intruder in my house. In fact, he didn't react at all. He just stared.

For maybe five seconds. Then something clicked in his eyes and they turned on. They registered my presence, acknowledged me. But the bastard still didn't seem surprised.

Or discomfited, if the gathering smile on his face was any indication. "Ah," he said, as if I were a friend who'd arrived with a pepperoni pizza rather than a cross-time killer with a poison-dart gun. "I *knew* you'd come."

If that claim had been uttered by anyone else, I'd have said it was bullshit. From Glenn? I believed it.

"Then you know why I'm here," I said. It wasn't a question.

Glenn nodded. "Of course."

"Because you're just that good," I said, hoping his answer would give me a glimmer of insight into why he was just sitting there.

He leaned back in his chair. "This is personal, I take it?"

*Goddamned right it is.* "You might say that."

"It would have to be. They wouldn't trust anyone who wasn't utterly committed."

It sounded like he was angling to know who "they" were. If so, I wasn't going to tell him. Because if I screwed up somehow and he got away, and he knew their names . . .

But he didn't ask me about them. Instead, he said, "Have you considered the repercussions of killing me?"

"Obviously." What did he think I was, an idiot?

"I mean in detail?"

It was a trick question. "Of course not. Nobody can predict the effect your death will have on future events."

He chuckled. "Nobody . . . ?"

"What are you saying?" I asked. But I *knew* what he was saying, didn't I? He was Glenn, after all.

"Well," he said matter-of-factly, as if he were talking about school taxes instead of temporal mechanics, "I've computed the effects. All of them. Within so slim a margin of error it might as well not exist. And you know what I found?"

Part of me didn't want to know. But the other part craved the answer, wanted to learn what price I'd be paying to end his miserable existence.

Not that it mattered. No matter how horrendous the results, I wasn't going to go back to my time without doing what I'd come to do. That horse had left the barn a long time ago.

Besides, whatever he said would probably be a fabrication, a ploy to save his skin. Or at least an exaggeration of what would actually happen.

Still, I wanted to know.

"Well?" Glenn asked.

"I have no idea."

He swiveled his computer around so I could see the screen. It was a matrix full of green, blue, and orange numbers I couldn't decipher.

"It's right here," he said. "And it's telling us the effect of killing me will be . . . *nothing*. As in nothing at *all*. Everything you know and cherish will continue to exist," Glenn said, just to drive the point home. "And everything you hate and fear and loathe will continue to exist as well.

"Except, you know . . . *me*."

It seemed unlikely. I said so.

"Not as unlikely as Hollywood would have you believe. You've been trained to see time as this infinitely delicate, infinitely fragile thing. Pull one little thread and the whole thing falls apart. But that's not how it is—at least, not usually. Time's a resilient son of a bitch. If it's not too much trouble, it wants to go in the direction it's gone in before. Sometimes even when it *is* too much trouble."

"Why wasn't I told that?"

He laughed. "How should *I* know? It's hard enough sometimes figuring out what *I'm* thinking. But what does it matter how unlikely it is that time will remain unchanged? Bottom line, you're not going to inspire chaos by offing me."

"I'm not."

"Not in the least."

I didn't get it.

If I'd had a reservation about killing Glenn, he'd done his best to remove it. He'd made it possible, if I could take him at face value, for me to kill him without a second thought.

But . . . *why?* Why would he make it *easier* for me to punch his ticket?

"Why am I telling you all this?" he asked, as if he could read my mind—a possibility that sounded farfetched even for him. "Seems a tad contrary to my interests, doesn't it?"

"A tad, yeah."

"So you now know what will happen if you end my . . ." He chuckled. ". . . *sorry* existence. But there's something you *don't* know—and that's what will happen if you *refrain* from killing me."

"If I refrain . . ." I echoed.

"That's right. If you *don't* kill me . . . because, let me tell you, that'll be one *hell* of a party."

My instincts told me that he was stalling for time. But why? If he could foresee everything, he could have taken measures to stop me long before I got a clear look at him. He could have had someone gun me down as soon as I opened his door.

But he didn't.

So it was possible Glenn had a problem—but time wasn't it.

"What *kind* of party?" I asked.

"I can show you," he said.

He turned his laptop around and tapped out a command on his keyboard. Then he turned it around again so I could see its screen, and a video began. Or rather, a series of videos.

They showed me terrible things. The kind of scenarios I'd expected Glenn to show me as evidence of his need to survive. People dying by the thousands, in the cruelest ways imaginable.

I couldn't watch it all.

"This," I said, "is the future we're going to have if I *don't* kill you. That's what you're saying?"

He winced. "It's actually a little more complicated than that. But for all practical purposes, sure. That's the future you'll have if you let me keep breathing."

"So by killing you . . ."

"You avoid all this."

He had put another nail in his coffin. It was as if he *wanted* to die.

But something bothered me. "You just said time is resilient. Yet that timeline full of catastrophes . . . that's a legitimate outcome too, right? So why doesn't *that* one snap back to its orig—"

"Whoa," Glenn said. He held a hand up. "Just whoa. Let's think about this."

I was grateful for the help. Wary, sure, but undeniably grateful.

"Okay," Glenn said, "you're assuming every timeline has equal . . ." He looked to the ceiling for a moment. ". . . we'll call it *standing*. But that's not so. There's a primary timeline—the way it happened, without our tampering—and a bunch of secondary timelines."

"So the primary timeline is the one where I kill you and nothing happens. The one where all the bad stuff happens—"

"Is a secondary timeline."

I got it. But just to make sure, I said, "If I kill you, none of the bad stuff happens. And I don't cause any ripples in time that will create other problems. A win-win for anybody who wants to do away with you."

"Exactly," he said triumphantly, as if we had climbed a mountain together and finally reached its peak.

Then it was time.

Except for one little thing. But not so little that it didn't keep me from putting a poison projectile in Glenn's neck.

What if . . . I'd misread Glenn? If he was the kind of guy who was willing to die for the sake of preserving the future . . . maybe he wasn't the kind of guy who *deserved* to die.

But what did *deserve* have to do with it? This was war—a

war with the greatest menace mankind had ever known, or close enough. And I had the chance to win that war with one shot.

I raised my pistol and pointed it at Glenn.

But I was still thinking.

If Glenn was the nice guy he seemed to be, maybe what he was up to in the future—Cockeysville and all—maybe there was more to it than met the eye. Maybe it had to happen to prevent *worse* things from taking place.

Which, it occurred to me, might be exactly what Glenn wanted me to think.

"So what are you waiting for?" he asked.

Things were moving too fast for me. I had to slow them down.

"Listen," Glenn said, "if you're feeling queasy, I can help you out."

"How's that?" I asked.

He shrugged. "I could take one of your darts and scratch myself. That's all it would take, right? Just a scratch."

I looked at him. "You're going to kill *yourself?*"

"Don't get me wrong, I don't want to die. But now that you're here, it looks like I'm going to do so. So why not make it a little easier?"

"How's it going to be easier? It's the same toxin. Your throat's still going to close and you're still going to suffocate to death."

Glenn shook his head. "I meant easier on *you.*"

"So I don't even have to do anything."

"Not really, no."

"Just hand you the projectile."

"If you like."

I laughed. "That's a good one. I just give you a poison-tipped dart. And you don't use it to take me out. *Right.*"

Glenn sighed. "We can always go back to Plan A."

I nodded. "Yeah. Plan A. I think I prefer Plan A."

Just then I heard a whooshing sound, like someone had opened a window and let in a damned hurricane. For the first time since I'd arrived, Glenn looked concerned.

"They're coming," he said.

"Who?" I asked over the whooshing sound.

"Well," he said, "let's just say not *everybody* stands to benefit from my dying. So they're moving to prevent it."

He reached over the back of his laptop and touched a button on his keyboard. Instantly, it showed me a view of the street in front of his house, where a bunch of people were pouring out the side of a van.

Suddenly, I knew who *they* were.

They were Glenn. *All* of them. Eight or nine of him from various stages in his life, all older than the one in front of me. And they could only be there for one reason . . .

*To stop me.* Because if I killed the Glenn in front of me, these others would never exist—and their attitude about that prospect was obviously different from plaid-and-denim Glenn's.

"If you're going to do it," he said over the whooshing sound, "now's the time." He leaned forward. "To tell you the truth, I've never died before. I'm kind of wondering what it'll be like."

It was shit like this that made him so different from everyone else. What made him so infinitely *dangerous*.

I pulled the trigger on my pistol and a poisonous dart hit Glenn in the chest. He looked at it for a moment, as if he was just curious. Then it started to make his throat constrict.

I thought about the girl from Cockeysville, the one who had meant so much to me. But even that wasn't enough to make me enjoy the way Glenn died. It was that bad.

As soon as he slumped in his chair, the whooshing sound stopped.

And I was back on the platform in the lab, in the twenty-first century. Grimsley and Cross were looking at me expectantly.

"Well?" said Cross.

"We're good," I told her.

And that's how it happened.

No—that's how I did it. "How it happened" makes it sound like I had no part in it, like I was just a pawn.

That's how *I* killed Glenn.

Turns out he was right, for the most part, about the effect his death would have on my present. It didn't bring on any terrible catastrophes. I mean, I'd know it if it had. After all, I remember the way it used to be.

But he wasn't *completely* right. Apparently, even Glenn could make a mistake. Which is why, unless you live in Maryland, you've probably never heard of a place called Cockeysville or anything terrible happening there.

Because now it *didn't*.

That's good for a lot of people, me included. You see, when Cockeysville didn't die, neither did *she*.

What can I say about Amy Lewanski that doesn't include her time in Tijuana?

Amy is yet another fiery redhead who wants me ded ded ded. She's taken her MFA in creative writing from Antioch University and used it to graduate from writing about other people's horrors to writing horrors about me. Her neighbors will say to the news crews, "she was such a nice young woman, always smiling," while the backhoes are digging up her yard looking for evidence.

To her I bequeath a posthumous alibi. The photos are in a locked moneybox, buried on Catalina Island. Sorry, I can't be more specific until I know I can trust you.

# RHINO
## by Amy Lewanski

IN THE BRONX ZOO, IT IS RAINING. EACH RAINDROP settles into the lock of the Indian Rhinoceros exhibit, filling the keyhole, loosening screws, and the gate creaks open. One of the rhinos pushes the gate all the way open. There's only a single muddy bank in the way of a flowing river. These rhinos have only ever had water poured for them. Curiosity fills the hearts of every rhino in the exhibit and they leave their manicured lawn enclosure and take their first steps to freedom in years. The rain has filled the Bronx River to the edge of the bank and the rhinos slowly step into the rushing water. The cool water rushes around their toes and the three rhinos jump and race through the mud and water, enjoying the feeling of cool, free ground under their giant rhino feet. They move like gentle thunder south and west, stopping only to drink and eat.

It's raining in Riverside Park. Glenn walks along the path, enjoying being alone, watching the rain dimple the gray water of the Hudson River. There weren't a lot of other people out, the rain was keeping most people in their apartments. Just a few brave athletes out, perfecting their form. Glenn's extremely lanky frame makes short work of the long paths and he sits down on a mercifully dry bench. A small stand of trees and bushes hide

him from the breeze and most of the rain and turns the bench
into an almost completely secluded haven. The river keeps flowing, runners run, parents watch their excited children jump in
every puddle.

The Hudson River may be full of sludge and pollutants, but the
sweet rhinos have only ever had zoo water. They don't know the
difference. These sweet giants consume gallons of sludge, and it
slides into their stomachs and trickles into their bloodstreams; it
fills their hearts and lungs and creeps into their brains, and their
grey skin stretches with each breath, and their little, dark eyes
open wide.

"Glenn" they breathe, his name filling their mouths and resting on their giant tongues. "Glenn." These three rhinos don't
know who Glenn is, but suddenly they see him in their mind's
eye and they want to be near him. They want his long arms to
pet them, run his artistic hands along their backbones. Whatever they were before means nothing to them now, for they only
need Glenn. The biggest rhino shifts his weight from leg to leg
and raises his enormous head. Glenn is north of them, he can
feel it. He walks up onto the grass, leaving the river to his left
and pools of water fall off his back and legs and collects in the
grass before running back down to the river. He takes off up to
the park, leaving large compressed circles of grass behind him,
his feet crushing anything beneath him.

The second and third rhinos follow his departure and then
they also thunder after him, like small gray buildings hurtling
past a moving train. Their feet hit the ground like miniature
earthquakes, knocking children over and sending dogs into furious barking. Cyclists crash into trees and benches, staring at
these rampaging rhinos. Rhino number two flattens a diminu-
tive tree in its mad haste to find Glenn.

"Did you see . . . ?" A mom with a sleeping toddler in a stroller
asks her mom friend.

"Did I see what?" Her friend says, standing up from straightening her child's hat.

"The . . . rhinos?"

"We're in the upper west side of New York City, Hannah. There are no rhinos here," her friend says firmly. There are no rhinoceroses in New York City except in the zoo. And they are nowhere near the zoo. The two moms and their toddlers continue their walk, not noticing the squelching divots of rhino feet in the grass nearby.

Glenn relaxes on his secret, dry park bench. The rain is now a light mist. He still has most of his very large bottle of Pepsi (with real sugar) to finish. The view is perfect, still serene, still quiet. Glenn can hear echoes of children's laughter from the playground. The ground under his feet rumbles slightly.

The three behemoth rhinos trundle and rumble through the park leaving a ripple of devastation behind them. A child starts crying.

"What's wrong, peanut?" his parent calls to him, anxious.

"A rhino knocked me over!" the distraught child hiccups between wails.

"You're safe, don't worry, there are no rhinos here." The parent soothes the still-crying the child. His sobs slowly peter out and he returns to his games, with a dark shadow of a racing rhino looming in the back of his mind.

Now the rhinos can smell Glenn: the smell of sugar, caffeine, phosphoric acid, men's shampoo, the warm fresh scent of clothes from the dryer. Their rhino hearts swell with excitement. Soon they will find Glenn, the person they need. They will find him, and their great noses and horns will nuzzle against his broad shoulders and chest and he will scratch those places right behind their ears that not even their zookeepers knew about. The infectious sludge they drank from the river is pumping harder and harder through their monstrously large bodies as they continue their thunderous journey to Glenn.

Glenn is calmly sipping his Pepsi. The quiet is soothing, as is the easy scroll of his phone screen as he reads updates on his friends and family's lives. Every victory is given a resounding like, every tragedy he files away to reach out and talk with them later. A friend posts a joke thread, and Glenn begins crafting a very silly response. He laughs to himself.

The ground shakes a little more, and Glenn finally looks up, mid-sentence. New York has never had an earthquake that he knew about. He checks news sites for information about shaking ground. Nothing. He thinks he is just imagining things; maybe the traffic is particularly fast today. At the very, very bottom of the news reports for the City, there's a tiny bulletin.

*A flood of calls from members of the public in the Upper West Side's Riverside Park report a horde of rampaging rhinos. Reporters sent to Riverside Park report no visible signs of rhinos. The local zoos have denied comments at this time.*

Glenn goes back to his friend's jokes thread, wondering why anyone would call in fake reports of rhinoceroses. He sips his soda. The ground rumbles beneath him.

The frantic pace of the rhinos slow. They are thirsty, each of them at the same time. They don't know why it's weird they are suddenly so thirsty. But they are. They change course and veer to the Hudson River. The cold, gray sludgy waters call them. The three rhinos dip their large, majestic heads to the rushing waters and lap up great mouthfuls of infectious water. The water slides and slips down their throats and into their stomachs and once again the pollutants pull into their bloodstreams and creeps to their brains and all they know is Glenn and they must find Glenn. Glenn will pet them, Glenn will give them scratches, rub their giant shoulders until they think they are puppies. Glenn will love them better than their zookeepers ever did.

The lead rhino lifts his head again. Glenn's scent is stronger now. More than just sugar and caffeine, there's the skin smell of humans that calls them. It is more intoxicating than the sludge from the river. It is better than anything the zookeepers or vets ever smelled of. They take off, galloping through the park. The ground shudders beneath them. Grass crumbles into the mud beneath their feet, sticks snap and stones roll towards the river.

All three of the behemoth rhinos are running at breakneck speed ever north, their minds intent on Glenn. They know Glenn is ahead of them. They know he is there. They know he will love them unconditionally.

The ground is moving like there is an eighteen-wheeler barreling down the highway right at Glenn. He now can't ignore it. Something is up.

He puts down his soda bottle and it immediately falls over, sending waves of dark Pepsi flooding across the small stones and wet grass in front of his private bench. A few weeks from now this small patch of grass will be a little brighter green from the extra sugar the Pepsi gave.

*This isn't right,* Glenn thinks to himself. *What is shaking?*

To the left of his little bench there is a strange sound, huge gasping inhales for breath but like rocks were rolling in the base of the lungs. The thundering sounds like feet pounding the wet ground now. He stands up, reaching his full tree height and looks around. Nothing he can see, but he is still partially hidden by the little bushes that frame his secret bench. The wind picks up and the scent of the Hudson River sits on Glenn's tongue, all acid and sharp and somehow grainy and dingy at the same time. And the breeze brings another smell, one that sits under the river stench. Glenn can feel it almost more than smell it. It's a warm, farmy smell, like hay and giant hearts pumping warm blood slowly through enormous bodies. It was calming, outdoorsy, and totally wrong for New York City.

There is a scream, a chilling sound down the park from Glenn, then horrified shouts erupt seconds later. People are yelling. Glenn's calm morning is broken in two.

"What the hell! My new bike!"

The thundering sound continues, getting louder and louder. The screams continue.

"Someone stop those things! This bike IS NEW!"

"Stop them!"

"Call the police!"

The shouts Glenn can hear have taken on a hysterical note and he isn't quite sure what is going on. What on earth could damage a bike without the sounds of a car hitting it? Was there a car in the park? Was Glenn in danger? Where were the sirens if it there was a dangerous driver destroying the park? Just one long step and he can peek out from the little trees. He moves, and he stumbles back in confusion.

The weirdest sight is in front of his face. The Hudson River on the right, tall brownstone city buildings on the left, the green, damp park between him and three stampeding rhinoceroses. The sound of their enormous feet is a rumble in his ears and the force of their feet on the ground shakes into Glenn's own feet. The three rhinos are only feet from Glenn and their large gray sides heave with their breath and their big eyes find Glenn and he can feel their focus settle on him and the rhinos slow to a walk.

The rhino in the lead plods forward to Glenn and extends its head until its large horn lightly touches Glenn's torso. Gently, it pushes against Glenn until he has to take a step or fall over backwards. The other two rhinos move to Glenn's sides and their big calf eyes stare up at him wetly. He can almost see little hearts in their eyes. The two on his sides also press in. He is the center of a rhino triangle.

Glenn stares at the three enormous rhinos surrounding him, their heads bow slightly to touch him with their noses. The screams from further away stop, or at least Glenn is no longer listening. He can feel his own heartbeat, and hear each inhale of breath, but louder than his own needs is the loud exhale and shifting weight of the rhinos surrounding him. He thinks they are kind of like horses, big but placid with loud breathing and the rhinos just staring. There's a strange feeling in Glenn's fingertips. He thinks that maybe the rhinos want to tell him something, but of course they can't, because they're rhinos. The rhino at his chest makes a low sound deep within its giant throat. He lifts his hand, pulling it from the gentle crush of the rhino pyramid surrounding him.

A buzzing hum fills the air, right underneath the frequency a human usually hears. The rhinos ears all prick forward. Glenn feels as though magnets have been turned on in his hands and his body. He reaches his hand out, tentatively, to the rhino in front of him. He places his hand gently on the animal's nose and three things happen all at once. One, the humming buzz gets louder, and Glenn's ears fill with the noise. Two, the rhino he is touching closes its eyes like it's the happiest it's ever been. Glenn swears it smiles. Three, the other two rhinos lunge. Not technically at Glenn, or the rhino he's touching, but at the hand that is touching the rhino.

All three rhinos start making a whining noise like they want something and he moves his hand and slowly strokes the rhino's nose and it begins to wiggle out of pure joy. The other two push harder and harder on Glenn's arms, until he is petting two of them at once and the third one stamps its feet and snorts and exhales large angry breaths. It is pushing, pushing at Glenn, pushing him away from the other rhinos.

And the other rhinos are pushing back against the first pushy one, but they're using Glenn as a battering ram and their little whiskers are tickling his skin where their pushes are moving his shirt and his jacket.

The rhinos' hearts are pounding in their huge chests, the sludge from the Hudson River coating their lungs and their arteries and their brains and all they want is Glenn all over them and just them, they can't share him with the other two rhinos at all. They do not want to share. One shakes its vast head, it doesn't want the red hot sludge but it's too late, the sludge lives in the rhino now and the shaking only knocks Glenn around against the other rhinos. He protests, yelling wordless shouts as the horns and heavily muscled necks slam into his side and he feels a rib snap and the head keeps moving and Glenn is on the ground.

Glenn is scared and confused, on the ground, his hand sinking into the muddy trampled grass. The rhinos above him threaten to swarm him, he can barely see the sky, and it's still dark and gray and the clouds look like the rhino skin and the rhinos keep snorting loud angry bursts of air and he can feel their hot breath on his skin and it smells like the Hudson River and then something crumbles and it's like the rhinoceroses are screaming. The rhinos are angry, angrier than they've ever been and they can't be angry because they've escaped from the zoo and freedom tastes like fresh running water and smells like grass and feels like Glenn petting their noses softly but whatever is inside them infecting them has taken hold of their animal hearts and brains and they are animals again and suddenly the other rhinos are trying to take their tiny patch of land with one terrified human in it and their eyes narrow and the only things left in the world are the other two and all three rhinos slam their hard heads together. One of them will win the ground beneath their feet.

They do not notice that the ground beneath their shifting, slamming feet is Glenn, even though he is what they want. In their loud, violent movements, they do not notice he is trapped under. In their maddened state, they do not notice the sounds of them trampling him in their need to be the only one Glenn pays attention to.

The poor, sweet, dumb rhinos, poisoned by the Hudson River, have no idea what they are doing. They do not know why they are called to Glenn. All they know is that they need him even as he is ground into the soft grass beneath their behemoth feet. The rhinos start crying as Glenn's last lungsful of air reach their great noses . . . their brains cannot handle what is happening, what they are doing. The poison is sucking its way through each and every vein and slips further into their hearts but there is nothing left for the poison to hold on to, and great steaming, burning poisonous tears fall and hiss on the grass beneath them. They don't even notice the horrified screams of the other humans around them or the wail of sirens approaching.

People all over the world closely follow the case, with protesters crowding the space outside the building. On one side of the sidewalk is a group angrily defending the rhinos, for they are endangered, wild beautiful creatures. On the other side is a group angrily defending Glenn's family's right to closure over the horrible death the rhinos inflicted. Ironically, both sides yell 'murderer!' at the lawyers and the witnesses and the rhinos whenever they pass.

The trial takes weeks. National news channels flock to New York. International reporters flock to New York. The police have to set up barriers between the protesters and the news cameras so the crowd crushes no one. Inside the courtroom it is no quieter. The rhinos are corralled in a front corner of the courtroom, breathing loudly. Their fresh straw wild animal smell lingers in the air even after they leave each night. Their giant, wet eyes stare at the crowds in confusion, and even the most hardened audience member feels twinges of compassion for the great beasts. The lawyers and the witnesses don't keep the room quiet, often devolving into yelling matches. When this happens, the rhinos startle, and they move, jostling the wood and metal around them. They add their loud, low voices to the yelling and the ceiling rings with shouts and animal yells of distress. When the judge bangs his gavel for silence, it quiets the humans but the rhinoceroses stay panic stricken, and zookeepers help their huge charges calm down with little treats and pats on the nose.

The arguing lasts days. Glenn's friends and family and the people watching the case like vultures stare at the rhinos' lawyer and the members of public giving testimony. The family members who speak and vouch for Glenn's character don't believe that this is what their life came to. In none of their dreams did they expect that they would be on the stand in a courthouse, arguing that an endangered animal killed Glenn. But here they are. The rhinos most definitely murdered their beloved Glenn but the people in the courtroom only care about the rhinos. The defense has medical reports of vile poisonous sludge in their systems, causing them to act out and to harm the environment around them, including Glenn.

"These are endangered species. We cannot punish them."

"Also they had Hudson River sludge infecting their brains. They couldn't control their behavior."

"They're animals, they can't be controlled."

"What about the property damage?"

"They're animals, it's in their nature."

"Glenn was a treasured member of the community and a pillar of his family, He deserves justice. These animals are at fault."

"They didn't know what they were doing! They were *poisoned*!"

The judge bangs his gavel. "I find the rhinoceroses not guilty," he says in a booming voice. The rhino's lawyer, appointed by the zoo, raises her arms in victory. The jury cries. Glenn's collection of friends and family members sit in the hard courthouse seats. "This case is acquitted on grounds that the defendants are rhino, and this is out of my jurisdiction."

What can I say about Jenifer Purcell Rosenberg that people aren't already whispering about her?

I mean, I could talk about...nah, better not. There is that time with the koi pond... whoops, statute of limitations is still running. The fire truck was just harmless tomfoolery, an acquittal is at least a 50/50 chance. (Sorry, that should be "truck on fire".) And I'm sure the video footage of her chasing after people to kill and eat them has a perfectly reasonable explanation. She has a great passion for researching her family history, but I'm thinking that she keeps looking to see if there's someone who has done worse things than her— considering her ancestors expelled the Jews from England in 1290, you can only imagine how bad her own peccadilloes must be.

To her I bequeath my own family history (perfectly safe to use with relatives at Hanukkah dinner) and a bottle of SPF1000 sunblock.

# WAKING THINGS
## by Jenifer Purcell Rosenberg

ONCE, I WAS PART OF YOUR WORLD. I WAS THERE with you, forever loyal, throughout the years. The myriad of late nights, the groggy late mornings, the caffeinated early afternoons. I was ever your companion, there for you when you were ill, when you were tired, when you were too busy to leave our home, when you were on the road. Every visitor, be they friend, freelancer, feline, or delivery person, knew me well. We were nearly inseparable. I was a legend in my own right.

I was your bathrobe.

I don't know how long I was with you before my own sentience began to form. It may just as easily have been months as decades. The first thing I became aware of was junk food. Oh! The glorious junk food! It fell about me as you focused on your screen or page, and I absorbed it. Oils from chips, dust from Cheetos, delicate drops of precious sugar-sweetened cola, all were shared with me, and became part of who I was. Over time, I also encountered amazing grilled meats, cheeses, and, through the proximity to your friends, wine. All of the delectable wine, I loved absorbing it!

As this sustenance helped me to grow stronger, my awakening continued apace. I became aware of discussion groups, websites, coding, and comic books. I took in knowledge and an appreciation for art, along with my fair share of ink. I developed a love of trivia, and could quote television programs and films, albeit without yet possessing an audible voice. I was soon an aficionado of puns. Life was grand! I felt that you and I were inseparable! I imagined my stripes were an extension of you, lending you camouflage against the backdrop of furniture and comics.

Of course, there were some sad times. Occasionally, those who visited would turn away from me, hiding their faces as they spoke. They always wished to speak to you, but could not bear to see me as they did so. A few of your old friends made jokes about me, and my feelings were crushed when they suggested you find a plush blue replacement. Apparently, the feeling was that brown with multicolored stripes was simply not fashionable. Perhaps silk with a print, they suggested, or the latest chunky chenille varietal. My fabric is "horribly outdated", apparently. Those colors are "SO SEVENTIES!" I was distraught.

Then one day, the unthinkable happened! Your wife, who always hated me, plotted to expel me from your presence. You were presented with a replacement for me, one in a fashionable classic black, with a hood. You fancied that you looked like a boxer when wearing it. I was cast aside. Shoved into a tall kitchen bag with remnants of ribbon and gift tape that stuck to my frayed edges, I was hauled outdoors and pitched by the curb. To add to my despair, you wore my replacement while discarding me. Had I tear ducts, I would have wept. I could only, however, feel the sorrow of abandonment. My senses are all an awareness of my surroundings without the sensory receptors enjoyed by humans. I simply know.

Just as I knew that other garments had been granted a second life through donation to charity, while I was assigned the fate of being sent to a landfill. I was apparently not good enough to donate. Had I been, I might have at least had some semblance of the life I shared with you. To be sure, I would have been laundered, possibly mended, and subject to things such as fabric softener instead of salt dust and corn crumbs, but it would have been far preferable to the raccoons and pigeons. The only other garments with me were a t-shirt so threadbare you could read a comic through it, and an old stained sock with a hole in the toe. I had been forsaken!

For what felt like an excruciating eternity, I was trapped within the confines of that bag, yearning to be set free and return to the life I once knew. I found myself plotting revenge against my new rival, the hooded robe. My rage sustained me, but it also made me bitter. I did not know how I could escape my situation and return to where I belonged. One dreary day, fate took hold, and the weight of water upon tons of discarded waste caused a massive shift in my section of the landfill. I felt a presence near me, and it was not like the presence of the vermin that scavenge for food and nesting material. It was a consciousness similar to my own. I dragged myself out of my fantasies of being returned to my Glenn, and I allowed myself to pay attention to my surroundings. I was being regarded by an eye of cracked acrylic. I could have sworn the faded yellow stuffed rabbit attached to it actually moved when it sensed me. Then, the unthinkable happened! The rabbit spoke!

"Hey, buddy. I'm Bunnana. It's good to see another Waking Thing out here." As much as I had felt adoration when I was a part of my former life, I had never considered that speaking was an option. Could I have asked to be kept? Could I have intimidated my rival into falling into the cat box? If only I had known!

I attempted to reply to the rabbit called Bunnana. "*Mmprfmllpp.*" Well, it was something, anyhow.

Bunnana grinned. "Hey, no worries, buddy. It takes a while, especially when you don't have a mouth. Try talking out of your pocket."

I sent all of my will to speak to my left pocket, and sure enough, I made a coherent sentence! "I am glad to meet something like me!" I said.

The bunny chuckled and waved a plush paw "Aw, that's cool."

In my discussions with Bunnana, I discovered that, although we were rare, the sheer amount of garbage produced by such a heavily populated region meant that we could still be found. Bunnana was the most common kind of Waking Thing: toys beloved by children and discarded either when said children grew older, or their parents intervened. I was in the second most common category, which was articles of clothing that were loved and then discarded. There was a pair of basketball shoes not far away, and we often heard them yelling "Three pointer!!!" as they relived their glory days. The books, records, and comics tended to keep to themselves, and were often deposited in little groups together. Other items were few and far between, jewelry and such, as well as things that had accidentally been tossed away.

Bunnana began to keep track of everyone, and had a few intelligence operatives—dolls that had learned to climb. We began to realize that it might be possible to escape after all!

First, several of the dolls helped to excavate a mannequin that had once been a regular fixture in the window of a piercing shop in the Village. When the shop closed due to raising rents, the mannequin, known as Rexy, went on to live with the shop's former owner. When rent became too much for her, she was forced to give up Rexy. We were lucky that Rexy had come to our landfill! This was our ticket out!

Bunnana then set the next part of the plan in action. A backpack, a hat, the exuberant basketball shoes, a concert t-shirt, some designer jeans, and I all got settled on Rexy. We talked happily about going back out into the world and finding our people again. Bunnana had several operatives go through and find all of the cash they could scrounge in the heaps of refuse. A couple of the dolls came back with a wig as well. Not a Waking Thing, but it would help Rexy to look a little more human. Bunnana and a few other toys climbed in the backpack, and we were off! Climbing out through debris, singing together (Bunnana knew some lullabyes, but Rexy knew some amazing music from the old shop.), and finding our way out.

At one point, a man in a bulldozer saw us making our way across the landfill and shouted "Hey, kid! Get outta there! It ain't safe!"

We'd done it! We'd passed for a human!

It took a while to find our way back to an actual town. We hadn't realized how far from inhabited areas the landfill had been. At least we weren't on a barge somewhere, though. We made it to a dingy little shop that smelled of plastic and bug repellant. The shop was called 99 Cent Discount Haven. We had to get supplies if we were going to all get back where we belonged. Bunnana had a whole list. We got some plaid pants and a hot pink shirt for Rexy, along with some humorous socks that looked like sharks, some slip-on sneakers, a new hat, and some sunglasses. Rexy also insisted on some gloves to cover the plastic appearance of mannequin hands. We got a couple baskets made from woven plastic strips, some laundry detergent, a hairbrush, sewing kit, baby wipes, and some dryer sheets. Our next stop was a laundromat.

Rexy went into the bathroom and changed into the new clothing after cleaning off the landfill grime with the wipes. The rest of us, backpack and basketball shoes included, were put in a nice washing machine with detergent. We were washed twice just to be sure, and then put in an enormous dryer with the sweet smelling dryer sheets. We came out clean and dry. Rexy asked a man nearby where someone could go to stay without ID, and he gave us directions. It wasn't hard at all to get the room. Bunnana's operatives had found us close to two thousand dollars that people had somehow managed to throw away.

Apparently fashion dolls have a good nose for cash. Rexy had spent decades being sewn into and taken out of outfits on display in the shop window, and had picked up on some sewing skills. Bunnana's left eye was secured, the tear in the backpack's side was repaired, and all of my little imperfections were shored up in matching threads of green, yellow, orange, and brown. I felt like a brand new bathrobe!

At one point, Rexy ran out and came back with some fine-tipped brushes, some paints, and some frilly fabric swatches. While the rest of us watched the television and caught up on what had been happening in the world while we were in a giant pile of trash, Rexy bathed the dolls, gently brushed out and styled their hair, and touched up the paint on their faces. Finally, each doll was given a fresh and fashionable new outfit. Rexy was a creative genius! We knew from all of the shared stories that most dolls ended up in the trash because they were no longer welcome in a home. Usually, kids were deemed too old to play with dolls, and that was that. Although the love from their humans had made

them Waking Things, most of the dolls did not want to go back
to where they came from, for fear that they would be rejected
again. Rexy had refurbished them so that they could be donated
to children who did not have a lot of toys. Every toy except Bunnana wanted to go this route: to be loved by a human who would
keep you in their world. We all knew what that had been like.
It could be that way again for our friends. Rexy arranged them
nicely in a basket and took them to a shelter we had passed on
our way to the hotel. As far as I know, those toys are now happily
owned and loved. That's all we really wanted, you see.

Well, except Bunnana. That little rabbit wanted revenge.
Cold, hard, grueling revenge. Enough nights of being taken away
to help the child wean off of his lovey had left Bunnana on the
couch in front of the television. Apparently, the parents of Bunnana's human were into scary movies about people being pos-
sessed by spirits of the dead. Bunnana figured we were capable of
possessing people as well. So that was the plan. But, while Rexy
gathered the necessities for human possession, the other Waking
Things needed to find their peace as well.

The designer jeans were easy. They knew which laundromat
they were taken to, and on which day, for wash and fold service. It was easy to slip them into the dryer with the right group
of clothes. We were all thrilled to think about how happy the
human who belonged to the jeans would be upon their return.
The T-shirt was put in a basket with a note that said "For Dave"
and hung on the door of a converted brownstone. Rexy sat in
a corner café across the street pretending to sip a latte for two
hours, waiting to see the reunion. It paid off! The next person to
enter the building was indeed the T-shirt's Dave. Many excited
expletives were heard when the shirt was found. We'd heard
that Dave's vindictive ex had taken the shirt and thrown it out.
Now it was back where it belonged. Sadly, we could not track
down the human who belonged to the basketball shoes. Luckily,
Rexy found a man on the street who was thrilled to have a new
pair of shoes, and the shoes were grateful to have a new human
of their own. We followed suit right down the roster of Waking
Things that had escaped the landfill with us.

We got to the point where it was just myself, Rexy, and

Bunnana. The time to enact vengeance for our little bunny friend was upon us! We found the train to the neighborhood where Bunnana had been thrown away, and after wandering in circles around houses that all looked the same for a while, we found the right red brick row house. Following the instructions we had rehearsed, Rexy rang the doorbell and shoved the human man inside when he answered the door. Waking mannequins are incredibly strong! I bet you didn't know that! We got the man into the basement, drew a chalk summoning circle on the floor, and placed him in the circle. He was pretty easy to maneuver, because he passed out when Bunnana called him a trash-loving tool. We sprinkled him with a mix of herbs that had been soaked in special oils, and Bunnana started shouting an incantation he had seen on some television program. The summoning ring glowed blue for a second and then, nothing. You don't want to know what a stuffed rabbit having an all-out panic attack looks like. Trust me, it isn't pretty. Bits of fluff everywhere!

Rexy figured that we must need some fire. People in the old piercing shop had always been talking about hot wax and candles. We left Bunnana to guard the human, and went in search of candles. A look through the house proved that we were doing the right thing. There were a handful of pictures of the child human, and most of them also featured a content-looking stuffed rabbit. Our friend was clearly too treasured to have been thrown out by the monster we had down in the basement. We started going through drawers. We came up with half a dozen birthday candles, a barbecue lighter, some oven matches, and some powder incense with charcoal tablets in what appeared to be a teenager's room. Rexy also noticed another herb in the room, and thought it might help in our future operations with humans, too. We went down to the basement. Yes, I know, I am a bathrobe. It's true, I am. Who do you think had the pockets we put all the supplies in? I was an integral part of this mission, and I would never have had to be had I not been cast aside by unfeeling humans!

Rexy crumbled the charcoal and sprinkled the incense powder over it, encircling the outer edge of the summoning circle. The birthday candles were broken up and sprinkled with this, and then Rexy saw a box on a shelf in the basement labeled

"Glittering Honeydew Wax Patties," so those were also crumbled and added to the ring. Bunnana sat in the circle on the neck of the human this time, grumbling something about a thorax. Rexy lit the circle and stood back. At first, there was just a small tendril of smoke and a slight orange glow as the charcoal began to catch, but soon, it started to pop and hiss, and the rich scent of the incense began to fill the air, along with the sharp odor of gunpowder, and the fake, waxy aroma of glittering honeydew patties. As the room filled with smoke, we could hear Bunnana screeching the incantations again, but this time throwing in several expletives. In addition to the orange glow from being on fire, the circle began to display a rich violet color, and there was a strange hum followed by a pop. The voice shrieking incantations went from being high and squeaky to being deep and articulate. The transfer had worked! Bunnana had become human, and the person who had thrown our friend away was now a faded plush bunny with a cracked acrylic eye. Success is sweet!

The man who was now Bunnana. . .Mannana?. . . stood up and shook his fists in the air. "I'm a frickin HUMAN!" he shouted.

We heard a loud, unpleasant beeping sound filling the house. "Crap! It's the fire alarm!" Rexy said. We scrambled around and found an extinguisher. The doorbell started ringing upstairs, and the bunny-inhabited human went to answer it. We shut the basement door and worked on containing the smoke. "It's all clear!" came the call from upstairs. Our friend, still carrying the yellow plushie around, came back down the stairs. "I told them I accidentally burnt some glittering honeydew wax patties, and they told me they hated those things and left. I've outsmarted the fire department!"

The little yellow rabbit looked up at the human and shook its fist.

"My friends," said the man, "I am now to be known as Marcus, and this little guy here is now called Bunnana!"

"Pleased to meet you, Marcus!" I said. The little rabbit plush fainted. I guess a talking bathrobe was just a little too much. But, you know, that's what makes it so great!

Rexy and I left Marcus and Bunnana to catch up, and we went

in search of Pearl, who had once been the proud owner of my mannequin friend. We looked at a map of the Village, but it was not a simple grid like the majority of the City, and we kept getting turned around. Since Rexy hadn't seen much but the immediate neighborhood, it wasn't terribly easy to figure out which way was which. Finally, my friend recognized some architecture, and we were in the right neighborhood. The old piercing shop was now a high-end coffee venue with a variety of gluten-free confections and vegan delights. It made me realize how much I missed all of the caffeine and snack food. I knew they wouldn't have prepackaged, preservative-laden sponge cake here though. I absorbed a little bit of spilled triple caff almond latte with a shot of smoke flavor and maple as we went inside. It was . . . interesting. The venue was filled with young people trying desperately to look simultaneously unkempt and meticulously styled. They all looked at me longingly. Several took out their smart phones to share my image with their friends. I heard one woman gasp "Sooo retro!" I fluffed my terry, and half the room sighed. That's right. No hooded boxer robe could manage that.

Rexy asked the young person at the counter if they knew where we could find Pearl. "The older homeless lady who hangs around? She's usually sitting a couple blocks over at the city green triangle. You can't miss her."

It turned out that there were several triangles, all with a little patch of green and a couple benches, an anemic shrub or two. They were meant to keep the City from being nothing but concrete and glass, I guess. We finally found the right triangle, though. There was a skinny woman in her seventies with bright purple hair smoking an unusual looking cigarette with some teenagers. She looked up, and her eyes widened, filling with tears. She coughed. "Wow! This is some potent stuff! I could swear I was seeing my Rexy in a vintage terry robe!"

The teenagers were staring, mouths agape, at the magnificence before them. "Miss Pearl, I don't think you're imagining it!" said one of the kids with her. Rexy stepped forward. Pearl took a puff from the cigarette and held her breath. The teens started tittering with amusement. Humans, as it turns out, are incredibly weird.

Rexy was thrilled, and shouted "Pearl! I finally found you!"

Pearl said "holy crap!" and handed the cigarette to one of the kids. She got up and gave Rexy a hug. I absorbed some tears. That's what it's like to love your waking things, man.

Pearl didn't really have a home anymore, but she had an entire network of people who were kind to her and helped her out. She'd been a neighborhood fixture for so long that the people who had rent control and were still around gave her a couch to sleep on when the weather was bad, or a bite to eat when she was between her meager Social Security checks. She even had a friend named Jacques who colored her hair. We were on our way to that friend's apartment now, as he had been a regular at the old shop. He let Pearl in, and jumped when he saw Rexy. "I always knew that mannequin was watching us," was all he had to say on that matter.

Pearl and Rexy spent hours catching up, as Pearl was practically the neighborhood historian. Rexy remembered everyone she mentioned, and seemed happy to know about them all. Then Pearl dropped the bombshell: she was dying. The clinic doctor said the problem was inoperable, and so Pearl had decided to do what she could to live life to the fullest. Rexy had another idea, though, and offered to be Pearl's new body. One that could not age or get sick in the same way. Jacques had been listening, and said that he could help.

While the ritual with Bunnana and Marcus had been to switch which body the consciousness was in, the ritual with Pearl and Rexy needed to be to put both consciousnesses together in the same vessel. Jacques loved reading, researching, and collecting old manuscripts, and he saw something once where a statue in a church had become a Waking Thing, and some priests put the consciousness of a dying monk into it by accident while trying to get the statue to heal him. The great news was that Jacques had incense and candles on hand, and it was not hard to set up the scenario. No summoning circle was needed this time, just a table to put Pearl on, surrounded by candles, and some incense to burn in front of Rexy. Instead of only consciousnesses merging, though, the craziest thing happened! The bodies merged into one human/mannequin hybrid!

Oh, I've forgotten my manners! Meet Pearlex! I'm sure you've been wondering who it was that shoved you into your kitchen when you answered the door, Glenn! Now you know why my friend doesn't look exactly human. Half mannequin! Pearlex was kind enough to bring me here after the merger, so that I could finally have justice for being thrown away like some piece of garbage!

It's been a few months since I became a human with the heart of an outcast bathrobe. The procedure wasn't much different from the process of merging Rexy and Pearl. While they now have a merged body and consciousness, though, I am now the dominant consciousness in one body. I was able to jump from the robe and free myself from the possibility of being discarded again—though I did have my former self framed and hung on the wall. Glenn's wife rolled her eyes about that, but ultimately said "whatever." Glenn is in here, and I readily use his knowledge to be able to interact with others, but I plan to let him grovel a bit more before I give him a chance to take the driver's seat.

Pearlex moved back to the Village, and has an arrangement to be a street performer that appears to be a statue and then moves when people least expect it—apparently very lucrative when tourist groups come through. We keep in touch via video chat. I heard from Marcus, and he is very happy in his human life. He was extolling the virtues of craft beer when last we spoke. I, personally, have taken an interest in wine and have laid off of the cola in favor of artisan coffee. Many of Glenn's friends have commented on his change in beverage choices, but nobody suspects they're really talking to a bathrobe.

What can I say about Paul Kupperberg that his Tinder profile doesn't cover?

He's written well over a thousand comic stories, many of them memorable and some of them actually good. Killing beloved characters is nothing new for him, having previously killed off Archie Andrews in a hail of bullets and getting Eisner and Harvey award nominations for it. The cover of a comic he wrote was even turned into a postage stamp, which is ironic because his picture has been hanging in post offices for years. His love for Jerry Lewis is larger than the entire country of France.

To him I bequeath my collection of Wheelie and the Chopper Bunch comics.

# THE DAY OF KILLING ENDLESSLY
## by Paul Kupperberg

I'M DOUGLAS SIMPSON, THE INSULT AUTHOR. FANS line up, waiting to take a zinger from me. Not a signing or convention goes by where I'm not asked to personalize books with insults or straight up profanity. Sure, a lot of it's an act, but there's plenty of times when it isn't. When I was a kid on the streets of Brooklyn, we called it "kidding on the straight" and I might have played that a lot with Glenn. He was, after all, a soft target.

The first time I killed Glenn, it was an accident. It was the evening of the first day of Shore Leave, the annual Maryland based science fiction and *Star Trek* convention. I'd arrived at the hotel late and in a foul mood thanks to JetBlue's inability to move an airplane from Point A to Point B in anything resembling a timely fashion. I'd managed to drift off for a brief, pleasant nap in the airport shuttle bus that marginally lightened my mood, but that disappeared when the front desk informed me that they had no record of my reservation. By the time that was straightened out, I had missed a panel and half of a meet the authors event, which was a bust for me anyway since no one on the convention staff could locate the box of my books that was supposed to have been shipped to the venue.

After the dealers room closed for the day, I declined invitations to join some of my fellow authors for dinner. All I wanted was a solitary burger and drink or three at the bar to settle my frazzled nerves, then go up to my room and sleep off my mood.

I forgot how quickly the bar filled up. In the time it took to place my order and it being plopped in front of me, the place had gone from near empty to over capacity with fans and cosplayers. There was an abundance of Starfleet officers, Klingons and Ferengi, *Star Wars* X-Fighter pilots, and other military, paramilitary, and fascist military uniformed warriors and wenches from scores of science fiction and fantasy franchises. I didn't usually write the militaristic stuff, although lately, I hadn't written much of anything except for whatever television or movie novelizations I could land. Those and the royalties from recent reissues of some of my older series were keeping me afloat while I looked for an idea for something new and original. I was in the sixth year of my search.

I don't know what it is about conventions, but after a couple of drinks the cross-franchise flirting and mating dances commence and sometimes it's not a pretty sight. I gobbled down my dinner, hoping to get out of there before things got uncomfortable, or worse, before a friend or fan wanting to chat could corner me. Tomorrow I'd chat. Tonight I just wanted sleep

"Hiya, Doug. Hey, you didn't save any burger for me."

The last bite of my dinner, which, by the way, had been cooked to delicious perfection and had brought me, with the help of a second vodka on the rocks, to a fine, settled place in my tired brain, was poised before my lips when I heard the overly cheery voice drop down on me from a height of some six feet, eight inches. It landed on my head like a gift from a passing seagull. I winced.

"Hey," I said, putting a fake little happy chuckle in my voice that never fools anybody except Glenn. "How you doing, Glenn?"

I turned to find him looming over me, eyes shining with happiness, grinning through his beard, like a giant, demented elf. Glenn is always grinning, or maybe he's just grimacing from oxygen depravation because of the altitude. I never could be sure. I didn't begrudge him that he always seemed so happy, but at times, I just wasn't in the mood for that much man-perkiness.

"Oh, brother, am I beat. We drove down from Jersey this morning, and the traffic was terrible," he said. Even as he spoke, the Klingon commander next to me was paying his bill and sliding from the bar stool. Glenn swiveled his hips in and took his place. "And I think I did something to my back unloading all the boxes of books."

"Yeah, that sucks, but I'm beat too. I was about to go upstairs—"

Glenn half rose from his newly acquired seat and levered himself across the bar like a toll gate in front of the harried bartender. "Gimme a Diet Coke, willya, and another one of whatever my friend's having."

"No, man, really, thanks, but I can't. I'm passing out here—"

Glenn cranked himself back upright.

"Aw, come on, just a little while. I haven't seen you since last Shore Leave. We never get a chance to talk."

"Ever think I might plan it that way?" I said with a Groucho wiggle of my eyebrows. I didn't want to hurt his feelings. Well, not too much. Anyway, Glenn, like anyone who knew me, was well aware of my slash and burn sense of humor and was, anyway, too well-intended himself to recognize half my insults.

I'd already signaled for the bill. I decided to use cash instead to expedite my retreat. I worked out my tab and tip in my head and had enough money in hand to drop it and run as soon as the bartender laid it down.

"Funny, Simpson. Hey, did you hear? Annie Dillman just sold her trilogy to Marco at Tor."

My bill came. It was the bartender's lucky night. I was two bucks over my estimate.

"Great, good for her, so I'll see you in the morning, okay? I'm going to sleep."

"C'mon," he said, starting to rise from his seat an instant before I hopped off of mine. I guess his center of gravity was off when I clipped him in the chest with my shoulder because he looked startled and toppled awkwardly back onto the stool.

"Sorry, man," I said.

He just stared at me with a wide-eyed look of surprise. Even though Glenn was sitting and I was standing, we were still eye to eye. And his eye didn't look right. Neither did the other one. They were dull and staring and his mouth hung open.

"Glenn?"

I started to reach to shake his arm, but that's when I saw the bloodied tip of an angel's wing sticking out of his chest. The wing was some sort of white, sparkly diaphanous material, probably Spandex, I remember thinking. It was draped and formed around a wire aperture made of cut and bent wire clothes hangers, the tips of two cut ends twisted together to form its peak. It was part of the costume worn by the young man sitting with his back to Glenn on the next stool, a black leather-clad warrior from the *Angels of Hell* series. It was, in fact, a beautifully made costume. It would have been perfect if he'd only thought to wrap the sharp ends of the wingtips in some electrical tape.

It was an appropriately freakish end for Glenn, taken down by cosplay while in the middle of being annoying. He'd toppled back against the little accidental spear must have slipped between his ribs and thrust up through his heart and out his chest. He was wearing a dark silk shirt, but as I recalled from forensic research for some mystery stories I'd once written, puncture wounds like that didn't bleed very much. The heart, and the flow of blood, stopped almost instantly.

I jumped up in horror.

Immediately, a major in the Imperial Guard took my stool.

I looked around in a panic. The place was shoulder to shoulder with fans and guests, all at maximum volume. Everybody was busy with their own conversations or flirtations. Besides, if you didn't look too closely, all you'd see was Glenn sitting at the bar with a goofy, far off expression that wasn't too different than his usual resting face.

I left as fast as I could through the mass of humanity. Throwing shaky waves and sickly grins to friends and fans but not stopping. Not looking back. Waiting for someone to scream or shout.

I finally broke through the crowd and was out in the lobby, gasping for breath and making a beeline for the elevators. I kept my head down until I was safely in my room, a "Do Not Disturb" sign in place and the door triple locked.

Since I'd already broken one commandment—"Thou shalt not kill!"—I shattered a second one—"Thou shalt not use the criminally overpriced hotel mini-bar!"—and downed three of the little bottles of vodka before I stopped shaking.

Once I calmed down, once the immediate shock and horror had worn off and the vodka had turned my bloodstream into a warm, comforting flow of alcohol, I realized that I was, in reality, neither shocked nor horrified.

Okay, look, you've got to understand about Glenn. He's a nice guy . . . well, *was* a nice guy. He was Johnny-on-the-spot. He wanted to be helpful. And he always, I know, meant well.

You know about "meaning well," don't you? It's that thing the road to Hell is paved with.

I seldom mean well, although there's no corollary that says the road to Heaven is paved with snarky cynicism. I only barely tolerate friends and suspect everybody else of something, I'm not sure what, but give me time, I'll figure it out. Overly helpful people especially set my teeth on edge. They're up to something, I just know it. Nobody's that nice for no reason.

Fortunately, I'm free to let my angry flag fly.

I opened a fourth little vodka bottle and lay back on the bed. It was too bad Glenn was dead, but it wasn't like I'd killed him. Not, you know, directly. Or on purpose. It was entirely an accident. Accidents happen all the time. Glenn could have died in any one of a thousand ways.

I fell asleep, drunken images of many little Glenns, dead by many different ways, dancing in my head.

I was jolted awake by the shuttle bus from the train station jostling over the speed bump in the hotel driveway. I sat bolt upright, my mouth pasty dry and the rest of me sticky with sweat. My suitcase was at my feet, and my fellow passengers were bustling around me, getting ready to disembark.

*You're still in Kansas, Dorothy!*

It had been a dream. Glenn was alive.

"Wow," I said out loud, and then chuckled. I didn't usually have such vivid dreams and Glenn had never played a role in any that I could recall. It wasn't as though he was on my mind. Sure,

I'd been after him for a couple of months to fix a bug on the website, but that was a Post-It note reminder on my computer monitor, not a capital offense.

Still, as I climbed down from the shuttle and rolled my bag to the front desk, I couldn't help feeling a slight twinge of disappointment. By the time I reached the clerk, I'd forgotten all about Glenn and my dream.

"Welcome to the Hunt Valley Inn, sir. My name is Brad. Are you checking in?"

"Yes, I am," I said. "I'm with the convention. My name's Simpson. Doug."

Brad smiled professionally and turned to his keyboard, typing in my name. He waited. He frowned at the screen. He typed some more. His frown deepened.

"Might you be registered under a different name?" he inquired.

"I don't think so. Simpson's the only name I've got."

"Mm yes, no. There's no registration under Simpson, Doug."

"That's weird."

"Did you make the reservation yourself or did someone make it for you?"

Glenn, I thought. He'd volunteered to act as liaison with the convention for all the authors in our publishing hub.

I gave the clerk Glenn's name, but that just lead to some more of Brad's head shaking. Yes, there were several other names linked to that reservation, but, no, *mine* was not one of them.

"Just like in my dream," I said.

"Pardon me, sir . . . ?"

I shook my head, trying to chase away a tremendously stupid thought.

"Nothing," I said. "I've just been writing science fiction too long . . ."

By the time my reservation problem was sorted out with the help of the manager, Mr. Gutierrez, I missed my panel and half the authors meet and greet, which I spent, again as in my dream, trying to find my missing box of books. I was a little distracted this time, though, trying to convince myself I was just suffering from one hell of a case of déjà vu, and by the time I'd relived the entire afternoon, the awake me needed those afterhours drinks more than dream me ever did.

I knew I was being ridiculous. This was just some bizarre little brain fart I was experiencing. A few drinks to short circuit the weirdness, then some dinner to get my blood sugar back to normal, and I'd be fine. Just fine.

Then, just as I was about to finish the final bite of my perfectly cooked hamburger, having convinced myself I was merely overtired and stressed, I heard these words drifting down from far above my head:

"Hiya, Doug. Hey, you didn't save any burger for me."

*Thump!*

I woke up on the shuttle bus, mouth pasty, sticky with sweat.

"This isn't funny," I said with a moan.

My seatmate, Denise Hammersmith, creator of the *Marines of Venus* series, looked at me and said, "What's not?"

I shook my head. "Nothing. I was just dreaming."

Denise inclined her head in the direction of the hotel. "Get your dreaming in now, Doug, because from here on out, it's a total nightmare." She laughed and deployed from the bus like jumping from a plane.

I was slow to follow. All of a sudden, I was in mortal terror of meeting . . .

"Welcome to the Hunt Valley Inn, sir. My name is Brad. Are you checking in?"

I gulped. "Yes, I am. I . . . I'm with the convention. My name's Simpson. Doug."

Brad smiled. Brad typed. Brad waited. Brad frowned. Brad typed some more.

"Might you be registered under a different name?"

"*Gnnnghh,*" I sputtered.

"How do you spell that, sir?"

I gripped the edge of the polished granite countertop to steady myself. It was almost exactly the same, word for word.

Then I remembered something else.

"Uh, is there a Mr. Gutierrez here?"

Brad smiled. "Yes. He's our manager on duty."

"I was afraid of that," I said slowly, "but if you'll get him, we can clear this up in two minutes flat."

Two minutes later, I was walking in a zombie-like trance to the elevators, my keycard clutched in my fist. I didn't know which I found more disturbing: being trapped in a delusion, or the fact that the delusion was such a cliché story trope. The still rational part of my mind knew I wasn't reliving the day over and over again. I mean, I routinely wrote about events and situations that bent and often broke the boundaries of scientific possibility, but that was fiction. In reality, physics had this nasty habit of being pretty damned consistent, one of those consistencies being that time ran in a continuous flow and didn't go *whee!, whee!, whee!*, all the way home in loop-the-loops. I *knew* the difference between fact and fiction.

At least what the differences were *supposed* to be.

I dropped my bag in my room, dunked my head in a sink of cold water, toweled off, and made it to my panel right on time. Glenn was sitting in the front row of the audience, arms folded across his chest, grinning happily. One of the speakers made a point about the importance of social media in book promotion, and as I started to respond, Glenn rose from his seat, raising his hand as though asking permission in third grade, and proceeded to correct the other panelist's point.

Already on edge, I tried cutting him off, barking into my microphone, "Glenn, if we'd wanted to hear your opinion, we would've had you on the panel."

"Thanks," he said, and without a pause, picked up his chair and brought it around behind the speaker's table, plopping it down next to me.

"Excuse me." He reached across me and dragged the microphone over in front of himself and picked up right where he had left off.

I wanted to kill him.

When I walked into the panel room for the author signings, I found my table bare. Bob Berger's table was across from mine, and he was happily tidying his stacks of books and adjusting his signage.

"Have you seen my books?"

He glanced around behind the tables and said, "Nope. No unclaimed boxes around here."

"Crap," I said. "I thought somebody was going to order for all of us from the printer."

"You can check with Glenn. He was in charge of putting in the order."

*Glenn.*

I *would* kill him. With my bare hands!

And because I now *wanted* to kill Glenn, I decided to steer clear of him. I knew the way this story went: break the cycle of Glenn dying so history can stop repeating itself and tomorrow will be the day *after* Groundhog's day. So I passed on the bar and ordered up room service. My burger, a double vodka—my use of the prohibitively expensive mini-bar had disappeared with the dream, so . . . win!—and a movie on free hotel HBO, followed by a good night's sleep should be enough to calm me down.

I ate. I sipped my drink. I watched the first thirty-two minutes of a movie that I'd meant to catch when it was in the theaters but had missed. The movie was every bit as good as I'd hoped and I was already into the story when the house phone rang. Without thinking, I picked it up.

"Hiya, Doug. It's Glenn. We been looking for you. Don't move! We're coming right up."

"No!"

I jumped from the bed. I don't know who "they" all were, but I knew once "they" planted themselves in my room, I'd be stuck with "them"—and Glenn!—for hours.

"Don't! I'll meet you downstairs, in the lobby." I slammed down the phone before he could argue.

Rather than wait for the elevators, I swung open the stairway door and started jogging down the two flights to the lobby. But I'd taken less than half a dozen steps when Glenn swung around from the next landing, taking three steps at a time with his impossibly long legs.

"Hiya, Doug," he enthused. "Just thought I'd escort you downstairs."

My fingers closed around the steel handrail, gripping it hard. "Because you didn't think I'd remember the way?"

He laughed. "I know you're not that senile," he chuckled. "Yet."

"Will senility involve forgetting you?"

"Oooh! *Touché*!"

"You're a freaking pain in my *touché*," I growled. "Look, are we going downstairs or not?"

"After you, good sir," he said with a bow at the waist and a sweep of his inhumanly long arm.

I stomped past him, shoving his arm out of my way like a turnstile. Glenn said, "Whoops," and stumbled back down a stair, but with his double-length leg stretched up over three steps, he was off balance and when he fell he kept going, bouncing like a movie stunt dummy down the concrete steps. When he finally came to a stop on the second floor landing, he was all twisted up like a Raggedly Glenn doll and as still as death.

"Crap," I said. I went back to my room and went to sleep.

Glenn just wouldn't stay alive. I was never the direct cause of his death, but I was always present for it. He died slipping on an ice cube in the vending room. He was decapitated several times, first by a falling ceiling fan, then when an arborist trimming the trees outside the hotel lost control of her chainsaw, followed by a sheet of plate glass that slipped off the back of a truck when the driver jammed on the brakes, and another piece of glass another time when the window of the Applebee's where we were eating shattered from a freak stress fracture.

Glenn fell off roofs, into empty elevator shafts, and tumbled down stairs. He walked in front of cars, vans, trucks, buses, golf carts, lawnmowers, and a runaway hotel service cart. He was electrocuted by frayed extension cords, the coffeemaker in his room, a blow dryer, toasters, microwaves, and a faulty microphone in a panel room. He was crushed by falling debris, crumbling facades, and toppling décor. He suffocated after accidentally inhaling a David Gerrold autographed tribble and he drowned in the pool, the Jacuzzi, the bathtub, a toilet, the sink, in the lobby fountain, and in a bucket of mop water. He bled out from a cardboard paper cut across the jugular and was impaled once on an ice sculpture in the restaurant and another time on a 1:6 scale display model of the needle-nosed Icarus spacecraft from the original *Planet of the Apes* movie.

I lost track of the many deaths of Glenn. Frankly, after I-don't-know-how-many-times, I woke up on that shuttle bus knowing what was coming and realized I had grown numb to the whole thing. Whoops, there goes another Glenn. What was the big deal anyway? Sure, there was dead Glenn, or parts thereof, all over the place, but so what? There'd be another one tomorrow, alive and just like this one. He was like a roll of giant, goofy paper towels, endless and disposable.

I was, needless to say, losing my mind. I decided, however, to believe it was all real. I'd rather think I was stuck in an impossible temporal loop than insane, but either way, death, or at least Glenn's, ceased to have any meaning. I guess I hadn't been prepared for a delusion of such existential depth and it lead me to ponder both the meaning and message of Glenn's life and deaths. Was I here to prevent Glenn's death in some cosmic offer of redemption to mend my selfish ways? Or, equally plausible in a psychotic delusion like this, I was here to *kill* Glenn, who had somehow come to represent . . . *something* in my life of which I had to rid myself.

So one night, when I was tired and Glenn was taking too long to die, I decided to test my thesis. In this one, I'd joined my fellow authors for dinner. We were on our way back to the hotel, crossing the sky bridge from the MTA station on the other side of the highway, while Glenn was about to go into his twenty-eighth consecutive minute talking about search engine optimization.

I glanced down at the traffic zipping by beneath us at a steady sixty miles an hour. I looked at Glenn, who'd paused to make an important point about hash tags. The others kept walking, still nodding on autopilot at whatever he was saying, and I thought, "Why not?"

I let out a roar and ran straight at Glenn. He saw me coming, looking first confused, then starting to grin like he thought this was some sort of joke. I think he may have still been grinning, wondering what the joke was as he plummeted to the tarmac below. I heard the blaring horns and the screeching brakes and the sickening, wet thud of impact but I checked over the side to make sure anyway. Yep!

Ike Rosenstein was the first to reach my side. He grabbed my arm and took a wincing look below.

"What the—!" he exclaimed. Then, leaning in close, he whispered, "Thank you."

*Thump*!

I woke up from my nap on the shuttle bus, disappointed, yes, but something else too. It wasn't exactly happiness—that would remain elusive as long as I was stuck in this endless spiral—it was more like a feeling of contentment. Seeing Glenn smeared on the highway like a gory Rorschach test had been cathartic. Knowing I'd sent him there was satisfying. He was, for whatever reason, at the heart of my current woes. Killing him had felt so . . . good. And, like potato chips, I couldn't murder just one.

I left my suitcase with the bell captain and set off in search of Glenn. I found him in the dealer's room next to, as if by fate, a display of Klingon weapons. He was correcting the Bekk First Class cosplayer's Klingon pronunciation when I sauntered over, so I busied myself examining the swords, knives, and battle axes for sale. Most of them were strictly decorative, made from painted balsa wood and leather. But they also carried some high end, forged metal pieces, including a custom made fourteen hundred dollar spiked ball and chain that I put on my American Express card.

"Hey, what'cha got there, buddy?" Glenn asked when I approached him with it.

"I wanted to see what it feels like doing it hands on."

"What *what* feels like?" he said, confused.

I hefted the ball and chain and said, "You'll see."

Okay, I know it's wrong, but I enjoyed it. I, who hadn't been in so much as a fistfight since I was twelve years ago. But there was something primal, visceral about bashing someone's head in, especially knowing that was no consequence or guilt. And it was Glenn, you know? Oh, there were a few times when I caught that "Why me?" moment in his eyes before I brought the hammer (literally) down and I'd almost hesitated, but momentum and habit helped carry me through.

Hotels during science fiction conventions are a potpourri of opportunities for mayhem. I made a game of it, the object being to see how long I could go without repeating my method. A maintenance man's toolbox alone kept me busy well into the triple-digits. Most cosplay weapons and accessories were too flimsy to do any real damage, but that wasn't anything a little creative thinking couldn't overcome.

Modesty prevents me from enumerating the endless ingenious ways I found to eliminate Glenn. Modesty, plus if I ever broke out of this cycle, I planned on using a lot of them in a new book. The idea came to me while I was relaxing watching Glenn struggle to free his head from the pool filter. Not the hackneyed repeating day gag. But I could use the killings. The story was still hazy though, but over that endlessly repetitive day, it slowly began to take shape and solidify. It was slightly outside my wheelhouse, but after half a dozen years of having to animate other peoples' creations, it was like giving birth: painful, but then you look at the result and see that it was worth everything.

I had Glenn to suffer for my art and I appreciated his ongoing sacrifice. Still, sometimes I was so preoccupied thinking about the book that I almost forgot to kill him. One time, I had to double back on my way to the elevator for the night and return to the lobby to strangle him with a cord from the venetian blinds. I felt like I'd let him down with such a simple, inelegant murder. I tried making up for the neglect the next time with something splashy: a pyrotechnic electrocution during the concert by Latinum Lobes Of Love, the Ferengi cover band, but it felt like a hollow gesture.

The feeling persisted. Stab. Push. Suffocate. Strangle. Yada yada yada. My heart just slowly bled itself of enthusiasm, to the point where I'd wake up on the shuttle bus dreading the next few hours. To battle the tedium, I invented a new game I called "Get it Over With." The aim was to get inside and kill Glenn as expeditiously as possible in order to, you guessed it, just get it over with. My record was three minutes and forty-two seconds, but that required leaving my suitcase in the bus and trampling poor Denise Hammersmith to the ground.

Momentum had become my enemy. I was killing Glenn by rote because, like the mountain he resembled, he was there.

It had been forever since he'd died accidently. Since, in fact, I'd begun taking a personal hand in things. And he'd almost made it through the evening untouched by my hands that time I went back to strangle him.

I started wondering what would happen if I just stopped?

*Thump!*

Startled awake. Shuttle bus. Dry mouth. Denise Hammersmith.

"Might you be registered under a different name?"

"You can check with Glenn. He was in charge of putting in the order."

"Glenn, if we wanted to hear your opinion, we would've had you on the panel."

"Hiya, Doug. Hey, you didn't save any burger for me."

Before shoving the last bite of delicious hamburger into my mouth, I turned around and let my eyes travel skyward. I smiled.

"Hey, Glenn. How you doing, my friend?" Before he could answer, I turned to the Klingon next to me and said, "Excuse me, commander, but I noticed you were about to leave anyway, so I was wondering if my friend could have your seat."

"Sure thing, no problem," he said and let Glenn in with a salute.

Glenn was looking at me strangely.

"What're you having, Glenn? A Diet Coke, right?" I signaled the bartender.

"Uh. Yeah." He peered at me through shiny lenses. "You feeling okay?"

"Couldn't be better, bud. I just worked out the kinks for a new original novel. First one in six years." I saluted him with my drink.

"That's great." He looked around nervously. "So, you're not, like, punking me or something . . . ?"

"No, man. I'm just . . . oh, hey!" I leapt suddenly to my feet and lunged towards him.

"*Yahg*! I knew it," he shouted.

But I reached past Glenn for the black-leather clad Angel from Hell sitting on the stool beside him, brushing aside his sparkly, diaphanous angel's wing with its deadly tip.

The guy started to protest, but I said, "Sorry, but it almost poked my friend. You should wrap up those pointy ends, you know?"

The Angel felt his wings and looked surprised. "Wow, yeah, will do. Thanks for the head's up."

Glenn was looking at me with a mixture of suspicion and fear.

"Why . . . why are you being nice to me? Don't be nice to me. It makes me think you're up to something."

"I'm just in a good mood," I said, risking a dislocated shoulder to reach up and pinch his furry cheek. "I'm at Shore Leave with good friends and I've got a new book to write. All's right with the world."

"Okay, but don't smile at me, either," he said with a shudder. "It makes it worse."

"Glenn, bubbalah! I wouldn't dream of harming a hair on your precious oversized head," I said. "At least, never again."

What can I say about Peter David that thousands of Twitter users haven't already accused him of?

He's the ringleader (I would normally use mastermind, but that word doesn't really apply to him) of this conspiracy to commit multiple murders of me. Best known for his legendary run on Mark Hazzard: Merc and author of The Powerpuff Girls Plus You Club: Hide-and-Go Mojo, he's the person who somehow thought that "giving the audience what they want" was "give them my corpse" and pushed it until these words were in your hands. This is a passive-aggressive way of telling me it's time to update his web site so he can talk about all of the other projects he's done at http://www.peterdavid.net.

To him I leave a copy of all the incriminating files I found while recovering the data from his crashed hard drive. They will be released to the public on . . . well, why spoil the surprise?

# THAT'S ALL, FOLKS
## by Peter David

GLENN SLOWLY BLINKED HIS EYES, TRYING TO determine exactly where he was. It was quite dark, though, and he realized he was going to have to give his sight some time to adapt to his surroundings.

The first thing he became aware of was that there was water lapping somewhere near him. Very near. That struck him as odd, though, because he generally could smell water when he was in proximity to it. For instance, when he went to the beach, the saltiness that wafted through the air was very distinct. If he was near the Hudson River, an aroma of garbage typically commanded his nose's attention. Here, though, there was nothing except the sound of the water . . .

And moans.

They sounded very distant. He had no idea where it was coming from, but there were certainly a lot of them, an almost infinite number. They weren't saying anything: just chorusing groans, as if he were on the "Haunted Mansion" ride down in Disney.

Could that be where he was? In some forgotten section of the park?

No, that made no sense. He and Brandy weren't scheduled to go to Disney.

Where was Brandy, for that matter?

And where in hell was he?

His eyes finally began to adjust to the absence of light. He could see the river now. It was a couple of feet away from him. He was also able to discern stony walls all around him. He was definitely somewhere subterranean, that was for sure. But how had he gotten there? He was hardly a spelunker.

Then he realized that the low, distant moaning he had heard earlier was coming from the river itself.

He had been lying down, but now he forced himself to his feet. He looked down and was confused to see that he was wearing pajamas. How the hell had he gotten out of bed and wound up in a cave while he was sleeping?

Was he dreaming? He didn't think so. When he slept, his only sense engaged was his vision. Here, though, all five of his senses were involved, including a distant, dank smell. None of this was making any sense at all.

Slowly, treading carefully in his bare feet, he made it to the edge of the river and look down. He couldn't believe what he was seeing.

Glowing, distorted bodies of human beings were floating within. A hundred, a thousand of them, just lying there and moaning as if they were permanently trapped in some endless hell.

Then he heard a faint splashing from off to the left. Something was coming toward him. It was a boat. It looked like a gondola from Venice, except far less stylized and charming. The gondolier was a tall, robed man, pushing it along with a rowing oar. Glenn couldn't make out his face because a hood was draped over it, leaving nothing but shadow visible within.

"Holy crap," Glenn said as understanding dawned within him. "That's Charon. You're Charon!" he called more loudly. "The boat keeper on the River Styx!"

Slowly Charon nodded, his face remaining shadowed.

"My wife loves Styx! Brandy is gonna die when she hears . . ." Then, slowly, his voice tapered off as he understood his predicament. "I'm dead, aren't I."

Once more Charon nodded, and then he spoke. His voice was soft and tremulous, and Glenn had to strain to hear it. "Yes. Yes, you are."

The boat bumped up against the shore where Glenn was standing.

"How did it happen?" Glenn asked. Then he attempted to answer his own question. "I know. It's the new tenants upstairs. They spent half a day lugging a piano up the stairs. I bet it came crashing right through the ceiling and landing on me while I was sleeping. Did I have any famous last words? I always hoped that right before I died, I would say one of those things that people always remember. Like John Adams saying, 'Jefferson lives,' not knowing that Jefferson had already died. Or Oscar Wilde supposedly saying, 'Either this wallpaper goes or I do,' which actually weren't his last words, but that's pretty memorable."

"I am not sure how you died," said Charon. "It is most puzzling. I dislike being puzzled."

"Do you usually know?"

"Yes," said Charon. "But your passing is strange. There are many conflicting means of your death and I cannot discern which is accurate."

"What do you mean?" Glenn was finding this to be more and more confusing.

"Well, in one case, you have a heart attack. That is a fairly simple, typical way to go."

"I guess, yeah,"

"But I also perceive that you were trampled by rhinos."

"*Rhinos?* Was I at a zoo or something and fell into a pit?"

"No, you were in Central Park, reading."

"That doesn't make any sense."

"Except," Charon continued, "you were also drowned while in college. And killed by a haunted house. And electrocuted by an employee of Thomas Edison . . . "

"*Thomas Edison?!*" It was making absolutely no sense. "Is there no consistency at all?"

"Just one. Your hair is always in disarray. Disheveled."

"Yeah, well, I guess that's fair," he admitted, running his fingers through his mop of messy hair. "But how in the name of God could I die over and over again?! This is just ridiculous! For that matter, why did I wind up in the ancient Greek version of the after life? I'm not Greek!"

Charon shrugged. "Perhaps the Greeks simply got it right, and all your other religions were incorrect."

"I guess. Although I was kind of rooting for the version of heaven from *Supernatural.* 'The Dark Side of the Moon.' You ever see that program?"

"We do not have television here," he intoned.

"Really? Wow, this is going to suck hard. So . . . do I get into the boat and we ship off?"

Charon extended his hand. "Payment."

"Oh, right. That's why in the old days they would put coins on people's eyelids. Lemme check . . ."

He reached into his pockets, rummaged around and was pleased to discover two pennies. He extended them to Charon and the boatman extended a hand that Glenn was startled to see was a bony hand devoid of flesh. It curled around the coins and then opened. The two pennies were gone.

"Nice trick," said Glenn as he stepped into the boat. It wobbled slightly as he settled down into the single bench. "Boy, Brandy's gonna hate missing this."

"Her time will come," said Charon.

The boat began to move.

Glenn leaned back and began to sing.

"*I'm sailing awaaay. Set an open course for the virgin sea.*

"*I've got to be freeee. Free to face the life that's ahead of me . . .*"

"What is that song?" Charon sounded genuinely interested.

"It's called 'Come Sail Away.'"

"I like it."

"That's probably because it was recorded by a group called Styx."

"Hunh. That does make sense."

"By the way," said Glenn, "why aren't I upset that I died? I mean, I feel kind of . . . okay with it."

"Almost no one is upset. The atmosphere of this realm helps to do away with all useless emotions, so you are satisfied as you transition to the next world."

"But what about them?" He indicated the moaning souls beneath the water upon which they were gliding. "They certainly don't sound satisfied."

"Those are religious enthusiasts. The type who spent their lives convinced that they would be chosen to rise up to the heavens during the end times. And they spent much of their lives endeavoring to convince others to join their cause. They are trapped beneath the waters because they cannot accept that they were wrong."

"Oh, I get it. The kind who supported Trump because they were convinced he was going to bring about Armageddon."

"Exactly so."

"Well . . . good," said Glenn. "Idiots."

"Don't be so sure," said Charon.

Glenn did not like the sound of that, but then immediately decided not to worry about it anymore. His life was over. He didn't need to worry about anything else that happened in the land of the living because he had departed it.

He took a deep breath and let it out slowly. He felt as if a massive burden had been lifted from his shoulders. He never realized how utterly oppressive life was.

He started singing again, picking up where he had left off.

*"On board I'm the captain, so climb aboard*
*"We'll search for tomorrow on evvvvry shore*
*"And I'll try oh Lord I'll try to carrrrry on."*

That was when the boat began to rock abruptly.

Glenn gripped the side, startled, not expecting any sort of chop on a placid river. Charon appeared startled as well, standing carefully to avoid being pitched out.

"Now what?!" Glenn shouted.

"I am not sure," Charon was clearly startled. He staggered slightly, using the oar to prevent himself from tumbling out of the boat. "This should not be happening. I do not . . ." Then he suddenly pointed accusingly at Glenn, his skeletal hand trembling. "You! You are the cause for this!"

"How am *I* the cause?!"

"All your contradictory deaths! Your presence is causing the underworld to come apart! It is arraying enemies to stop you!"

"What kind of ene—?"

A thunderous roar that simultaneously, oddly, sounded cute interrupted his question. The water began to roil. Something was coming toward them, something that was displacing the water.

Something massive loomed out of the shadows in front of them.

It was a giant mutant cyborg hamster.

Glenn stared in wonderment. "Now *that's* something you don't see every day."

"Get out! *Get out!*" howled Charon. He brought his oar around and slammed it into the side of Glenn's head. His head ringing, Glenn toppled out of the boat and fell into the River Styx.

No longer were songs from the liked-named group filtering through his head. Instead the moaning was all around him. Glowing hands were coming from everywhere, grabbing his legs, his arms. Glenn tried to cry out but the moment he opened his mouth, the blackish water seeped into his lungs. He felt as if he had massive weights tied to him, and he sank and sank and . . .

And woke up.

Glenn sat up abruptly and looked around himself in shock. Sunlight was filtering through his bedroom window.

Brandy was glancing in through the door, smiling. "Someone slept in today," she said. "I've got breakfast on the table if you're interested."

All Glenn could do was nod. He was afraid to say anything, terrified that the River Styx was the reality and this, the dream. "Love you," he managed to whisper.

"Love you, too," she said, and vanished back out into the hallway.

He flopped back into the bed, touching his chest and legs to make certain everything was real.

He was alive.

He couldn't believe it.

"Thank God," he said in that same, whisper. Then he sent off a prayer to God or the gods, thanking Him or Them for having made his passing merely a dream. He was so grateful, because there was so much left to do in his life. And now that he had been given a second chance, he was definitely not going to screw it up.

That was when a large crack cut through the ceiling.

He looked up.

The ceiling collapsed and a piano fell through it.

"Aw shit," said Glenn.

As last words went, they weren't especially memorable.

They were, however, remarkably typical.

# POST (MORTEM) SCRIPT

What can I say about JK Woodward that won't get him in trouble with his parole officer?

For starters, as the cover artist, he's the only person associated with this book that didn't actually kill me—just threatened me a whole lot. (I now presume the JK stands for "Just Kidding.") He's remarkably well-adjusted for someone who not only has been working in comics for 13 years, but has been working with Peter David for all of that time. He will be happy to know that my mother was very pleased with the painting, saying that she's seen that expression on my face many, many times . . . which I suspect is a veiled reference to how I look when she's talking to me.

To him I bequeath my saved Photoshop actions and filters. I'd bequeath my Alex Ross books, but a cursory look at his work proves he's already got them.

And finally, you, the imaginary reader. What do I bequeath you?

I leave you this, from Ecclesiastes: People don't know when their time will come any more than fish taken in the fatal net or birds caught in a snare; similarly, people are snared at an unfortunate time, when suddenly it falls on them.

No one knows when that day or that hour will come, not even the angels in heaven.

So take care to leave as little unsaid as possible, leave as little unfinished as you can, for time and fortune happen to us all.

And also for you, who took such pleasure in my multiple demises, I hope you die slowly, over years and years, like a cat playing with a mouse in a trap.

Slowly. Slooowly. Oh so slowly.

It'll be a drawn-out affair, and I hope it's going to last a long, long time. I hope you slowly wither, become feeble, probably start to drool, and get progressively shorter.

Take it from me—there are many worse ways to go.

—Glenn Hauman
Wildwood Cemetery

# WELCOME TO CAMELOT!

You thought you knew about King Arthur and his knights? Guess again!

Learn here, for the first time, the down-and-dirty royal secrets that plagued Camelot as told by someone who was actually there, and adapted by acclaimed *New York Times* bestseller Peter David. Full of sensationalism, startling secrets and astounding revelations, *The Camelot Papers* is to the realm of Arthur what the *Pentagon Papers* is to the military: something that all those concerned would rather you didn't see. What are you waiting for?